THE MAN FROM MITTELWERK

M. Z. URLOCKER

Published by Inkshares, Inc., Oakland, California
www.inkshares.com

Edited by Adam Gomolin and Pam McElroy
Cover by Tim Barber
Interior design by Kevin G. Summers

ISBN 9781950301416
eISBN 9781950301423
LCCN 2022930119

First edition

Printed in the United States of America

I would always remember his frantic eyes, just before my
world exploded in blue-and-orange flame.
I had to know. Was he still out there?

PART I

CHAPTER 1
The Tunnels

Nordhausen, Germany
April 11, 1945

We faced only feeble resistance in taking Mittelbau-Dora. My men and I were among the 1,500 soldiers of the U.S. 104th sent to secure the camp's perimeter by late-morning. I was a captain and that allowed me the freedom to scout the mission.

We'd been moving across German lines without break since November. Every day was a blur. All a man could do was worry about the day in front of him and hope to hell to make it to the next.

We passed the tunnel entrance, and then the gatehouse. That's when the dregs of the Nazi guards, too old, too ill-equipped to mount a serious challenge, salvaged some pride and fired a few rounds into the spring sky. Then they threw down their weapons.

Some soldiers were having a laugh behind me. "These guys are older than my dad," one dogface said as the guards raised their hands and fell to their knees.

Germany was losing the war and everyone knew it, especially the Germans.

Mittelbau-Dora was a high-value target. G-2 reports said there was an underground weapons factory, directly beneath the camp in a series of tunnels. We had to get a look before the Russians did.

My source went a step further, reporting that Himmler had authorized some new scientific work down there, something they called *Wunderwaffen*, the so-called miracle weapons that would win the war for Germany. Above ground, we were liberating POWs. Underground, well, who knew what would happen?

I led my men to the side of the camp gatehouse and gave my orders. We would secure the prisoners' barracks, half a klick up the gravel road. We marched ahead through puddles, into what looked like an abandoned lumber camp.

We were at alert, weapons raised and ready, moving ahead in column formation. We saw no prisoners. I signaled to the radioman to check in with Divisional HQ. "Tell them we're moving forward. No hot contact so far." I still had time.

All morning, there had been a foul smell, heavy in the air. The closer we got to Mittelbau-Dora, the worse it was. Pigs? Slaughterhouse? Unclear.

Up ahead, two GIs from another squad were bent over in a ditch, a fifty-foot fire pit with wood stacked alongside and smoke floating near the ground. Something was off. It didn't fit with a wood fire in a pine forest. One of the soldiers gave me a cursory salute as we passed, pale like he was about to faint; the other one retched. The dwindling smoke of the near-extinguished fire burned my eyes and I rubbed them. When I opened them again, I understood.

It wasn't a wood fire. The stacks were bodies of prisoners piled like logs. God, what were we up against? We'd heard rumors, but in war, you never knew what to believe. I froze in my steps and somebody bumped into me. I barked orders.

We ran to the barracks to search for survivors, and that's when we discovered how bad things were. I'd been a cop in Detroit. I'd seen the bodies from the Purple Gang's street wars. But nothing prepared me for this. They were stick people. More than a hundred of them. On bunks and the floor, packed in tight. The smell was putrid, worse even than the sight.

These weren't the Jews, Gypsies, and homosexuals who ended up at Auschwitz and other Nazi death camps in Poland. Their red triangle badges indicated they were politicals, sent to the tunnels to be worked to death. They spoke mostly French, some Russian, some German. I counted seventeen dead in the bunks. One man whispered: "*Merci, les Américains.*" His throat was full of fluid and he sounded like he was drowning. Then he dug a harmonica from his pocket and started to play *La Marseillaise*. He got five notes out on the rusted Hohner before he ran out of breath, choking. The fellow behind him patted his shoulder blades with the strength of a baby. I doubt the Frenchman was much older than I was.

It was 11:40 hours. Getting late. I had to embark on my mission—something my C.O. only vaguely understood and my men knew nothing about. I turned to Baldwin. "The camp is secure. I need you to take care of this."

"Cap, we barely started," he said in his staccato way. Baldwin spoke like an automatic rifle. Rapid bursts. Short pauses. Made sure he always hit target. "Twenty more buildings. Who knows what we'll find?"

"We scouted the whole area. There isn't a German soldier worth worrying about for ten miles." I glanced at my watch. "Stay put and do your best for these men."

"Where you gotta be . . . sir?"

We'd been through a lot together, and if someone had to know, it would be Sergeant Baldwin. But the risk was too high.

"I've got some orders. A joint operation in the tunnels. That's all I can say."

"Your brother and his secret ops? Keep me out of it."

I knew what he meant.

Leon Baldwin had joined the 104th in December, transferring in from the First Division. The Big Red One was a strong unit and I was glad to have him join. He was a small, wiry guy from Atlanta. When I first met Baldwin, I wondered how he passed the army physical and whether he actually ate, because there seemed to be nothing to him physically, except unlimited energy. But he proved he was all soldier and a natural leader. He also knew when to steer clear.

"Battalion aid will be on its way," I said. "Don't feed anybody anything. Liquids only. Tag 'em if they can't sit up or speak, move 'em outside if they're able."

I turned and made my way. I was to rendezvous with British intel inside the tunnels at twelve-hundred hours. Jordan had infiltrated the site a few weeks earlier, working undercover for the Office of Strategic Services, the top U.S. spy agency. My mission was to get Jordan out and let the Brits exfiltrate any German scientists and equipment of value to the Allies.

That was the plan, but nothing was easy. Now that the Nazis were near defeat, cooperation between the Allies was getting rough. Each country was in it for its own interests. All I cared about was Jordan. It was too late to worry about anything else.

I jogged back to the tunnel, alone, gravel flinging from my boots. Once I passed the gatehouse, I hit it double-time, like a drum solo reaching a crescendo. After what I'd seen at the prison camp, I didn't want to think about what the Germans would do if they discovered a spy.

I hit the entranceway and nearly skidded in front of the two American MPs at their post in front of a jeep. They looked like a couple of linebackers right out of college.

The MPs were dwarfed by the entrance to the tunnel, a rectangle built of concrete wide enough for two locomotives, with two sets of railroad tracks underfoot. The Germans had built wood scaffolding overhead, draped with a camo net, making the entrance invisible from the air.

"This is a secure area," the first one said, stepping forward.

"JIC-Two," I said. JIC referred to the Joint Intelligence Committee. The "Two" I threw in to set them back on their heels. "I'm following up on a report of incendiary devices, if you boys want to join me." I drew my pistol.

"Ah, that's all right, sir." He saluted and his partner stepped back, staring at the ground.

Twenty paces into the tunnel, it was a new world. Wet. Colorless. It was all black and gray. No vegetation, no birds, no sign of life at all. Carbide lamps hissed overhead, releasing a faint garlic smell and lighting the tunnel in a yellow haze.

I ran down the tunnel, my shadow shortening as I approached each lamp and then elongating again. My footsteps echoed off the distant walls and sixty-foot ceiling, sounding like a squad. It was cold enough to see my breath. The tunnel seemed to go on forever until it opened up onto a central area three stories tall, carved out of solid stone. This was *Mittelwerk*, an underground factory spread throughout five miles of tunnels dug in an abandoned gypsum mine.

The floor was smooth and level, embedded with perfectly laid small-gauge rail tracks. The walls were set uniformly straight with sharp right angles. I had to give it to the Nazis; they built the place to last a thousand years. It was like an underworld Ford factory, stretching out as far as you could see. No woody station wagons here, though. At Mittelwerk, they used prisoners from Mittelbau-Dora as slave labor to build the V-2 rockets that bombed London and the Belgian port of Antwerp. We didn't know what other weapons they had built down here.

I could see the Nazis' vast ambition laid out before me. They planned to conquer the world, enslaving people to build the very weapons that would destroy them. There must have been thousands of people working here just days ago. Now it was quiet as a Detroit snow fall.

I shook my head to get clear. I listened for a moment. Nothing.

I was to meet my contact at Bay 47. I didn't even know his name. British officer "F" was all they had signaled. I'd be temporarily under his command as part of a program called T-Force. There was a four-minute window to meet him. If one of us didn't make it, the other had to decide whether to go in alone or call the operation off.

I squinted to read the map Jordan had prepared. There were two long S-shaped tunnels, A and B, that ran parallel, connected by a series of numbered chambers every thirty meters.

I made a short right turn into Tunnel B and started running again. It was lined with a dozen workshops, each one numbered and labeled. There were half-built rockets, hundreds of control panels, helmet-shaped gyroscopes, motors, and tools laid out. Not a worker in sight, as if they'd all gone on lunch break and never returned. I ran almost a mile until I came to what I was looking for. A white "47" painted in two-foot numerals on the rock wall at eye level. *Danke* for German orderliness.

Bay 47 was the final stage of the plant. I passed two giant specimens of fully assembled V-2s. One was erect and spanned nearly the full height of the tunnel. Another was loaded horizontally on rail cars. The fins alone were taller than I could reach.

The scientists behind the V-2 were far ahead of the Americans. No one had ever thought on such a grand scale. The V-2 traveled five times faster than the speed of sound. It was a weapon of sheer terror.

I thought of the civilians we'd met in Antwerp, in northern Belgium. They had endured two months of V-2 pounding, going about their lives knowing there would never be a warning. The V-2s flew so quickly they were silent until they struck, leaving a crater the size of a city block, four stories deep.

I paused to examine the map. Next to Bay 47, the word "descend" was written in Jordan's neat handwriting. I looked around. No signposts here. You had to know what you were looking for. Then I saw it, the rounded top of a metal ladder that led down an almost-hidden shaft to a lower floor. I felt relief that I'd found it. I climbed ten steps down the ladder to a landing where I faced a black metal door with no number —*Dunkelwerk*, the secret lab within the secret plant. The dark factory.

Jordan never explained what the Germans were doing at Dunkelwerk, only that he had to infiltrate it and slow them down. Now that I had seen the scale of Nazi brutality in the camp, I had to wonder what he thought he could achieve.

I glanced at my watch, the silver one that Jordan had given me. There was a metallic taste in the back of my throat, and things felt shaky for a second. It was 11:58. I had two minutes. The smell of sweat and disease from the prisoners stirred my stomach. We were going to make it. We could get out alive. But where was F?

I breathed silently and listened for enemy soldiers nearby. I was cold now. It was noon and I hadn't eaten since battle breakfast at zero five hundred. I heard nothing but water dripping. I waited the four-minute window. No F.

Christ almighty.

I waited another two minutes. That was the limit. T-Force operated with no backup rendezvous or timeslots. These were single-shots. Get in, get what you needed, and get out before anything could go wrong. Timing was so tight, it was a miracle when the operations worked. A no-show or a dead scientist, that was the norm.

I should have called for backup. I could have brought Baldwin into it. I could have done it five different ways.

I had a bad feeling. It was like when you knew there were enemy soldiers just beyond the next ridge. You hadn't seen them, or even heard them, but you just knew.

I looked at my pistol and checked the clip.

Jordan had goaded me the first time I had used a weapon. We were boys and our dog, Boxer, had been missing for a week. There was a rabies scare all summer. Jordan found her, disoriented and snarling in the woods behind the farm. Jordan said we had to take care of it ourselves. He loaded the clip and then handed me the old Springfield rifle from the barn. "You have to kill it, to protect the farm," he said. "You have to be brave."

He never had to tell me again.

I slipped open the door to Dunkelwerk.

A narrow corridor opened up into a well-lit chamber. The air was still and it smelled of carbolic, like the army hospital at Camp Adair where I had trained. I didn't know what to expect. But not this. It looked like a laboratory that had been hit by a tornado. Papers littered the floor. Filing cabinets circled the room, drawers yanked open, contents spilled. Was I too late? Maybe Jordan had gotten out on his own. Or had the Germans fled and taken him as a bargaining chip?

I looked for any sign indicating that people were still around. I could make out steel cabinets and racks of electronic equipment, vacuum tubes, wires, and complex instruments.

A strange looking wood-and-steel chair stood at the center of the room, with a tangle of wires running up its back. I could see that there were posts in the ground where other such chairs had been, evenly spaced out across the lab. There had been a dozen of them, but now there was just one, under a bare light bulb, like a barbershop that had fallen on hard times. I counted a dozen gurneys around the perimeter. I pulled the sheet off the nearest one. It held two emaciated, identical, naked corpses. I almost jumped. What the hell was this place? What had Jordan gotten himself into? What had he gotten me into?

I walked counter clockwise around the periphery slowly, trying not to make a sound. A soft scraping near the entrance acted like an electric shock. I ducked behind one of the large metal cabinets and held perfectly still. I counted to ten. I heard nothing more. I peered from behind the cabinet. Still nothing.

My eyes were drawn toward a large wooden door at the far end of the room. Two German guards emerged, shuffling and talking loudly. Their hands were full, and their rifles were slung on their backs. The first was straining under the load of two metal gas cans that sloshed as he walked. The oily smell of kerosene filled the air. The second, who looked barely twenty, held a bundle of long brown tubes in his arms like firewood. It wasn't hard to work out what they were up to. Hitler had given the Nero Decree: burn everything that might assist the Allies. This was a complication I didn't need.

"Halt," I called. I pulled my Colt M1911 and aimed at the closer of the two. "U.S. Army. Surrender."

The two soldiers swung to face me, and the second one dropped part of his load. I braced for an explosion that didn't come. The first turned pale as the moon and then there was a large, growing damp spot in his pants.

"Hands high," I jerked my left hand and pointed it upward. They gently put down their wares.

"*Wir geben auf,*" the first one said. They were giving up. No surprise there.

"Mausers down," I said. "Slow."

I approached them, leading with my pistol.

I was close enough to smell the sweat and urine.

I thought about what I'd seen earlier, the survivors, the fire pit, and the bodies on the gurneys around the lab. They knew what went on at Mittelwerk. They were part of it. I wanted to blow it all to pieces.

Something in me snapped.

I heard two gunshots, then two more. The bodies were on the ground. I had felt the recoil in my arm and the ringing in my ears. Had I pulled the trigger? It was as if a film had jumped a few frames and I had missed what happened. The Colt was in my hand and four casings were on the ground.

I holstered and stood stunned for a moment. They deserved it. Now I was as dirty as they were. God help me.

I sniffed something sour and then a thin hand gripped my face from behind. I struggled until cold metal touched the back of my neck.

"So, you are the brother?" the voice behind me said.

"What brother?"

"Turn around." He gave me a shove and then his eyes appraised me from top to bottom. "I know you." He blinked. "You are Jordan's twin."

The man with the pistol was younger than me. He wore a lab coat with a dark wool sweater and tie underneath. He had thin brown hair and steel-rimmed glasses that magnified his eyes and gave him a mousey look. He had a pencil neck and the face of a teenager, but he had a Walther P38 pointed at my chest and that tipped the scales.

"*Herr Doktor Panzinger,*" he called out. "*Der Bruder ist hier.*"

A second man appeared, coming from the same doorway as the soldiers. He was taller, a few years older, and wearing a tight gray SS uniform beneath an open white lab coat. His left collar tab showed four silver pips, indicating *Sturmbannführer*, major. Wavy hair, warm eyes. He moved with the confidence of a movie star accepting an award. He held a heavy book in his hand, a volume of *Birds of America*.

I might have been able to tackle one of them, but now my odds were much worse. Still, they could lead me to Jordan.

"Good that you have arrived," the major said. "I always like to meet healthy twins." He saw that his book had caught my eye. "Audubon was brilliant. Far ahead of his time." He tapped the cover with his index finger. "Not a German, but not an American, either. He was a true scientist." He tapped again. "Even today we have a lot to learn from him. I am working on a new translation."

"Where's Jordan?" I said.

"Of course, of course. Your brother is fine." He looked at me as if I were an old friend. "We knew you would come. You are the older brother, yes?"

I nodded.

"Yes, like the barn swallow, you have a sense of family duty. Whereas Jordan, he is more of a . . . he is like an American swift, always in flight." He slid open a brown cardboard packet of cigarettes, tapped one and lit it. "Very dangerous work, spying." He exhaled a plume of smoke and watched it swirl in the still air. "He denied having a brother. But we found the photo. Naturally, we were very interested. Would you like to see him?"

I nodded slowly, doing my best just to breathe. I didn't know how we'd get out, but finding Jordan would put me halfway home.

Panzinger said something in German I didn't understand. His sidekick with the glasses went back through the door and rolled in another gurney. Jordan was stretched out on it, strapped down. The first thing I saw were dark stains on his white shirt. Then I saw him. He was emaciated; his face waxy and gray, with dark rings around his eyes. He wasn't as far gone as the prisoners in the camp, but something had been extinguished in him.

My heart fell like a parachute drop, a sudden fall and then a slow float to the ground. This couldn't be my brother. What they had left was more of preserved specimen than a human. He looked up at me and there was terror in his eyes. It was Jordan all right. He tried to reach out his right arm toward me.

"What have you done to him? This is torture!" I was shouting.

"With some rest, he will be fine," Panzinger said. "Jordan has made a real contribution to our project." His eyes were bright and he smirked as if he had just solved a tricky mathematics problem. He nodded. Panzinger's helper nodded, too.

Jordan's face twitched and his shoulders twisted sideways uncontrolled, like a snake. "Jack, you made it." His eyes bounced like pinballs, jumping from me to Panzinger, to the equipment at the center of the room.

I ignored Panzinger and moved closer to Jordan. "I'm here," I whispered.

Jordan clutched my hand. His head whipped from side to side, feverish. "You have to destroy it. All of it," he said.

"We need to get you ready for the experiment," the assistant said. "Jordan can sustain another round." His eyes were excited. He picked up a clipboard and skittered over to the control panel beside the chair.

"You're surrounded," I said. "There's no way out for you."

Panzinger flicked his cigarette to the floor and ground it with his boot. "Research on twins has been the keystone of our work here," he said. "We shall perform one more test, now that you've arrived."

He swept his right hand toward Jordan as a signal to his assistant to proceed. "It takes only a few minutes." He looked at his watch, then he glanced at the chair with the wires sticking out. "By comparing results on two identical bodies, we can determine the correct—"

The lights flickered and we heard the low grind of iron heaving under a heavy load. Tanks overhead. The rumbling of caterpillar tracks echoed through the chamber. Maybe Sergeant Baldwin had a change of heart. I had to stall for time.

Panzinger looked up, acknowledging the arrival of an American tank corps. "Oh," he said, undaunted. His eyebrows flashed up and down. He was still smirking. Nothing threw this guy.

"Your brother tried to fool us with his endless equipment delays, but we got what we needed." He looked over at the other man and flicked his chin. "Finish it," he said.

His assistant looked disappointed. "*Herr Doktor*, we should wait for the other—"

"No more waiting!" he shouted. Then his calm returned. "Now we go to the backup plan." He stripped off his lab coat and jacket, throwing them to the ground, and he pulled on a heavy wool overcoat. "Gather the documents."

They wanted the same thing I wanted, to escape with their lives. "You won't get there without me," I said. "The Red Army is within three kilometers right now."

At the mention of the Russian Army, Panzinger's assistant froze. Every German knew. There was no surrender to the Russians.

"You have a way, Captain Waters?" Panzinger gazed at me as though I'd suddenly become interesting.

"Leave us here and I'll give you a way out," I said.

The assistant twitched. He was perspiring.

"What do you have for me?"

"I know exactly where the American and Russian troops are located. I scouted the area this morning," I said, holding out the map.

He took it from me, noting the Russian positions immediately without revealing his destination. "We need to get north of the forest," he said.

"Take this route." I traced a path on the map. "But your chances of getting out alive are fifty-fifty at best," I said. "You'd be better off surrendering to my unit."

"I appreciate your candor, Captain Waters." To look at Panzinger, you'd never know the war was lost for Germany and that he was surrounded by two enemy armies. "I agree with your assessment," he said, handing back the map. "But we have our plans and they do not involve show trials held by the enemy. I'll leave you here to make your own way."

"You've got to help my brother," I said. "Please, give him something."

"It is just a question of time as he leaves the stasis zone. He will be fine within a few minutes. One officer to another, you have my word." Panzinger nodded and seconds later, they were gone.

I turned my attention to Jordan and began unbuckling the straps. "Jordan, we gotta go." His eyes were cloudy.

"I can't fix this . . . Leave me."

"You're gonna be okay," I said. "I'll get you out of here."

I heard a metallic click and smelled a brief whiff of tobacco. Then a heavy blanket of kerosene. That lying bastard . . .

A deep rumble emerged from the chamber. There was a whoosh of hot air and a crack like a mortar shell as the air caught fire in a giant explosion. I saw Jordan scream, and I watched in disbelief as the wall in front of me was blown out and a steel girder fell, missing me by a few feet. For a split second, I watched the smoke and debris swirl in front of my eyes, and then a pulse of orange flame lifted me high into the air while huge chunks of stone and steel fell from above. I felt like a twig in a windstorm.

I fell to the ground and everything was silent. I saw the tunnel walls collapse but I heard nothing. I thought of Boxer, twisting and howling when I had fired into her. It was right to kill her. She was mad with rabies. Better off dead.

Then everything went blue, then orange, and finally black.

That was the last I saw of my brother.

American Evacuation Hospital
Nordhausen, Germany
April 15, 1945

When you come out of a coma, it doesn't happen all at once. It's like emerging from a long dream. The only difference is the dream keeps pulling you back.

That's how it was for me, anyway. One minute, I was in a tunnel below Mittelwerk, and the next minute . . . I was a little fuzzy on all of that. There was an explosion. Then darkness. But I couldn't leave the tunnel, not without Jordan.

That's why I kept getting pulled down. I had to find out what had happened. I would spend days, years, exploring the darkness. It was beautiful and quiet, like swimming underwater at night. The air was cool and moist. I would spend a lifetime down here if that's what it took.

But every once in a while, I'd hear something. A ripple on the surface would pull me up to the real world.

I heard a voice in the distance, soothing as a summer rain.

"You'd like San Moreno," she said. "You could come visit, when this is over. I bet you'd like that."

It sounded swell, and I wondered why I hadn't thought of it myself.

I felt something warm and soothing on my face. The smell of Barbasol shaving cream. Then there was a soft scraping and suddenly I was back on the surface. I opened my eyes.

"Look who's awake," I heard her say.

I blinked. I wasn't sure if I really wanted to be here. I looked at her and I saw her high cheeks, the roundness of her lips. Not a nurse. A uniform I didn't recognize.

She had a straight razor in her hand. She wiped it on a cloth, dipped it in warm water, and went back to work. She drew the razor across slowly, gently along one cheek, then the other. She followed the curves of my chin with the razor, never pressing too hard, never cutting. The strokes were long and soft and luxurious. She wiped me down, and it felt like teasing.

"My name's Faith," she said.

I thought I was still dreaming. Or maybe she was a ghost or something worse. I didn't want to appear foolish, so I said nothing.

"You've had a lot of people very worried," she said, holding the back of my head with her left hand while gliding the razor above my lip. Her hand was warm and I wanted her to keep it there forever. To never let go.

She leaned forward and whispered into my ear. I felt her breath on my face.

"Everything's going to be okay."

Then there was a crash. Someone had dropped a metal tray and it clattered on the floor. I heard a bottle roll, and someone cursed. I looked past Faith and took in the whole room. A sea of hospital beds, as big as a football field, filled with the dead and dying. Doctors and nurses and equipment and charts and someone rolling a trolley. The noise got louder and I saw the whole room in chaos. Men wearing lab coats were approaching. It was too much.

"I can't do this," I said. "Not yet."

"I'll be here when you're ready," she said. She squeezed my hand.

I smelled the sweetness of her perfume. I clamped my eyes shut. I went back down into the darkness, into the tunnels again.

I had to find Jordan.

CHAPTER 2
The Watcher

San Moreno, California
Thursday, June 29, 1950
Early afternoon

The plastic Hawaiian dancer swerved from side to side, glued to the dash. I was driving to the meet. Every song on the radio sounded dissonant, like they were playing two different songs in two different keys. I punched the buttons to find something and gave up when the news came on. I gripped the side of my head with my right hand and steered with my left.

I turned into my parking spot near the bank and put the car in park. For the umpteenth time that day, I thought back to the tunnels. I could picture them—gray, cold, and silent. But I was losing the details. What was it Jordan had said to me? All that came to mind was the sweat dripping down his face and the blood spattered on his chest as he silently pleaded for something. I never figured that out.

My head hurt. A ray of pain went through my skull like it wasn't my own.

I need to stop thinking about the war, I told myself.

I got out of the car and sat on a rusty park bench with time to kill.

I was out on surveillance, awaiting the arrival of a powder-blue Cadillac driven by a known deadbeat named Hal Sanford. If there was one thing you got used to in the army, it was sitting around waiting.

A spotted towhee flitted past me, its feathers orange against the blue sky. As I followed its flight across the park, I pulled out a pack of Hermanos, glanced around, and lit up. The smoke was sweet but harsh and burned my throat in that familiar way. In a few minutes, things would calm down. I scanned nearby vehicles to stay sharp and pass the time.

There was a green Chevy Fleetmaster with a "Jail the Hollywood Ten" bumper sticker parked on the north side in front of the Pacific National Bank. The driver had slicked-back hair and was staring at the bank. I couldn't tell if he was hoping for a loan or casing the joint.

In front of the Chilli-Villa, a blue-and-white '49 Ford F-1 panel truck idled, a Dutch Boy Dairy sign on the side. The sign looked orange, or it might have been a trick from the light. The driver, in a navy uniform with bright-blue piping, was chatting up two women at the restaurant's service door. Women love a man in uniform, even a milkman.

They looked like sisters or cousins in matching white aprons. The older one brushed hair from her eye and looked to the ground, avoiding his gaze. Her smile fractured. War widow, I surmised. The younger one was oblivious, hoping to catch his attention. When she did, her laughter filled the air, and he smiled like Liberace. *There's something between those two,* I thought. He turned toward his truck, his smile vanishing as he swung a crate into the back. I couldn't see it working out between them. He was damaged goods.

I took note of everything as I watched the parade of humanity around me. Interpreting gestures and emotions, layering in hidden motives. It didn't mean anything to me except as a way to keep my mind off other issues. Just like smoking Hermanos. I took in another deep pull and let it out slowly. I was starting to feel it.

It had been five years since Mittelwerk, and I was still looking for Jordan. I wondered what he'd think of me now, the way I was living. What would I tell him? *I'm doing all right, brother. How 'bout you?*

After I landed stateside, I took the train to Interlochen, ahead of Jordan's memorial. I couldn't accept that he was dead, so I stayed on one more stop to Traverse City. I walked three blocks to buy a pint and caught the next train south. In my haste, I lost my return ticket. The conductor waved it off. "Glad you made it back, son." With that, I drank myself into a stupor that went on for months.

I disappeared in Detroit. I couldn't go back to being a cop. Not after what I'd been through. So I rented a room and worked construction. I had loads of new friends, drinking buddies, that sort, and worse. I never told anybody what happened in the tunnels of Mittelwerk. How could I? I still didn't understand it. And I sure as hell didn't want anyone's pity.

Now it was a new decade, and we were all doing great. At least, that's what they told us. New schools and neighborhoods were popping up across the country. America was awash in new TVs, manufactured food, and a made-to-order red scare to keep everyone in line. Senator Joe McCarthy was peddling enemies in our midst—communists—and people were buying it like penny candy.

Well, maybe not everyone. Every frontline soldier had seen and done things he couldn't speak of. Every family lost someone. And there was nothing that Spanish jugglers on Ed Sullivan or fifteen-cent Lucky Lagers could do to change that.

Sometimes it felt like another war was on the horizon. I'd heard on the radio last week that a Russian spy was arrested in New York. An army sergeant named Greenglass who had worked at Los Alamos on the bomb. He spilled everything to the reds. The gall. Now he's spilling more to the FBI. In Germany, we knew exactly who our enemies were.

Soldiers buried their memories, like they buried their friends, deep as they could. Hoping the pain would fade over time. And if it didn't, maybe after a few years, a guy could save enough money to buy a cabin in the woods, take up fly fishing, and, one day, as likely as not, blow his brains out.

Like I said, I was doing all right. I didn't even like fly fishing.

I hit bottom, though, drinking myself away in Detroit. It took me half a year to straighten up and save some money. The whole time, Faith kept writing. It was the one bright spot in my life. She'd believed in me even when I hadn't. Eventually, she repeated her invitation to visit her in San Moreno. I had to see if there was something there or not, so I motored west and promised Faith I would never fall back to my old ways. That was more than a year ago.

Now we had a business going—the Robner & Waters Detective Agency. We'd solved some insurance cases and were starting to build a reputation. Today had been a slow morning at the office, which was not uncommon. Still, I had my daily rituals, flipping through pictures of Jordan, making my weekly action list, writing letters to congressmen and low-level army officials for support, making supervised visits to military records offices to search the Spinners, files labeled "Service Personnel Not Recovered." As Faith reminded me, I was making as much progress as a monkey tackling Shakespeare.

I took another puff and the chaos of the world melted away just a little in the afternoon sunshine. I was tired and stoned and I didn't care.

I started the morning at 4:00 a.m., as I had every day for nearly two weeks, hanging on the wire for an overseas phone call. I was chasing a lead from a Red Cross shortwave broadcast. The rollcall of displaced soldiers included a GI found in Berlin, comatose and disfigured. When the phone call finally came from Geneva, I couldn't hear a thing for all the static. I shouted for them to telegram the vitals. Four hours later, it came in a three-squib, station-to-station message relayed by Western Union in Los Angeles: Five feet four, blue eyes, 58kg.

A dead end. I slammed another drink. It wasn't even 8:00 a.m.

Faith arrived at the office at 9:00. She sniffed the air, looked at me, and turned to leave. But not before we had an argument.

She wanted us to drive up to San Francisco over the weekend, see some old friends of hers, layabouts Patty and Paul. Poets or artists or something. I'd forgotten about her plans and organized a gig on Sunday.

"So I have to cancel?" She crossed her arms. She was looking at me with her head tilted to one side.

"I'm sorry, honey."

There was a long pause. Finally, she shrugged. "Well, if you're with Mick, at least you'll stay out of trouble."

Mick had a charming, easy-going vibe, but he had his finger in all kinds of pies. For some reason, Faith thought of him as my guardian.

She wasn't wrong. She wasn't wrong about any of it.

We'd built our little agency together. It was meant to be a precursor to marriage. A test run to see if we could work together. That part was fine. But there were cracks. And every day I saw them getting deeper. I wondered whether I should patch them up or reach in with a crowbar and tear it all apart.

I was getting warm, sitting on the bench in the sunshine. The pleasant feeling was boosted by the jag from the Hermanos. It made me nostalgic, so I reached for my wallet, slipped my right thumb behind my P.I. license, and pulled it out.

It was a black-and-white photo of Jordan and me, taken long before the war. We grew up on a farm in Paradise Township, Michigan, a few miles from Kingsley. The picture kindled a lot of colorful memories. We were standing in front of our father's International farm truck in the bright August sun. Brush cuts, big eyes, shirtless in dungarees. Absolute friends, arms over each other's shoulders, knowing this last bit of summer freedom was coming to an end. I was all smiles, looking up. Jordan posed seriously, head tilted. Jordan was on a scholarship to study languages at Yale. I never understood that. I'd wanted a job, and so I was headed for training with the state troopers in Lansing. We shared the carefree optimism of young Americans about to enter the world.

Back then, I would challenge people with the photo to see if they could tell who was who, but now I didn't talk about Jordan. He was lost and I was still here and I couldn't get over it.

I stared at the photograph. None of the promises in that picture came through. There wasn't a day I didn't replay in my head what happened in the tunnels and what I could have done differently.

I leaned back against the park bench, closed my eyes, and drifted until the town clock struck three. I hoped Faith had cooled off.

A loud crack cut the air like a gunshot. It flew straight into my brain. I jumped to my feet, a sharp pain in my temple. My vision shimmered and the color drained from everything. For an instant, I saw the face of my nightmares. The man in the SS jacket. His face gaunt, like a skull. He stared at me and laughed.

I shuddered and squeezed my eyes tight. I thought back to Faith at the evac hospital in Nordhausen, when she whispered in my ear. I wondered if things would ever be okay again.

I took a deep breath and opened my eyes. There was my target. A powder-blue '42 Cadillac four-door pulled in behind the milk truck. It was his car that had backfired. His brakes squeaked and blue smoke poured out of the exhaust. Sanford had let the Caddy go like an unpaid bill.

That's why we'd arranged the meeting.

I followed Sanford at a safe distance as he made his way to the Bella Vista Inn, across the street. The hotel bar, the Galley Room, was a typical upscale watering hole with a big mahogany setup in the center; dim, red velvet booths around the edges; and thick drapes that obscured the windows. It was a private place to pick up, break up, or crack up, whatever the situation called for.

I gave him a minute, then strolled in and took a seat at the bar, close to the entrance. I dropped two quarters on the bar top for a beer. Best to leave a big tip in case I needed the barman on my side. As planned, Faith was sitting at the far booth, facing the door, so Sanford wouldn't see me when he sat down opposite her.

Faith wore her red Hazel Bishop lipstick. Her hair was down. She was a knockout in her white blouse and a black-and-red paisley accent scarf, playing it up for Sanford. It was a variation on Mutt and Jeff, army interrogation. Faith was the friendly start. I was the heavy, on call. If Faith touched her right cheek, that meant I was to step in. If she brushed back her hair, I was to stand down.

Sanford had been a jocular client in the rag trade, but he turned shy once our bill was presented. He had a problem with disappearing inventory, which we cracked within three days. His dresses were walking out the door, two layers undercover with the night shift employees, a dozen or more every night.

Now his bill was six months overdue, and he wasn't answering my phone calls. Faith had figured out a plan to get paid. She understood his type and got her hook in by suggesting they meet for a drink at a hotel.

Within two minutes of Sanford's arrival, she brushed back her hair. I wasn't happy about it, but it was the plan we'd agreed to, so I donned my hat and left. I tried to catch her eye, but Faith was a pro—once she made her call, that was it. Was she still angry from this morning?

Twenty minutes after I got to the office, Faith returned, too. I was sitting at the spinet tucked in the corner, trying to remember some long-lost jazz chords. My parents made me take lessons as a kid and I used to torment my teacher by playing boogie-woogie instead of Brahms.

I turned toward the door. Faith's hair was tied back, her usual business style. She walked toward me and leaned across the piano and pulled a small packet of fifty-dollar bills from a Pacific National envelope, letting them flutter onto the keys, one at a time. Eight of them. That was more than we'd earned in all of June. Her eyebrows were raised high. She slowly pulled away her scarf and it looked like she had burst two buttons on her blouse. She winked. "Sanford came across, in full."

She put her hands on her hips and beamed. "I told him he either walked with me to the bank to get the cash immediately, or I would drive to Inglewood to tell Mrs. Sanford why her husband worked so many late nights."

Her eyebrows danced. "His eyes popped out even further than yours did." She flicked the scarf at me.

I felt my face get hot and I started to stammer an objection, but she just laughed.

"Jack, don't be such a prude. You should be proud of me. I used what I had to get leverage. That was brains, not body."

It was hard working with someone you loved. The relationship seemed to always get in the way of business. Or maybe I had it backward.

CHAPTER 3
Our Man Palumbo

A little while later, a man knocked loudly on the door before he stuck his head inside. "Anyone in?" he asked.

"Nobody here but us chickens," I answered.

Faith shot me a dirty look, which I deserved. I shrugged it off. I wasn't trying to be rude. Sometimes it just came naturally. It was one of the reasons Faith wisely divided our duties. Her background as a reporter gave her a friendly disposition when dealing with clients. She got them to open up through genuine curiosity. I closed them with the cold expertise of a war-hardened ex-cop.

I'm Faith Robner," she said, getting up and extending her hand. "What can I help you with, Mr. . . . "

"Palumbo, John Palumbo," he said. "My friends call me JP." He reached out and shook Faith's hand. He had five years on me. Hard years. Craggy face, short hair, gray on the sides, straight posture, crisp dark suit with a wide hand-painted tie decorated with sailboats and palm trees. Ex-army, I figured. Officer type. The tie didn't work. He was past the age where he could pull that off.

She pulled him into the client sitting area. We had a small black lacquer coffee table, three chairs, and a bronze art deco lamp. Faith steered Palumbo to the client chair. It was a nicely padded leather armchair designed to put the client at ease. It was also positioned so that he had to turn one way to speak to me and the other to speak to Faith. That made it easier for Faith and me to observe a client and communicate in our own private language of secret glances and subtle hand gestures.

"This is my partner, Jack Waters," Faith said.

"It's quite a delicate situation," he said.

"They always are," Faith said. It was the standard opening for anyone who visited our agency. No one came to a private investigator because they were proud. They came because they were ashamed, in trouble, or desperate. Maybe all three. But Palumbo's words didn't match his demeanor. He didn't seem like a man who was easily ruffled.

"I run security up at CTS Aerodynamics," he said. He removed a gold card-case from his inside pocket and handed us each a card.

That got my attention. Half a dozen companies had popped up in the San Moreno valley in recent years, building new planes, engines, radio equipment. And since the war, they were growing at an even faster clip, doing both military and civilian work.

"And is this a professional engagement or something more personal?" I asked. We didn't take divorce work if we could help it. Our area of expertise was insurance investigation, fraud, arson, and the like. But June had been lean, and I knew that if Faith hadn't gotten Sanford to pay up, we were mere weeks away from late-night photo sessions at the no-tell motel. I didn't know if I had it in me to backslide to the minor leagues again.

"Strictly professional. I'm very happily married." But as he said it, his eyes fell on Faith in a way that suggested otherwise.

"New to the area?" I asked. He turned to me, and Faith gave me a look of relief.

"Yes, that's right," he said. "I've taken a new role at CTS. A transfer and a promotion. My family will be moving out here in September for the new school year. So right now, I'm living out of a suitcase and flying back to Nevada half the time. We have a facility there, as I'm sure you know. We do a lot of our ground tests on the salt flats. And I've got to hire a new man to take over my old post."

Faith's expression had hardened. I could see something didn't sit right with her.

"Mr. Palumbo, what can we do for you?" she asked.

"Straight and to the point," he said. "I like that in a woman." Palumbo's eyes were on her again, so she kept an engaged look on her face. I rolled my eyes for her. Palumbo thought her smile was meant for him and that was fine. She worked it to her advantage. Nothing ruffled Faith when it came to landing a client or working a case.

Palumbo turned to me. "I'm sure you've seen the reports in the newspapers. Communist spies out to sabotage our country."

Faith started to laugh, but she turned it into a cough by the time he turned toward her. "Summer cold," she said.

I nearly bust a gut at that, so I held my breath tight. Faith liked to joke that the red scare was good for business. It was becoming a national mania.

"It happened in England, too." Palumbo seemed defensive. "They caught that scientist, Klaus Fuchs," he said, pronouncing the name like a curse. "You get me?"

"Yeah, worldwide," I said.

"Exactly. We work on quite a few military contracts at CTS. Top-secret clearance, you know. And I've got to ensure that we are one hundred percent secure against any foreign threats."

"You want us to do background checks?" I asked.

"We do that already. I'm not concerned with employees. It's outsiders I'm concerned with."

"What is it you had in mind?" Faith asked.

"I'd like you to conduct a security drill. I want you to attempt to breach our security. Use all the means at your disposal to identify weak spots, so we can fix them."

"You want us to break into CTS?"

"Exactly." He smiled steadily at Faith. "But of course, it's not a break-in. It's under my authorization. I want you to find the holes in our security and then write it up."

"Write it up?" I asked.

"Yes, give us a report so we know exactly how we can strengthen our operations." He paused. I don't know what reaction he was looking for, but evidently we weren't living up to his expectations. "You're an army man, right?"

I nodded. Had been. Once. Maybe he saw the framed newspaper on the wall. Or maybe he'd read the story years ago and that's why he called on us.

"So you know what it means to manage a good defense. You've got to test it with a strong offense." His right hand formed a fist and he slapped it into his left hand.

The military had performed these kinds of training operations for years. I was wondering why I hadn't thought of this before. I saw Robner & Waters pulling out of our slump, getting out of arson for good. We'd hire security experts with military training.

"We've looked at doing this kind of operation before. But, you know, it takes a lot of manpower. It doesn't come cheap," I said.

"I came to Waters & Robner because you're a vet, someone I can trust." Faith raised her eyebrow at that. People came to us because a lawyer wanted them out of their office, or they found our ad in the yellow pages.

I quoted him a figure. It was more than twice what we got working insurance cases. Faith's eyes popped, but Palumbo didn't flinch. I wished I'd gone higher still. I imagined new offices, with a fancy reception area. Teams of people answering the phones. Reporters calling for interviews.

He reached into his jacket once more and took out a leather checkbook. "I'm willing to pay top dollar for top quality. That's what CTS deserves. Would it be all right if I give you an advance for seven days?"

I glanced over as he started writing and saw the check had the CTS Aerodynamics logo in red, as well as a seal for the Bank of Nevada. Faith frowned. I hoped I wasn't drooling.

Palumbo looked up, picking up his pen off the check. I mentally willed him to resume writing. "And Mr. Waters, I'm willing to pay a generous bonus for every vulnerability you can identify. You know how it is. Guards get their training and after a few weeks, they're reading on the job, skipping their perimeter tours. Our government contracts require that we're secure, and I want to make sure we're as locked down as Fort Knox." Faith gave me a look like she'd found a pair of old gym socks in my desk. Couldn't she see the goldmine CTS represented? I took in a sharp breath.

"We're happy to design a custom—"

"Where are you staying, Mr. Palumbo?" Faith interrupted.

"Please, call me JP. I'm staying at the Sundowner on Highway 14."

"We'd be pleased to work with you." She stood up and reached out to shake his hand.

I exhaled silently.

We were about to turn it around. A gold mine.

Palumbo stood up, pen and checkbook still in hand, looking a bit confused.

"This is a busy time for us, as you can understand, Mr. Palumbo. We're working on a similar operation for Hughes. Believe me, we've found quite a few irregularities already. You have no idea how sloppy they've gotten. We took the guided tour and just wandered off with a camera for an hour without anyone noticing."

I had no idea what Faith was talking about. Did Hughes even have tours?

"The FBI was very impressed," she said.

"FBI?"

"Oh, yes, standard procedure," Faith continued. "We're obligated to share everything we find with the feds. We've got to keep the commies at bay, right, Jack?"

Palumbo's eyes darted from Faith to me and then the door.

"We're . . . doing our part." I was improvising now, an actor who'd forgotten his lines.

Palumbo put his checkbook back in his jacket, and it was all I could do not to reach into his coat and yank it out. We needed to hire a whole team and I needed his check.

"So, how's next week?" Faith gave an eager look. "Shall we stop by your office to make the final arrangements?"

"Ah, no, I'm not quite settled here yet," he said. "I'm traveling next week."

"Back to Nevada?" I asked, my eyes pleading.

He nodded. "Yeah, family."

"Whenever you're ready, Mr. Palumbo, you get back in touch." Faith patted him on the arm, and he jumped like he was caught in a raid at an after-hours club. He walked out, with my dreams of business expansion trailing after him.

Faith shut the door and leaned back against it.

"Can you believe that guy?" she asked.

"Okay, what just happened?"

"You tell me, partner."

I thought for a moment. "Well, something wasn't on the level. The way he scrambled out of here when you mentioned the FBI."

"That's one. What else?"

"He's less married than I am. And the family in Nevada? That seemed fishy."

"No one stays in Nevada in July if they can help it. And an out of state check on Friday before the Fourth of July? That check would have been bouncing between here and Reno for weeks."

"Okay, you win. Does Palumbo even work for CTS?"

"There might be a John Palumbo who works there. But it's not this guy." She held up his business card. "These are cheap stock. Not the kind an executive gives out. And why would he have cards printed up for the San Moreno office if he hasn't moved here yet? Oh, and he didn't even get the name straight. He called us 'Waters & Robner.' That guy was nervous."

"You know, it has a nice ring to it—Waters & Robner."

She gave me her "don't even joke" look.

"So, what's the scam?" I asked.

"I saved you from serving two-to-ten for accessory to breaking into a top-secret military facility."

"Wait, what?"

"He's in the trade, and he's casing CTS. Only he's looking to hire a stooge for the recon job. Wouldn't even know they're doing it. Write it up like it's an internal report. Then he puts together a crew to do the break-in."

"What's he after?"

"Design plans? Equipment? Who knows? I'm sure there's a black market for everything they're working on. Industrial espionage. He could turn around and sell it to Boeing."

"Maybe the Russians."

"Russians, English, French." She shrugged. "Every country has an aviation industry, an air force, an intelligence agency. And no one wants to fall behind."

"And if we were caught?"

She snapped her fingers. "Palumbo's a ghost, and you're in San Quentin."

"And there I was thinking we'd finally have a good July."

"He gave me the creeps from the start."

"I figured he hadn't had lunch and was just hungry."

"Shut up, Jack." She leaned into me and wrapped her arms around my waist. "You're the only one who gets to look at me like that."

Maybe I was worried for nothing.

CHAPTER 4
Playing in the Band

"Honey, let's go out and celebrate."

"Celebrate what?" I had just settled in at my desk with the late afternoon newspaper.

"Don't be a stick." Faith pulled out one of the fifty-dollar bills from Sanford. "My treat." I warmed to the idea for a moment. And then she added. "We can stop by the Legion Hall. They'll have a band playing, won't they?"

"Could be," I said. I put down the newspaper. "Hey, we could go to Lorenzo's if you like."

She came over and reached her arms around my shoulders from behind. "Forget Lorenzo's. We can go there anytime. Let's go dancing. It'll be fun."

"I'll pick you up at eight." She leaned over and gave me a kiss on the cheek.

Thursday night was Jerry's semi-regular gig at the Legion. I think Jerry had more bands than friends. I sat in on piano for a few months with his Legion band. At some point, Jerry said he wanted to strip down the sound, and so me and the sax player were out of the picture.

We entered the hall from the back, and Faith waved to Jerry and Mick. She could thaw an iceberg with her smile. I was about to settle in at a table near the entrance, but Faith continued toward the front of the room near the stage and dance floor, finding an open two-top.

"It's your old band," she said, grabbing my hand.

I gave a wan smile.

She leaned toward me. "We can go someplace else."

"It's okay," I said. "We'll stay for a couple of songs."

Jerry was dressed in a brown checked Western shirt. He looked toward me and raised his eyebrows. His body was lean like he'd missed a few meals, and his hair was shaggy. He didn't go for the older big band sound, but he could deconstruct it and put it back together in a four-piece combo.

He picked the first few notes on his guitar, the intro for "I'm So Lonesome I Could Cry." I groaned. It was a good song, but Jerry played it too slow and it became a dirge. You could play it after everyone was up and dancing if you wanted to give the couples a slow number, but you couldn't start there. It was like taking a tractor to the race track.

I looked over at Mick at the drum kit. His red hair was hanging in his eyes, and he had a scraggly beard that matched. He shrugged, and they all fell into step.

Jerry introduced the next song as "an obscure B-side by Hank Williams on the Sterling label," which was code for Jerry sneaking in one of his own songs. In this case, "Wanting and Waiting." The audience brightened. They liked what they heard and the band picked up the tempo. One or two couples went out on the dance floor. Faith was swaying to the beat.

I thought back to when we'd all been in Jerry's basement in the spring, for one of his legendary improv sessions. It started in the early evening and sometimes went right through to the morning, before Jerry's girlfriend complained and told him he had choices to make if he wanted to keep living there.

Those jam sessions felt like a twilight. We were on the cusp of creating something new, combining jazz, western swing, and R&B into a new sound that was all our own.

Tonight, I was just a spectator. I gritted my teeth. They were playing it safe.

When the song ended, Jerry mumbled into the mic: "It's great to have some of our old friends here tonight." Mick hit the crash cymbal and Faith elbowed me in the ribs. Jerry turned back, toward the band. There was some discussion about what song to play next. Don, the bass player, started an old familiar riff. I could see it wasn't what Jerry wanted. But then Mick joined in and I heard Jerry say, "I guess we're doing this."

It was a twelve-bar blues number with a rolling rumba beat that got people moving. A few more couples scurried onto the dance floor. Without the piano, it didn't sound right to me.

"So?" Faith nudged me. Of course she recognized the song. We used to play it at some of the late-night jams.

"Jack, they're playing it for *you*," she whispered into my ear. I shook my head.

Jerry started clapping his hands over his head on the two and the four. Soon the audience joined in.

"If you don't get up there, *I'll* go up and play it."

Faith was a good dancer, but her playing piano was about as likely as me stepping up to the pitcher's mound at Gilmore Field. She reached as if to stand, and I had no choice.

I stood and climbed the steps to the stage. The audience clapped and I played a glissando across the keys as I sat on the bench. Mick let out a crazy drum fill, and it was like old times.

My fingers hit the piano keys with sharp staccatos, hammering out a progression of ninth chords for a jazzy sound. Don opened his mouth in a small 'o,' his eyes wide as he looked back at me. You weren't supposed to play anything but covers at the Legion. But it sounded good and Faith flashed me a moonbeam smile.

Jerry grinned and let his head back in a howl he only used when we were really cooking. With that, we were all in, consequences be damned.

The song evolved into syncopated Cuban blues, and I took the lead again. I was hammering the notes in double time, driving the beat. To my surprise, Faith stood up, pushed her chair back, and started dancing on her own.

The blue light on my hands became brighter, almost cataclysmic as I played a solo that ran the length of the piano. Jerry was shouting out improvised cheers in some made-up Caribbean patois.

We were all locked in to the beat. Jerry and Mick and Don and I, each adding our own contributions to the moment. I signaled once more to Mick, so we could take it back to where we'd started. He nodded to the beat and on the four, he played a Krupa-style tom fill, signaling a break in the tempo. With that I stood up and gave a bow. The audience clapped while Jerry repeated the intro in half-time, and Mick played a shimmering finale on the cymbals.

Faith rushed toward me and kissed me as I walked onto the dance floor.

"Jack, everybody loves you."

I squeezed her tight. After all this time, she knew me better than I knew myself. She'd set up the whole night just for me.

CHAPTER 5
The Flicker of a Smile

Friday, June 30, 1950
Early evening

The next evening, at Faith's place, I looked out the living room window. Clouds gathered overhead and I could feel the pressure building toward a summer storm. There were bursts of light in the distant sky. The low roll of thunder ten miles away in Loma Vista echoed throughout the valley.

Faith's two-room walk-up was about a mile from the center of town. There was a discreet side entrance, which I used for occasional late visits. I plunked myself on the sofa.

"You've got to decide," Faith said. I had nixed San Francisco, but Faith was making one final attempt to change my mind. "What if we drive up Monday?"

"I can't," I said. "We committed to a gig on Tuesday as well."

"So now it's two gigs?"

I turned my palms up. "It's a fundraiser. We're hoping the mayor will come by and we'll get some press coverage for missing soldiers. I was hoping you'd be able to help me."

"Sure. Reverberations from San Moreno will echo across the land, and Jordan will suddenly emerge out of some bus station."

I jumped up. There was a stunned look on her face. I felt like I was about to do something, either throw that stupid lamp we had gotten from the expensive furniture store, or say something I shouldn't.

She froze, staring at me as if I had pulled a weapon.

I put my anger aside and sat back down. Faith exhaled.

"Sorry," I said.

She resented how much time I was spending on my search for Jordan. She just didn't want to say it out loud.

Faith went to the kitchen to finish making dinner. She was a good cook and it was our custom to have dinner together a couple of times a week, ostensibly to review current cases. I grabbed a Lucky Lager from the icebox where Faith kept a few stubbies for me.

After a while, Faith came out. She had an apron on. She pushed back her hair with one hand, trying to put things in place.

"Chicken's almost done," she said. "Come here."

She opened her arms. She coated me in a tight embrace. There was something off about it. Like she was trying to prove a point. I noticed a bouquet of flowers by the window. I didn't recall seeing them earlier in the week, but Faith liked to keep the place nice.

We separated by an inch. Static electricity crackled on my shirt.

"What's this all about?" I asked.

"I shouldn't have said what I said." She squeezed me. "And I'm glad we got Sanford to pay up. We're a good team."

"That was your doing."

She looked up at me. "I worry about you."

"We'll go another time, in the fall. Patty and Paul will still be there, I'm sure."

She went cold. "It's Paula and Patrick." She pulled away from me. "You can't even get their names right."

She walked to the window and rearranged the flowers. Then she stuffed some newspaper clippings into a thick green folder on the bookcase nearby.

I sniffed the air. "Do you smell something?"

"Shit *la merde!*" She ran back into the kitchen. I followed.

Smoke filled the tiny room. Faith grabbed her oven mitts and pulled the smoking roasting pan out of the oven while emitting a stream of army-grade curses.

"You could—"

"Don't tell me what to do," she snapped.

"I'll leave you to it then."

A few minutes later, Faith came back out, carrying a plate with a piece of well-done chicken amandine and a half serving of charred potatoes.

"I'm afraid there were casualties," she said. "I did the best I could for them."

"You're not eating?"

"I'm going for a walk."

"You might need an umbrella," I said.

She turned. "I need what I need." I heard her slam the kitchen door a moment later.

I remembered meeting Faith for a drink at the San Moreno Inn, shortly after I arrived in California. I had just one beer—that was my limit those days—but Faith was quite spirited, consuming a couple of sidecars.

When there was a lull in the music, she leaned forward and said, "You're the man I want to marry someday." She looked me straight in the eye as she said it, like some kind of dare.

I didn't know what to say. Even after all this time, she still had the ability to surprise me.

Now it was a year later, and it felt like we were stuck in a pattern. Being in business kept us together, but it created an awkward dynamic. We were partners more than lovers. I never tried to hide who I was. But I also never tried to woo her. So things ebbed and flowed in an off-kilter way, never quite finding the right balance.

I cleaned up my plate and looked at my reflection in the darkened kitchen window. What was I waiting for?

I was startled from my reverie when I heard the bell over the screen door. Faith stepped in, dripping wet.

"Goddamn you," she said. She gave a flicker of a smile.

Sometimes it just doesn't pay to be right.

As Faith dripped her way across the apartment, the phone rang. She walked to the front hall and answered it. She listened for a moment.

"Yes, this is Robner & Waters." I leaned in the doorway wondering who would be calling this late on a Friday evening. "This is Faith Robner." Then a longer pause. "Yes, I understand perfectly. Please hold for a moment." She covered the phone with one hand and said in a cold tone, "Paging Mr. Waters."

It was Captain MacDonald of the Loma Vista police. It wasn't unusual to get a business call in the evening. We were used to nervous clients in need of handholding and insurance adjustors working overtime. But it wasn't often the police and certainly never the brass.

"How can I help you, Captain?" I tried to sound cheery, but the sharp look Faith gave me made it feel phony.

"We've had an accident over at the Blakely Estate. You know it?"

"Of course, sir." The name was vaguely familiar. I didn't concern myself with the upper crust social scene, but you couldn't live in the Loma Vista valley without hearing one story or another about the families that settled the area and continued to make money in oil, newspapers, or hotels.

"There's been a fire at the research lab." I had no idea what he was referring to, but arson was our specialty. Mostly because other firms stayed away, not wanting to wade through the ash and debris. Me, I enjoyed it. It reminded me of cleaning the pens as a kid. There was solemnity to it.

"You work with Pacific All-Risk, don't you?"

"Sure," I said. "I know Barton."

"Alan Hugo, the top man at Blakely, wants the best man on this case, so I floated your name. We'll contact Barton in the morning."

"Great," I said, happy to have a new case now that the mirage Palumbo had pitched was gone. Pacific All-Risk was a good firm and they paid quickly. "I can be in the office tomorrow."

"You're not getting this. We want you there now."

"I'd have to get the team together," I said.

"A routine case like this, I'd have thought you could handle it on your own."

"That's not how we operate."

"Let's keep this simple tonight, all right?" There was silence. "Given your service record, I thought you'd jump." Another pause. "If you don't want the job—"

"No, no," I said. "We can do it your way." I looked at Faith. She was in the kitchen, her back to me.

"That's good," he said. "I know you've got an application in with the department. If this works out, it could be just the thing to move your file forward to the hiring committee. It's a half-million-dollar policy. Sergeant Duff can pick you up."

I did the math. The higher the claim, the higher the investigation fee. Added to what Sanford had paid us, we could be back in the black by the end of July. "My office is at the Haven building, across the street from the San Moreno Inn. How about I meet him in the lobby in thirty minutes?" At that, Faith turned around.

MacDonald clicked off, which I took as a yes.

I knew he wasn't telling me the whole story. He dangled the lure of a nice payoff, but it didn't mean there wasn't a sharp hook lurking below.

Faith drove us back to the office in her Dodge Luxury Liner to pick up some gear. It was a round hulk of a car in pre-war rusting teal. The seats squeaked like an old spring mattress and rain dripped in above the visors. If we ever made any money, we'd get something new.

I gathered what I needed from my desk as she leaned against the wall. After getting soaked, she had changed into wide tan pants. Her hands were thrust deep in her blazer pockets, where I'd like to be. She was wearing men's clothes but she didn't look like a man.

I checked the cylinder of my Smith & Wesson, packed the .32 into a shoulder holster, and put back on my sport coat and hat. I'd told Faith about the fire and Pacific All-Risk at her place, but I had held back.

Looking at her now, I thought the picture was bright, so I decided to ease her into it. "Captain MacDonald said there could be a job, a regular job, if this goes well."

"Great," she said. "Why is the captain calling you? And why solo?"

"You heard me push back," I said. "Anyway, it's a good case."

"What am I supposed to do?"

"You can wait here or at your place. I'll find a reason to call you in."

"Jack, my name is on the door, but I always feel like I'm an afterthought. Why don't you be the Girl Friday for a change?" She turned away abruptly.

"What's going on?"

"Jack, take the job." She looked at her nails and scraped her left thumbnail against her index, wearing down a rough edge. "You want to stay here in San Moreno, work for the local PD, that's fine."

"It's for us," I said.

She turned back to face me. "No, it's not. I meant it when I said I can't be your Girl Friday." She looked back at the wall where the framed newspaper hung. Her front-page story.

"What am I supposed to tell my parents?" she asked.

"What?"

"It wasn't Paula and Patrick we were supposed to meet." The lines in her face were deep, like a mask. "I told you."

Her eyes were deep, black holes. I'd never seen her this angry.

"You've never even met my father. We were supposed to finally have dinner with my parents at the Top of the Mark."

"Faith, you can't spring this on me now."

"I never sprung anything. You're always so blasted and now you're getting up at 3:00 a.m. Half the time you don't know what's going on. Dad booked the train a month ago."

"You're talking stories."

"Jack, it's not me." She wiped under her eyes. "I see all the things you could be. A great detective, a brilliant musician, a wonderful father. But you're not living up to any of it. You're wasting your life." She took a deep breath. "I'm sorry about what happened to Jordan. I really am." She clasped her hands. "You've got to let it go."

Lots of people told me to do that. But I had yet to meet anyone who told me how. Jordan was a part of me. He always would be.

She looked up for a moment, bracing herself. Then she cast her gaze back to me. "I'm leaving Monday."

"Sure," I said. "Don't worry. I'll wrap up the case." I could be the peacemaker, if that's what it took. "And apologize to your folks for me."

"Jack, I'm leaving."

I stood motionless. I didn't breathe.

"Whatever this is," she said, spitting out the words, "a business, a romance, a rescue program . . . it's over. I'm taking a job in San Francisco. I'm going to fill in for a columnist at the *Chronicle*." She grabbed her purse. "There are things I want, and you don't even live in the same town as them. I'm sorry." She dabbed at her eye with the back of her hand. "I'm going home. If you need something, you can call me later."

She started to leave and then turned back. "I try to be everything for you, a cook, a maid, a lover. I can't do it anymore."

Her heels clacked on the tile as she walked out. I could still hear her footsteps echo in the stairwell after she shut the door.

When I lost Jordan, Faith was there and she saw me through. But now what did I have? I was one sorry sonofabitch. No wonder Faith walked out. I would have done the same in her shoes.

CHAPTER 6
Everybody Gets What They Deserve

I walked over to the wall and gazed at the framed *Loma Vista Record* with the 80-point headline: HERO SURVIVES TUNNEL EXPLOSION. It was dated April 20, 1945. The day I'd come out of the coma for good.

I never figured Faith for a quitter. Not after what we'd been through. And as long as she believed, then I was willing to go along, never looking too closely to see what was below the surface.

I reached my arm back and punched the glass, pulling my fist back at the point of impact so I wouldn't break my hand. The glass shattered and with it the illusion of everything I'd been working toward.

I never liked that news story. I wasn't a hero. I'd survived, but Jordan hadn't, and saving him was the whole reason I'd gone into the tunnels.

Faith was proud of the story. It was her first front-page scoop and it went national. She said it commemorated how we met. It helped us get the occasional client, but it was a lie. No one bothered to read past the second paragraph where Jordan was reduced to three lousy words: "missing in action," as if that explained anything.

Despite the promise I'd made Faith, I figured I could do whatever the hell I wanted, now that she'd bailed on me. I opened up my pack of Hermanos and pulled out a reefer. I glanced at my watch. I still had time before meeting the sergeant that Captain MacDonald was sending. I sat on the corner of my desk, pulled out my Zippo, and lit up for the second time that day. I held the smoke in deeply, the way Mick had taught me. The sweet smoke filled my lungs. It wasn't as good as a drink. It was better. It gave me a comfy cocoon in which to wrap myself and take my mind off what had just happened.

Mick had been the guy who first turned me on to this stuff. We'd been filling in a few times at Dynamite Jackson's on the Avenue in Los Angeles. We were one of many area jazz bands strutting our stuff on a weeknight hoping to break into a regular gig. Me, I never worried whether we'd make it or not. The band was just a lark, something to fill time after the day job. But for Mick and the younger guys, it was their only job and they wanted a shot at the big time.

After every set, I'd see Mick, Antoine, our trumpet player, and some of the others head out for a smoke. I didn't get it. Why go outside? But I followed Mick out one time and he let me in on it.

"You sure you want to try it?" he asked.

"What's it like?"

"You'll play like Fats Waller."

"Yeah, in your head," Antoine laughed. Then he took a big pull, held in the smoke, and started flapping his hands before letting it all out.

"I'm serious. It'll give you a groove," Mick said.

"Better take a couple of puffs then," Antoine said. He held out what looked like a hand-rolled cigarette, but it burned unevenly and crackled like a twig. "You need a *lotta* groove."

I was the old man in the band and they were always telling me to loosen up. Well, why not?

It put me in a groove all right. That old upright never sounded so good. It was like the keys were playing themselves and I was watching the whole thing go by. I could see the color of the notes and feel them as I was playing. It wasn't just the touch of the piano, it was something deeper. I saw the notes as light and shapes emanating from the bass, the guitar, the horns. The music was all laid out in front of me. Nothing bothered me that night. We kept the tempo, and whenever I took a solo, it wasn't that I was playing like Fats Wallers, I *was* him. I was Fats Waller, Hoagy Carmichael, and Champion Jack all rolled into one.

When the gig was over, I took the guys out for steak and eggs before Mick and I made the long drive back to Loma Vista. Then I asked him where I could get some more.

That was almost a year ago. The band drifted apart after a while. Antoine got a gig with a touring jive band that went up and down the coast. Mick was tired of the drive to LA and hooked up with Jerry, who wanted to create a new sound, one that dropped the horns and piano for electric guitar. "Jazz is dead, Jack. It's for old people." Yeah, people like me.

They let me play with them once in a while, but they thought I cramped their style and probably that was true. There was some stuff they got up to that didn't warrant having a detective around, private or not.

Mick was still a friend and he was the reason I got to play at the Legion Hall shows. And he was still my connection for Mary Jane. Since I'd burned through nearly the whole pack of Hermanos, I hoped he'd be there early at the San Moreno Inn.

But it wasn't just a groove that it gave me. It took all the noise and distraction away. I could concentrate for the first time in ages. I could look at a case, and connections would jump out at me. Cases became more of a game. Could I find my way through the maze? Hell yeah.

Most of all, it kept the nightmares away. At least I was so hopped up most nights, I forgot about them.

Forgetting was the main thing.

Ten minutes later, I was standing on the sidewalk in front of the Haven building as a light rain started and I listened to thunder in the distance. I looked up at the sky as I crossed Oak Street to the front of the San Moreno Inn. I felt the warm rain on my face and I took it as an absolution. There was still a world of possibility. Jordan was still out there and I would find him.

The red brick hotel had seen better days, but it was a regular spot for me. I liked the music and the dim lighting of the lobby bar. Inside, an eclectic crowd of up-and-comers, musicians, artists, beatniks, cheapskate business travelers, and the more liberal local working stiffs came to listen to music, argue, and dance. It made for an interesting mix.

Mick and Jerry's main band, the Del-Fi's, had a regular Friday evening gig and they were bringing in a younger crowd. Some of the older customers would head out as soon as the band started. But Harry, who owned the place, figured the younger kids drank three times what the regulars did, since they were on the dance floor working up a thirst, rather than nursing a twenty-cent draft all night.

The band played rockabilly and even though that wasn't my kind of music, it had an urgency. I was happy for Mick. They were writing their own songs and bringing energy to the place. When the band was cooking, you couldn't help feeling they'd found a new sound all their own. They gelled in a way that the Legion band never did.

I heard the neon buzz of the Eastside beer sign as I passed into the lobby and took off my hat. It was still early. A couple of out-of-town salesmen were leaving the bar, complaining about the Los Angeles Angels–Hollywood Stars game being called because of rain.

I scanned the room for Mick. He was easy to spot because he was the tallest person in the room. I saw him at the far end, scratching his beard as he horsed around with the equipment. It looked like the band had been called into service earlier than expected.

Loretta, an older blonde in rolled-up black jeans and navy Keds, was at her usual seat at the bar. She liked to dance. I never danced with her, but plenty did. No sign of Sergeant Duff. That was a break. I had time to get what I needed. I walked quickly to Mick and pulled out two bucks. "Sorry I can't stay for the show tonight." I passed him the folded bills.

"Plant you now, dig you later," Mick said.

"Thanks for bringing me on stage at the Legion. No trouble?" I asked.

"It's all good, man. The manager was helping unload a delivery in the back, so he didn't hear a thing."

"A lucky break."

Mick flicked his pink eyes to Manny at the bar and then hit the bass drum twice as a signal.

I followed Mick's gaze and walked over. Manny's head dove below the bar. Then he rose and started pouring a beer. Manny was a Mexican from Detroit. I'd arrested him for running three-card Monte near Eastern Market in '41 and he got a square deal because he was a juvie. I used to hang out at a bar he worked at after the war and when I dried out, we drove west together. As strange as it was for an ex-cop and a short con, we were both Detroiters, so we got along. He wasn't a kid anymore, but I tried to keep him straight, or at least less bent than he'd have been otherwise. I helped him get the bartender job. It turned out a little differently than I expected, like most things.

Manny's ping-pong eyeballs bounced between me and the beer, not always in sync.

I followed the script. "I left my cigarettes here yesterday." I laid my fedora on the bar.

Manny finished drawing the beer. He wiped the side of the glass with a red-and-white striped bar towel and slid it to the side. He looked below the bar and pulled up a cardboard box of bric-a-brac, the lost-and-found. "Turkish?" His eyes bounced again.

"No, Mex," I said.

Manny reached into the jumble of hairbrushes, a lighter, keys, and a Kafka paperback. His head popped up, followed by his eyes, then his hand with a pack of Hermanos, red. It was the best marijuana in town and would do fine by me. He slid the pack across the bar, concealing it under his hand. I glanced over my shoulder. Shifting my position to shield what I was doing, I swept the pack up and into my left pocket in one smooth motion. At the same moment, Manny snapped the bar towel with his left hand and released an innocent pack of Winstons from his right palm, dropping them silently onto the bar where the Hermanos had been a second earlier.

"No, not mine." I pushed off from the bar with the finger-tips of both hands.

"Okey-dokey." He removed the cardboard box, leaving the Winstons.

"Manny," I leaned in. "There's a bull on his way."

"Cheese and rice," he said.

"Don't worry, he's in the dark. I'll shove him off."

"You're A-1. Next bale is on the house."

"When do I get to stop looking out for you?" I grabbed my hat and stepped back into the crowd.

Mick and Jerry had a new bass player, Paul from Seattle. Instead of playing a double bass, he had an Audiovox bass guitar and a portable amplifier. He claimed it was going to change the music scene forever, but everyone else just figured it was so he could play louder.

Mick played a short fill and Paul hit a false start coming in too early. Jerry raised his hand to cut it off and then counted them in, tapping the rhythm on his electric guitar. It was a new song, an up-tempo blues number in a minor key. The crowd was thin and nobody was paying much attention yet. It wouldn't really get hopping until the second set. I stood halfway between the bar and the door.

They went once through the twelve-bar form with Jerry playing a nice bluesy intro on guitar. Then Mick hit the crash cymbal before bringing down his volume, and Jerry stepped to the mic. He was so thin it looked like he was holding on to the mic stand for support. But when he sang, his voice filled the place and it made for a haunting effect with the sparse arrangement. They didn't need the embellishment of a piano or horns for the kind of music they were creating.

There's a man down in the alley,
He's got a Colt 45
He's got a brother in Vegas,
Don't look like he'll survive
But there's one thing certain in this world,
Everyone gets what they deserve

Someone in the bar hooted in drunken approval and a few people clapped.

I had loosened up and I felt the pulse of the bass and drums washing through me. It was a great song. If I'd heard it on the radio, I would have waited for the deejay to name the singer.

Loretta was tapping her feet on the black-and-white checked floor. The bass player nodded to Mick, more relaxed now that they'd gotten going. Mick was in his own world, floating above all of it. Jerry maintained a distant look even as he peered straight through me. He looked almost happy, but that wasn't his style.

I saw the flashing red lights before I heard the car pull up, and it yanked me out of my musical daydream. When the car door slammed, Mick dropped a beat and I heard a bottle clank. I looked to Mick and gave a slow shake of my head. "Don't worry," I mouthed to him and signaled in a short, sharp hand chop.

A man in uniform barged in. He had the thick belly of a high-school football star gone to seed. And he limped. In five years, he'd be fat, and in five more, stooped and nearly bald.

Duffy put his hands on his hips and scanned the room like he was ready to collect from half the people in the place. If anyone saw him, they weren't making eye contact. I stepped toward him.

"Sergeant Duff," he said to me. He hitched his pants, leaned back, and looked around, his head bouncing softly to see if anyone dared look up. He loved the intimidation game. He reached out his hand, stubby fingers splayed. He had Popeye forearms and fists like pigs' knuckles. "Everyone calls me Duffy. You Waters?"

"Me Waters," I said. "Where Jane?" I pumped his arm and then cast my eyes down to the right. On his other hand, parked on his hip, his knuckles were white with scars.

"Funny guy, eh?" His chin rose. "Listen, peeper." His thumbs pulled at his belt again. "Just because the insurance muckety-mucks got you on the case, that don't mean nothin' to me."

"Look, Sergeant, I didn't mean anything by it." I looked down and reached into my right pocket, grabbing my deck of Luckies. "Smoke?"

I had two cigarettes out and flipped my Zippo open before Sarge could say *thank you*, not that it crossed his mind.

For a P.I., working with cops is an occupational hazard, so I had to keep him warm. You could work side by side for weeks, but when they went out for drinks, you were as welcome as a case of crabs. We got hired by the big insurance outfits so they could negotiate a quick settlement, rather than waiting months for some fire marshall's report.

I lit us both, and he eyed the inscription on my lighter:

Antwerp '44 - Köln '45 - Mittelwerk '45

"Army, is it?" he said.

"Yeah." I clanked the lighter shut and pocketed it.

I took a drag of the cigarette and the taste was smooth and warm.

We walked out the door. As I put my hat on, I heard Manny expel a sigh of relief. Mick let loose a chaotic two-bar drum fill as they went into the bridge.

Outside, in the cruiser, we rolled down the windows and smoked.

"I was at Okinawa," he said. "FUBAR from start to end."

"Tell me about it," I said.

"Bullets rained for eighty-two days." He turned briefly away, looking out the driver's window. "How you think I got this shrapnel in my leg?" He coughed. His eyes returned to mine. I didn't much care what he said. I recognized a phony story when I heard one. The glance away, to repack and shorten his story while trying to stay credible, the raised eyebrows asking, *Are you buying this?*, the left hand tapping on the dashboard, scurrying to the finish. And the telltale cough. Amateurs got nervous and choked on their lies.

I learned all this at the Detroit House of Corrections, or DeHoCo as we called it. In my first two years as a cop, I spent half my days escorting prisoners to the city's largest holding pen, a thousand-acre facility in the middle of nowhere. Lying is like breathing at DeHoCo, for cons, for screws, for lawyers, for prosecutors. I saw it all and I learned how to tell shit from Shinola and find the truth. It was all part of the game.

"My brother came home. He got a real good set-up," Duffy said.

I bit down on my cigarette.

"Nutralite. You know how much people spend on vitamins?" Duffy stretched his back 'til I heard cracking, then patted his belly. "I do pretty good, myself." He laughed and started the engine. "Don't foul this up and I'll do good by you, too, sport."

As we pulled away, the hotel door opened and Loretta came out, looking dejected. The music drifted into the street as the band finished the song and people were clapping and cheering. Maybe this would be the song that would finally get them a record contract.

"Everyone gets what they deserve," said Duffy. "Ha."

CHAPTER 7
Just Like Daddy-O

Loma Vista, California

We drove in silence down the Loma Vista county road. The rain was heavy, punctuated by the rhythm of windshield wipers flapping double time. Water was coming down the hills and pouring across sections of the road.

I turned on the radio and after it warmed up, Moonlight Sonata came on. It reminded me of how I used to fool around playing it on the piano. I had taken the first few bars, added some jazzy chords, and turned it into a torch song. Sometimes when a gig was slow, one of the guys would look over at me and say, "Moonlight, baby." That was my cue. They all thought it was Cole Porter, and I never corrected them.

Sometimes, Mick and Antoine would join in on the second verse. They gave it a light touch, with lot of space for the vocals.

Moonlight, baby
You're a part of me
Ain't nothing right
When you're away from me
I won't ever find

Any peace of mind
Until it's moonlight, baby

Of course, it was about Faith. I think she knew. Anything that had any beauty or meaning in the world for me was because of Faith. When I was in that coma, she saved me. It was the only way I knew how to thank her.

The car rutted on a pothole and jolted me back to the present. I glanced at my watch. It was coming up to nine. It was an easy case. I'd be done in two hours. We turned onto a bumpy single track that was marked by a granite milestone with a ceramic white sign, Blakely Estate. Palm trees on either side of the road swayed in the wind. After a few minutes, we came to a clearing with a wide circular drive.

It looked more like a rich kid's private school than a laboratory. A tall red-brick wall curved around the outside of the estate. A three-story stone tower stood in the center of two wings folded back slightly past 180 degrees to add an ersatz European look to the classic architecture of American money. A fence full of curved black iron decorated the three doors. A mill, a garden, and a tennis court stood to the left side.

"Get a load of this place, Waters." Duffy whistled. "Must have cost a fortune."

I raised my eyebrows but said nothing. The walls were chipped and crumbling, like a government project fallen on hard times. A birch sapling sprouted from the centerline of the tennis court. It was dark and well past working hours, but light shone from every window in both wings and the tower.

As he wheeled the car to the front, Duffy pulled a small notebook from his breast pocket and read off a list of who we needed to interview: Alan Hugo, the owner of Blakely Labs; his daughter, Beverley; a scientist named Schuler; Charlie Cordero, a local helper; and a houseguest named Asheton. Everyone else had left for the weekend.

Duffy slammed the car into park but kept the engine running. He stared at me, then pursed his lips into a tight, toothless grimace. It was a nasty sight, with a hint of violence and something worse.

"Oh yeah," he said, "and in addition to the fire, we got a body in the lab." Duffy slammed his arm in front of my chest and pushed open my door. I tumbled from the car.

Duffy gunned the engine and steered the car to the back, spraying mud. He opened his door as he rounded the corner and called back, "Meet me inside."

Rain was falling, cool and heavier than before. My feet sank into mud and I felt a chill. For an instant, I was reminded of being back in Germany on night maneuvers, but now I was on my own.

I walked up a half-dozen slate stairs to the door and rang the bell. A shadow appeared through the glass and the door opened. The woman standing there was young and looked like she was dressed for a party. Her curly black hair had been swept up into a poodle, but it was tumbling out and into her eyes.

She opened the door, looked me up and down, and said, "Well, if it isn't the fuzz." She said the word fuzz with a few extra Z's and the effect was like Lana Turner blowing a kiss. Her mouth was wide, her lips painted dark red. She tipped me for a moment, but I willed myself back to business.

I took off my hat, gave my name, and said I was with Pacific All-Risk, to investigate the accident.

"All the same to me," she said, only she slurred her words, so *same* sounded like *shame*, which was how it seemed to me.

I stepped inside, and she brushed against me to shut the door. She was warm. There was a smell of perfume, cigarettes, and juniper. Any two of these would have worked, but with all three, it went from alluring to annoying, a party that had gone on too long.

In the light of the hall, I could see now that she was young. Frizzy blue-black hair, a pale face. Her mascara was smudged. Her eyes were hooded, deep blue and clouded. Whatever was going on here, she was in over her head.

I asked her name. Her lashes fluttered and she looked down. "Beverley," she said. For a moment, there was a seductive smile. But then it carried on to a lopsided grin. She looked up. "I'm Beverley Hugo, heir to this broken-down palace." She swept her left arm in a stiff, rehearsed move.

She reached for the martini glass she'd left on the side table near the door, missing it by an inch. She looked over to see if I had spotted the lapse. I looked straight at her. She was a kid, maybe nineteen or twenty. She had the makeup and was playing the part, but she was only a few years past dress-up. She plunked herself with a thud into a heavy brown leather chair. I waited for an invitation, but then, none forthcoming, I sat, too.

I knew where she was at. I'd been there myself for a long time, so I didn't have a lot of patience for drunks. They either found the right path or they didn't.

"What do you do when you're sober, Miss Hugo?" I asked.

"I get up to lots of things, sober or otherwise." Her right index finger caressed the stem of her glass.

"Such as?"

She squinted and paused as her eyes looked left. She pulled her lips in the same direction, tilting her head. "Expelled from Miskatonic," she said.

Guilt was a door you could open. I let her stew for a moment.

She tried another angle. "That was a while ago. They let me back in." She broke into a smile and her eyebrows danced. "I'm studying physics, just like daddy-o," she sang it like a bebop scat. She was tight all right.

She was just another misfit from Miskatonic University, the East Coast dumping ground for the troubled offspring of the rich. There was always something off about Miskatonic. It was an old college in a remote town, too inbred for my liking. It surprised me to hear they had a physics department. If there was a school that still had a program in alchemy, I'd put my money on Miskatonic.

"Home for the summer?" I asked.

"I'm doing research for Dr. Panks, in our lab." She jerked her thumb vaguely behind her. "Mostly recording results and cleaning up. Nothing exciting." She paused, working out some gin-soaked idea. "Maybe now with Schuler's big discovery . . . " She tilted her head for a moment and a new thought took hold. "You should have heard what Schuler called Panks." She pointed her index finger in exaggerated fashion and she imitated a vaguely European accent. "'You're a Bolsh . . . a Brooks Brothers Bolshevik.'" She laughed. "What does that even mean?"

I wasn't playing ball. "And your mother, is she also a scientist?"

She nodded and looked down. "Mother's away, but I'll tell her you asked about her."

I let that one pass.

"Okay, so what happened tonight?"

She sat upright, angry and clear-headed. "You ask me, what happened to that b—"

The French doors behind her exploded open and a man stepped in, followed by Duffy. "Enough of that, young lady."

The man had a Van Dyke beard and wore a double-breasted, heavyweight gray suit. His hair was swept back. The burgundy-and-black striped wool tie of the Tomb, the top alumni club at Miskatonic, hung around his neck. Word was you had to be on your way to a Nobel Prize or a million-dollar business to be punched by Tomb. From the press reports I'd seen, Alan Hugo might score on both counts. He had a dark wooden cane with a sculpted silver grip in his right hand. It was the winged head of Mercury, the Roman god of travelers and guide to the underworld.

"I'm not interrupting something . . . am I?" Hugo asked. His mouth was a zig-zag: half-sneer for me, half-apology about his daughter. His eyes were as dark as ink pots. And he was short.

Hugo leaned forward on his toes and flicked his head at Duffy. The cop stepped front and center.

"Yeah, what's going on, Waters?" Duffy's fists were clenched at his sides. "I told you, no interviews unless I'm here."

"Gentlemen," said Hugo. He pivoted back through the French doors, beckoning us to follow him.

I had taken Duffy for a lout on the make. That wouldn't have been a problem as long as he didn't foul the insurance investigation. But now I was getting a different picture.

CHAPTER 8
A Great Deal of Genius

We were a little parade, led by a little man, marching down a big hallway. We emerged through another glass door into Hugo's office.

It was an average-size office for a head of state. There were two life-size marble statues at kitty-corners to the desk, one of a young man on knee, the other of a maiden peering into an orb. A large oil painting of a woman sitting beside a window was on the wall behind the desk. She looked like Beverley, but the simple white gown and long ringlet curls suggested the 1920s.

Out the window, I could see a few lights illuminating the lab and what looked like barracks in the distance.

The room was wallpapered in pictures of Alan Hugo. Hugo with Wall Street bankers in their spectator shoes, Hugo with local politicians grinning and holding checks, Hugo with Jane Wyman and that squinty-eyed B-list actor she married.

But one picture caught my eye. It was Hugo with FDR, framed side by side with a letter from the Sphinx himself. It was an unusual shot for two reasons. First, FDR is standing, which was difficult because of his polio. Second, Hugo is on the left, chin jutted and with a facade of a smile, shaking the older man's hand, as if he had deigned to grant the president an audience.

Hugo scraped his chair to get my attention and then sat behind the Queen Mary of oak desks. There was a brass lamp, a black candlestick telephone, and papers spread across the top. Duffy and I perched on small black leather wing chairs on each side.

Hugo ran his hand through his hair, pushing it back in place. "Who are you exactly?" he asked.

"Jack Waters, insurance investigator."

He gave me a look of contempt that could scare the paint off a wall. "I don't know how much of this you'll understand, not being a scientist. We're working on an important fusion project here and this work must continue. So I want you to settle whatever needs settling quickly."

Duffy turned in his seat toward me to add 40 watts of glare.

"Of course, Mr. Hugo," I said. Duffy resumed breathing. "Pacific All-Risk will settle, whatever needs settling, when I've finished my report. And my report will be settled, when I've had a chance to look around and all questions have been answered to my satisfaction." I could see Duffy's temple throbbing at 110 beats per minute, but he stayed silent.

"Such as?" said Hugo.

"Sergeant Duffy has given me the basics. And I'll be examining the lab shortly," I said, "but why don't you tell me what you think happened."

"What I *think*?" Hugo asked, his voice rising. "What I *know* is we've had an industrial accident. We have a lot of high-voltage equipment. Edison's lab caught fire all the time. Now, what is it that you want . . . to know?"

I pulled out my field notebook and pencil and wrote, *Edison, lab fire*, just to show I was playing along.

"What kind of work do you do at the lab? You have any chemicals or solvents stored there?"

He gave me a look, like I was the dumbest freshman on campus.

"This isn't some junior chem lab project. I'll have you know that I ran the most advanced fusion lab in the world at Los Alamos."

"So this is some sort of energy project?" I asked.

He lit up at that. Every bore loves a dummy in need of education.

"The work we do here is vital to several top government agencies. It builds on more than a decade of research that I've led. Calling it an energy project is like calling the Hoover Dam a roadside tourist attraction. My research will completely revolutionize everything we know about thermodynamics. We've developed a new form of a high-energy dissonance wave that can transmit and store power that was previously inconceivable. Imagine, the power of the Hoover Dam at any school, hospital, or manufacturing plant, costing pennies to operate. Think how that will transform society. One day, we'll be able to do things in science, medicine, and industry that have been completely impossible."

"What do you mean by 'one day?' Does it work or doesn't it?"

"Mr. Waters, it took forty years from Einstein's first paper on his special theory of relativity until scientists were able to harness atomic power in a meaningful way. He was a great scientist in his day, but what we're doing here is far more important." He looked toward the fireplace. "Every day we're getting closer. A new technology like this takes time." He turned back to me. "It takes time, money, and a great deal of ingenuity to do what we are doing."

"And modesty," I said.

Duffy shot me a dirty look.

"The people I work with, the senators and businessmen who have backed this project, they know me and what I'm capable of. So, when there's . . . uh . . . *a setback,* like we've had tonight . . . " He swallowed and looked down at the desk. "It's a sad fact of life that there can be accidents like this. But our work here is too important to let that slow us down. And that's not what Panks would have wanted anyway. Our greatest progress has come at times of great difficulty and this will be no different. I remember early in my research when I saw what Livingston was doing with his cyclotron at Cornell. I thought, there's got to be a better future than wielding two-ton magnets, and it would be up to me to invent it . . . "

Hugo continued with the college lecture filled with entropy, neutrons, and plasma, along with new terms—reverse field pinch, portal—all the product of something called a Tillinghast resonator. He threw in the occasional English word for dramatic effect. I was doing my best to stay alert. Duffy had given up completely, closing his eyes for a brief siesta.

"This is a new type of energy and we are only just beginning to understand it's vast possibilities. There's no limit to what we can do, but we have to be discreet about it. That's what I learned in the war from the Counter Intelligence Corps. It's a bet on the future."

He leaned forward, sharing a secret. "The physicists at Berkeley and Cornell get all the funding they want from the army. After all, they're working on improvements to existing designs, producing better A-bombs. But some of those professors were members of the party, back when communism was considered merely an academic eccentricity, like wearing patched corduroy jackets.

"With the work I did during the war, I earned the respect of men now in top roles in military and government agencies.

They know they can trust me. These days, that's every bit as important as the technology."

I learned a lot, though not what Hugo intended. This guy, now slouching back in his big chair, thought he was untouchable. But for all his talk and dreams, the project was stuck. When I tried to nail Hugo on the results of his work, he got deeper into scientific riddles.

"The thing you have to realize, the power of what we are doing, is that it's based on a fundamental break in the evolution of theoretical physics." His face was an intense knot of concentration. He was like a cult leader sermonizing in a radio studio, cranked on his own power. "This is a massive leap forward, leveraging discoveries in non-Euclidean geometry that enable us to transform matter into energy and back again in a way that is far more powerful and more stable than nuclear fission.

"Given the experimental nature of our work, I'm sure you can appreciate that I'm not at liberty to say more. But rest assured, the applications will be endless. We will create high-speed, fuel-efficient transportation. New cities will emerge. It could be used to desalinate oceans and turn the Sahara Desert into farmland. Fusion begets a new science that will change all of society." He had a look of exhausted satisfaction on his face. I thought he was going to roll over and light a cigarette.

F. begets the new sci. That, too, went into the notebook, underlined.

"But now you need a new scientist," I said.

"Waters, you don't talk to Dr. Hugo that way."

"Duffy," said Hugo. Again, a flick of his head. "Would you mind?"

Duffy stood up quietly and slipped out the French doors behind Hugo's desk.

"Listen, Waters, I graduated *summa cum laude* from Miskatonic at nineteen." He looked above my head at the bookshelves. "I was lecturing at Oxford a year later. And I was in the war, too, dictating terms to generals on both sides. I know your type, ex-GI. So, let me be clear: get on with it."

"Half-mill is it?" I said.

"What?" He sat up straight up now.

"Your policy with Pacific All-Risk. Half-million face value. I don't know how much of this you'll understand, being a scientist, but here's how insurance works. I'm conducting an independent investigation, and I do it on my own terms. I'm not subject to your or anyone else's orders."

Hugo sputtered, but no words came out of his mouth.

"Look, Mr. Hugo, I've got a job to do. The sooner I get it done, the sooner I'll be out of your way."

Hugo pushed his hair back again and grunted.

"There was a death in the lab, is that right?"

He spoke slowly, his posture rigid and his face tense, his anger still visible. "Kurt Panks." He took in a deep breath. "The man was a genius. He would have accomplished more than Einstein and Oppenheimer combined. That was clear in the '30s. It's a terrible loss."

"You have other scientists here."

"Sure, but . . . Panks had a rare talent, not just in physics but in other fields. We used to say he made the electrons sing." He heaved a sigh. "But like an orchestra that loses a great vio-linist, there's always a second string ready to move up. I will get him there, same as I did with Panks. I'm the conductor and it's my job to coax, scold, and wring it out of all of them." His face beamed as he brought the subject back around to himself.

"And your two maestros . . . what were they arguing about today?"

"Aren't you getting this? It's about the science. It's *all* about the science."

I looked at the painting. "Your wife's a scientist. Where's she in all of this?"

A cruel gaze crept over his face "Mr. Waters, I'm afraid your investigation must be running behind." His faced turned dark. "My wife has been dead for eleven years." He leaned back in his chair and glared at me like it was my doing.

I felt like a fool. I would have fired a rookie who made a mistake like that. What was it about this place that was throwing me off? I flipped through my notes as if that would get me past it.

"I'm sorry. I-I misunderstood something your daughter told me."

"Beverley has a dark sense of humor."

"And how long did Dr. Panks work here?"

"I set up Blakely Labs three years ago. We were founding partners, Panks, Schuler, and I. We worked together at Los Alamos. You could call this a spin out.

"There's an expediency we have as a private lab, operating outside of the charter and regulations of a government agency. We have an informal agreement to share our work with certain groups. And that creates a buffer, if you will."

"In case something goes wrong?" I asked.

"It's standard practice. Over time, I could see that more than government financing was needed. I had the contacts, so I took the lead on that. Panks ran the scientific side of things."

No mention of Schuler.

"What went on between Panks and Beverley?" I asked.

He bit on that. "My daughter's been through quite enough already. There's no need for her to be part of this." He thumped his walking stick twice on the ground and Duffy reappeared.

"I'm sorry, Mr. Hugo. I have a couple of more questions," I said. I waited but there was only silence. "Where were you this evening, after dinner?"

"I met this fellow, Asheton, a reporter for the *London Times*."

"A splash in the international press might help with the current round of funding. Is that it?"

"I hadn't considered it," said Hugo. "We were here in the office when the lights went out, and we heard an explosion."

"He was here with you?" I asked.

"Do try to keep up."

"And then?"

"He ran to the lab, even though I'd told him it was off limits. We all got there momentarily. There was smoke and some flames, but Panks . . . " He shrugged. "It was too late."

"And this reporter," I looked at my notebook, "Asheton, can vouch for you?"

"Of course." He snatched his walking stick and stood. "Duffy, show him."

Then he turned to me. "When you're done with your little tour, you write up your accident report, Waters." He was back onto his toes, leaning forward. "And if it's done properly, there'll be something in it for you, too. From what I understand, you and that partner of yours could use the money."

I was burning inside, but I kept my smile on tight to prevent my feelings from seething out. I smiled like the chump Hugo thought I was. I'd seen guys like him before: polished, in charge, and ready to take what they wanted. So I knew how to deal with him. In life, you either get pushed around or you push back. This guy, who thought he was so clever, so superior in his club tie, was hiding something. I was going to find it.

I nodded, pretending to be grateful for his concern for my financial health. "Sure, Mr. Hugo," I said. "I left the claim forms for you to sign at my office. I'll have my partner run them over. All right if I use your telephone?"

Hugo gestured to the desk, and he and Duffy strode off. I picked up the old candlestick telephone and dialed the five digits to her place, CHapel-207. Faith answered on the first ring.

"Hey, sweetheart, it's time to come in," I said, trying to sound positive.

She hesitated. "What's the situation?"

I spoke quietly and held the mouthpiece close. I could imagine Faith, her face bright, leaning forward, wanting to learn more. She loved her work, that's what made her so good at it. "Fire, dead body." I glanced over my shoulder and cupped my hand closer to the mouthpiece, as if I were whispering directly into her ear. "Probably arson gone wrong. Bunch of Los Alamos scientists running out of money and excuses."

"Los Alamos, my, my. Collect any good props?" she asked.

"We're on a short leash. Duffy is about to lead me around. There was an explosion, probably gas."

"What exactly are they working on at this lab?"

"Some kind of energy project, fusion. Guy's smarter than Einstein."

"Really."

"You know how I know that? He told me himself."

"You're not falling for that."

I could picture her smiling, leaning forward, eager to dive in.

"Jack, you're over-thinking. It's a paper mill. A bunch of investors ponied up and he staged a fire as an excuse to close down and take the money. The insurance payoff is his bonus for a con well done. You could close this case in your sleep."

"Maybe," I said. "But something's not right, even for a grift."

"Hey, wanna buy my car? It's pre-war, but runs on rocket fuel. Zero to sixty in four-point-oh."

Faith was always a step ahead. I guess God has a sense of humor about these things. If we worked side by side on the case, maybe I could turn things around. That was how I got Faith into my life. Now I needed to get her back.

"Okay, you're the brains of this operation." I drummed my fingers on the receiver. "That's why I need you. Four-point-oh. I'd like to see that. Look, bring the folder with those two-oh-nine forms. That's your cover."

"Don't worry. I'll be in top form, darling. I'll be there before you've bagged the last oily rag." She paused. "Remember, Jack . . . "

I held my breath.

"After this, I'm done."

CHAPTER 9
Visitor from the Past

Duffy was waiting in the hall.

"Let's go," he grunted. He walked ahead and punched open the back door.

Outside, a sign pointed right to Blakely Lab and another sign pointed ahead to staff quarters. A hundred yards to the right, down a flagstone pathway, a young patrolman in a black slicker stood outside the lab. He gave Duffy a sharp salute as we walked by. Duffy didn't even nod.

We entered the lab wing. The ceilings were twelve feet tall, the corridors wide and white. Buzzing fluorescent lights overhead made everything look green. We walked down the tiled hall past a black sign with white block letters that read "Machine Room."

It looked like a car had crashed into a museum. Two back windows were blown out. Clear glass fragments were scattered on the floor, along with a smashed porcelain sink, broken tubes, ash, and burnt paper. The sharp, bitter smell of an electrical fire and the stench of burnt flesh and hair filled the air.

A seven-foot steel rack of machinery in the center dominated the room. Ropes of red, black, and yellow wires flowed across it into a miniature skyline of broken glass tubes and candy-colored resistors. On the left, a wide console stood with a dozen black numbered dials, several round glass oscilloscopes, and half a dozen large black switches.

Maybe it was the fumes, but I had a screamer of a headache. There was a flash of blinding white light and I closed my eyes for a second and jerked my head back as if to break free. When I opened them again, Duffy was staring at me. I coughed into my hand as if everything was fine.

A sturdy dark brown wooden chair with its own set of controls sat a few feet from the console, connected by another rope of wire. Panks's body lay face down on the floor in front of it.

"There's the DB," Duffy said, nodding toward Panks.

My head pounded. I grabbed my Zippo, lit two Luckies, and handed one to Duffy. If you worked fatalities, you knew the drill when there was a dead body. Cigarette smoke would keep you from retching from the smell.

I bent down to get a closer look, flicking cigarette ash on the floor. Flies were already buzzing around and I swatted them away. I took a deep breath of tobacco, but still the odors of charred meat, burnt sugar, and alcohol filled my nostrils. There were burns to the back of his lab coat, including a large round hole in the left shoulder blade that revealed red and black charred skin. The black marks continued in a spiral pattern down his left pant leg. The left shoe was on the floor, charred and smoldering. The right leg was relatively clean. Right shoe, in place and intact, brown oxford lace-up.

His hands were blackened and his left fingers twisted. The top two segments of the ring finger of his right hand were gone. He'd been fried to a crisp. I'd never seen a lightning victim, but I'd heard tell of the injuries and this lined up. Electrocution.

After what I'd seen in the war, not much shocked me anymore. My head was throbbing nine bells, and I felt faint, but there was work to be done. I looked across to Duffy. "Okay if I turn him sunny-side up?"

"Your show," he said, expelling a cloud of cigarette smoke. Despite his bluster, Duffy stepped back a pace. Nobody likes this part.

I positioned my right knee next to his hips, my left foot at his shoulder. I sucked in the cigarette smoke as I slipped one hand under the shoulder and the other under his waist and levered myself at the knee to flip him.

As he rolled, I could see the body was wearing thick amber goggles with a broad leather band, like a pilot's headgear. The straps were brittle and the goggles slid off, falling to the ground as the head lolled toward me.

I felt as if the floor opened up and I was falling down a deep well. I looked up and the ceiling tiles were starting to spin. I knew I was in trouble. The cig dropped from my mouth, the lit end bouncing off my right hand. I stood up and grabbed hold of the chair to steady myself. Then I walked as straight as I could manage out the back door and into the rain.

I should have killed him when I had the chance. It wasn't Panks. There was no Panks.

It was *Herr Doktor* Panzinger from Mittelwerk.

CHAPTER 10
A Promise Made

I kept my head down as I lurched past the patrolman and turned right to go farther down the pathway. At the far corner, an archway with a light sat above another door. I headed toward it. I had to maintain my cool.

My footsteps made soft sounds on the flagstones but they felt like someone else's. I clenched my fists. I was outside, but Panzinger still haunted me. He'd ruined my career and destroyed my life. Worse, he'd taken away Jordan. I felt the bitter taste of bile rise up in me. I took a deep breath to calm myself—I couldn't think about that now—but I still wanted to scream.

I had a few minutes before Duffy would try to find me. To him, I was just another puking rookie. I had to pull myself together.

When I reached the archway, I turned back to check on the young policeman. His eyes were facing front. I reached up and unscrewed the lightbulb, my hands trembling. Then I grabbed the Hermanos out of my inner pocket, pulled out a stick, lit it, and inhaled. I coughed but I held it in.

It was working. After a minute, I felt calmer. I needed dope to cope. I laughed at that.

It started out, I'd smoke a little grass when I played with the band. I liked the effect it had. It put you right inside the music. You could feel the chords ripple right through your hands. I became a more daring player, making chord inversions and scale changes that I wouldn't have thought of otherwise. It turned on a different part of my brain, letting me make different connections. I liked the feeling. A lot.

Then it got to the point that I'd smoke half a joint when I shaved in the morning. Sometimes, I wouldn't bother shaving, but I'd still burn half a stick. After a while, I noticed I was going through a pack a week. I wasn't smoking to get high. I was smoking to feel normal.

I was caught up in my own thoughts, so I didn't register the sniffing sound. Then I heard a familiar voice to my right.

"You seen the lab? It's bad. No wonder you're smoking that." It was Beverley. She was sitting on a ledge under the eaves of the garage across the pathway, smoking. She stood up and flicked her cigarette to the ground. She walked over slowly and then looked me in the eye. "You wanna share?"

I was starting to float but I wasn't stupid. I touched my right hand to the damp brim of my hat and extinguished the roach between my thumb and index. I stashed the roach back into the packet and put the packet back in my inner pocket.

"What do you want?" I asked.

"You saw him," she said. "What a way to go. Burned alive on his own invention."

"Yeah."

"He was brilliant. And so driven. Nothing was going to get in the way of his work—not me, not anyone," she said. "We were just pieces of the machinery for Panks. I hated him for that."

She sat back down on a step and looked at the ground.

"And we were so close." She raised her left hand, her finger and thumb separated by a slim gap. "He was getting ready to test a new fusion reaction, to see if it would be enough to break through."

"Fusion begets the new science," I said.

I instinctively ducked before I knew what had happened. She'd thrown a stone that whizzed by my head. She didn't connect, but it was hard to say if it was a matter of intent or aim.

"You're as phony as a three-dollar bill." Her mouth was clenched in a sneer. "The cool-headed detective, pissing on everyone. But look at you. You're nothing."

I straightened. At tough-guy school, one thing I learned was that I shouldn't argue with her. I just had to take it. And she was right. I was nothing and I had no one. That hurt more than anything.

"I suppose you think it's funny, all these big ideas my father has. I was supposed to be next." She lit another cigarette. "Did you know Panks?"

"Oh, I knew him," I said in a rasp, catching my breath. "That was a long time ago." I knew him and I hated him for what had happened in the tunnels.

I thought I saw a movement to my left. Someone in the shadows. But as I turned to look, whatever it was disappeared. My mind was playing tricks on me. I had to focus.

Beverley had been right the first time. Panzinger was a bastard. I never forgave myself for trusting him. I was left with nothing for my end of the deal. I never saw or heard of him again until now. I had assumed he'd been arrested by the Americans or shot by the Russians, another casualty of war.

" . . . and then the explosion." Beverley's hands were raised to eye level.

"Explosion?" I hadn't been listening. "How do you know about the tunnel?"

"What tunnel?" Her face was ashen. Her eyes narrowed. "I was telling you how my mother died. That's the reason I got drunk. All I ever wanted was to be like her."

I had missed something. It gave me an uneasy feeling, like time had jumped a few bars ahead. So I played along, hoping to catch up.

"It was just like tonight," she continued. "A storm, an explosion. Charlie and I ran to the lab, but we were too late.

"I still see her and talk to her," Beverley said. A crow cawed and she turned to watch it fly overhead. "In the weeks before she died, Mother sang me a nursery rhyme, counting crows. Do you know it?"

She recited it softly, almost a hymn.

"One for sorrow,
Two for mirth,
Three for death,
Four for birth,
Five for waters,
Six for thee,
Seven for my mother who watches over me."

She stood up.

"Does that mean anything to you?"

I shook my head. It didn't sound right to me. "Never heard that one."

"She promised I'd be protected."

I had made a promise, too. Dead or alive, Panzinger would lead me back to my brother.

I knew what I had to do. I took a deep breath and tried to steady my mind before I went back inside.

Banging open the door with the palm of my hand, I walked straight past Duffy, who was leaning against the wall. He had an uneasy look, like he'd lost a bet. "Shall I dig in?"

He shrugged. "Sure."

"Gimme a smoke."

He fished one out of a pack of Camels and, with a match, lit it and passed it to me.

I puffed and crouched next to the body.

I started by patting the outer pockets of the lab coat and running my fingertips along the seams. Nothing.

Now it got squishy. I took another puff with my left hand as I fished my right hand inside the shoes, the pants pockets, the center joint. The inner left pocket yielded scraps of paper. I stood and examined the haul. Half a C-note, leaving only the right side of Franklin's face, and two train tickets for the 12:15 tonight to Los Angeles, with connections to El Fronterizo, the sleeper to Mexico City. Passenger names blank.

I handed the find to Duffy and got back down to my knees. I wasn't done with Panzinger yet. I needed to know for certain.

I ripped open the shirt. Duffy's mouth popped open, too. Yanking the fabric away from Panzinger's left shoulder, I saw what I had expected—a German calligraphy-style tattoo on the tricep, halfway to the elbow. It read "AB." Panzinger's blood type. SS members were routinely tattooed in this way to speed blood transfusions in battle. But above the letters was something else. The blue ink was faded and smudged but still visible. A twelve-spoked wheel of SS lightning bolts stemming from a black circle. Below the wheel was a scroll of text, but I could only make out part of it: "*aller Zeiten*." Forever.

The Nazis had a tattoo for everyone, but what this meant, I didn't know.

I stood up, brushing off my trousers. "Why don't you tell me what's going on, Sarge?"

"Think I know?" Duffy had the passive look of someone used to being at the bottom of the chain of command.

"Look, why didn't you say the duck was German?"

"I never talked to him," Duffy said. "He's dead, remember? Besides, he's an American now."

"What?"

"All these guys are Americans," he said. "War's over, sport, didn't you hear?"

"What are they doing here?"

"Hey, apart from football, I slept through high school. What the lab is working on doesn't concern you or me. You seen the body now, so write up the accident."

"There been any other accidents?" I asked.

"I told you, write it up."

I held up my palms. "Just for background."

"There was two college boys here from CalTech. They filed a complaint about safety. 'Unsafe handling of special materials' was what they wrote."

"Jesus," I said. "What were they talking about?"

"There's some questions you don't ask," he said. "Almost went federal, but the old man sugared them off." He held up his right hand in a fist and circled the air. "I was the other side of the equation, just in case. They whistle-geared outta here before anyone could wind their watches."

"I need to know what's going on."

"Waters, the captain told me about your file. Never you mind what he says about a hiring committee." He thumped his chest. "*I'm* the committee. I make the rules."

"Look, Duffy—"

"It's a good job in a good town. So I got two questions. First, you were a cop, right?"

"Yeah, before the war," I said.

"Good," he nodded. "Second, you know how to keep your mouth shut?"

I nodded. Sure, I could keep quiet. But it wasn't my strong suit.

CHAPTER 11
A Blinking Rat

I heard a muffled howl. Duffy cocked his head. The sound sang out, a low throbbing tone spiraling higher, more animal than human.

Duffy unholstered his revolver. He turned to me and jerked his head. I pulled out my .32 lemon squeezer, and we crept toward the sound.

We proceeded silently around a corner and down a narrower hallway until we were just outside the barracks. We stopped in front of the dining hall door, where the sound seemed to originate. The place was shut down. It smelled of cold greasy food. There was only a dim light coming through the round glass window in the door. I could make out the silhouette of a man sitting at a broad table, twenty-five feet away, with his back to us.

The moan went on, cutting into me. It called me back to the war, to the prisoners at Mittelbau-Dora.

Duffy nodded for me to go right. Then he signaled the count on the fingers of his left hand: three . . . two . . . one. He slammed his shoulder against the door to open it and bolted left. I moved hard right. We both aimed at the seated figure, his head buried in his hands, slumped over the table.

"Up, up, police!" Duffy shouted.

The man turned slowly and looked at us. His head weaved. He squinted. His face was wet, his mouth a crevice of pain. "You are not here to shoot me, I think?"

We held our weapons. He reached for his glasses.

"Professor, what are you doing here?" Duffy holstered his revolver and strode forward, then put his beefy arm around the man's shoulder. "I told you to stay with the others in the house."

"I-I had to be alone," the man squeaked like a teenager.

I holstered my piece but kept my distance, staying by the door.

"Like I told you before," Duffy said, "we gotta ax you some questions."

"That is okay." He squinted. "And who are you?" I could barely hear his whisper.

"I'm with Pacific All-Risk, the insurance company," I said from my position across the room.

"That is good, *ja*," he said. "My name is Dietrich Schuler." He walked toward me and held out his right hand.

I felt a wave of nausea. He wasn't twenty anymore, but he retained a lean, boyish face, like a young Valentino. I wanted to get out, but I shook his hand and watched for any sign that he recognized me. This changed everything. I stepped back a pace and let Duffy take the lead.

"So, tell us, professor, where were you when this thing happened with the fire and all?" Duffy asked.

Schuler blinked in surprise. "I was in my room, all evening," he said looking from me to Duffy and then back again. "Until I heard the explosion. Then I ran to the lab, with the others."

"Can anyone vouch for you?"

"Naturally. Charlie was there. He was in the barracks all night. Reading his Bible, as is usual."

I jumped in. "How long did you know Kurt Panks?"

"I worked with Kurt—Dr. Panks, I mean—a long time." He paused. His face stiffened. "We met at Los Alamos, years ago. He was a brilliant scientist. It makes no sense what happened."

"You met at Los Alamos?" I couldn't believe Duffy was buying this pack of lies.

"Of course, my accent. I came here at the end of the war," said Schuler. "I am American now, but I am originally Swiss."

"Oh yeah? And how did you know about Panks's research?" As soon as the words left my mouth, I regretted it.

"Fusion is my field of study," Schuler said. I could see he was appraising me. "Kurt published all his work in the journals. He was quite renowned."

"Look, the professor is okay." Duffy said to me. He turned his attention back to Schuler. "Do you think maybe it was the storm, the lightning that set off the explosion?"

Schuler looked up at the ceiling and then at me and then back up at the ceiling. His eyes narrowed. He scratched at his brow. He was working out the mathematics.

"No," he said. "There is a circuit breaker. It is extremely unlikely. Besides, the storm had not . . . " He searched for words. "The lightning, it was later."

"What do you think happened to Dr. Panks, professor?" Duffy asked.

"It makes no sense." Schuler shrugged. "He knew every circuit and every switch, the way a great musician knows his instrument. It is impossible for the Z-machine to blow up like that."

"So, it's not likely Panks made a mistake, is that it?" Duffy said.

"Correct."

"Who has access to the lab after hours?" I asked.

"It is an open facility for the research staff."

"And what's a Z-machine?"

"That is the project here," he said. "I leave it to Dr. Hugo to explain so all is clear." He barely acknowledged the *e* in the last word, so it sounded more like *klar*.

He was holding back, so I pushed harder. "What was your fight about today?" I asked.

"Fight?" His pitch rose. He glared at me.

"You and Panks."

"We were like brothers. We do not fight."

"Any ladies?"

"Kurt was a handsome man," he said. "Many women liked him."

"And what about him?"

"The Z-machine is the love of our lives." He shook his head. "No women."

"What about Beverley?"

"She's just a girl," he said.

"But there was something?"

"She had illusions." He sniffed. "It is dangerous to believe in illusions."

I flipped through my notes. "Wasn't she studying physics at—"

"That young lady is but trouble," Schuler interrupted. "She couldn't reach to Kurt's level. Or any of us in the lab. She has Mr. Hugo wrapped around her fingers, but her charms did not work with Dr. Panks."

"Look, *Frau* Dietrich," I slipped my jacket open with my right hand, flashing my holster, "what was the disagreement you two had?"

Duffy's mouth froze into a flat line.

Schuler blinked twice and then a thin smile appeared. He'd made me. "It was nothing."

"Sing," I said.

He glanced to Duffy, but got nothing. "Good," he said. "I had a new design."

"What design?"

"The Z-machine," he said. "The fusion reaction always ran too hot to be effective. I had a new way to do this, fanning out dozens of smaller resonators in parallel."

"Yeah, so?"

"This is the breakthrough Kurt needed since the '30s. We were to begin new experiments immediately."

"And Panks was impressed?"

"He was the boss, so it was as much his work as mine own." His shoulders collapsed like a circus tent.

"So he took credit for your discovery."

He pulled out a handkerchief and blew his nose like a trombone. "What is there to say, now that Kurt is dead?"

"And with the fire, is this fusion project over?" I asked.

"No, the work we can rebuild," he said. "It is not a problem. But no one can ever replace Panks."

Duffy was running three bars behind. "What are these experiments?"

My head was pounding. I pressed on. "Without Panks, what have you really got? Hugo says he was a genius."

"Oh yes, the Alan Hugo theory of scientific research. He's not the one who figured out the power design. That was me."

"So you say. I'm not so sure I believe you."

"You think you know so much."

"I know a lot about *you*, Schuler. You should remember that."

"You ask a lot of questions for an insurance man." He gripped his chin. "What is it you think you'll find here?"

"I want answers. About the past."

"Are you sure? I've seen men destroy themselves looking for one thing when they wanted something else. What is it for you? Revenge?"

"There was a time. Not anymore. You could say I'm searching for someone."

"Maybe then a chance to cooperate." He raised his eyebrows. "There are things I've learned that may be helpful."

"Yeah, like what?"

"Panks and I were very close. As I said, like brothers." He removed his glasses, fogged them, and wiped the lenses on his sleeve. "I think you know how that feels."

I closed my notebook and turned to leave.

Schuler opened his little book. He read a line in German, his voice delicate, as if trying out for a choir. "It is from Faust," he said. Then, as we made our exit, he translated:

"My heart's so heavy,
My heart's so sore,
How can ever my heart
Be at peace anymore?"

He paused for a moment. "We all want something, don't we?"

Once we were outside, Duffy started in. "Waters, what are you doing? This guy's a mouse."

"No, what you saw was a rat."

CHAPTER 12
Cold Coffee

I'm not sure which was stranger, finding Panzinger dead or Schuler alive. The fact that they had made it to America left me shaken. What were the odds they would end up in the same part of the world as me? How did they get here? What were they after? Questions were piling up faster than cars on Route 99. I walked back to the main house to see if I could find something to steady my nerves.

I entered the kitchen and started opening cupboards. I nearly jumped out of my shoes when a voice from behind me asked, "May I help you?"

My first thought was to wonder why Alan Hugo had an English butler. But when I turned around, instead of seeing a plump elderly gentleman in black tie and tails, I was greeted by a tall thin man in a rumpled suit slouching against the door frame.

"I didn't see you." I swallowed, my mouth dry. "Seen any coffee?"

He raised his eyebrow above his horn-rimmed glasses as if to signify an in-joke. "Ah yes, the second-best beverage for late-night writing." He stayed leaning and then thought better of it and took a step forward. "Asheton," he said. "Edmond Asheton, the *Times*."

I shook his hand and introduced myself. He was a year or two older than me. His suit was a worn gray tweed, his cuffs were stained, and he wore an English school tie that was slightly askew. I couldn't remember if it was Cambridge or Oxford, but it was intended as a signal for the well-to-do of English society, not American private detectives. He had an evenly trimmed mustache that was in contrast to the sandy-blond hair that fell in disarray upon his face.

"Insurance man, correct?"

"I'm an insurance investigator," I clarified. "But we work independent."

"Independently."

"What?"

"Never mind. Grammar isn't really your thing, is it? You Americans." He pushed the hair back from his forehead. "There's some coffee on the stove. Been there since this afternoon."

"Cold coffee's better than no coffee, right?" I found a mug and poured half a cup, gulping it down.

"How is it?"

"Best coffee I've ever had," I said.

"Well, why not then?" He pulled a mug out of a cupboard and I poured him a generous amount. He took a sip and made a sour face. "Bloody hell, tastes like battery acid." He ducked his head and in a low voice said, "Alan Hugo's trying to poison us all." He poured some cream and sugar and tried again. He winced and pushed the cup away.

"I've had worse," I said.

"And will do again." He gave a forced smile. "Everything all right? You look a little ragged."

I ignored his gibe and pulled out my notebook. "Mind if I ask you a few questions?"

Asheton sat down at the kitchen table and cleared away a place for me. "Not at all. Your Sergeant Duffy mentioned you'd be along."

"He's a bit touchy about who I talk to, so this is just background."

"Sure." He leaned back in his chair. With his hands cupped behind his head, Asheton had the casual look of someone who would rather sit and talk about work than do it.

"What is it that brings you to Loma Vista?"

"On assignment for a week. My editor is putting together a Sunday magazine story on the impact of European research science. He thought it would be interesting to get the perspective of American industrialists."

"People really go for that?" I asked. I couldn't picture it. Were English newspapers so different from our own?

"I have no idea," he laughed. "I was just happy to get out of Blighty. We're still rationing meat and butter. Makes you wonder who won the war."

"All right." I nodded to get on to business. "When did you arrive here at Blakely?"

"Arrived late this morning. Honestly, I think Dr. Hugo had forgotten about it. He was a bit flustered. His publicity man had left on holiday for the weekend."

I leaned back. "That seems odd."

He waved his hand. "You know how these boffins are. Only half in the real world most of the time." He leaned forward conspiratorially. "That's why he has a staff." Again, the smile fixed in place. "But his man Palmer promised me an in-depth interview, and I wasn't going to leave without it." He leaned back again. "I'd have been the laughing stock of the office."

"Hard to disagree."

"Yes—what?"

"So you got time with Hugo?"

"There was some confusion, but I managed to get an hour with him before he had to pick up his daughter at the train station. He explained what his fusion research could do."

"Oh, yes?"

"Well, I mean, who really knows, right?" He lowered his voice. "What do *you* think they do here?"

If I had a subscription to the *Times*, I would have thought about cancelling it. "Desalination, isn't it?"

He squinted and the lines on his forehead creased in disbelief. "Seventy miles from the coast?"

"Yeah, that's what I was thinking."

"Still, German engineering." He winked. "You never can tell."

Was he baiting me? "What's that supposed to mean?"

"You know the Germans. Everyone just taking orders in the war. You'd have thought the whole German army was just Hitler, Goebbels, and twelve million conscripts." He looked up at me, his rant finished. "Where were you stationed?"

"All over. France, Belgium, Germany."

He nodded vigorously, a dog eager to pounce. "You know what I'm talking about. Bloody travesty to have these Germans running around now as if they had nothing to do with it. Officer, right?"

"I . . . Yes, captain in the 104th infantry."

He whistled. "That's something. I was just a deskman, you know. Wrote press releases for the King's Regiment, out of Liverpool. Never saw anything more dangerous than a paper cut."

He was selling it pretty hard.

"Antwerp, that was the big push, wasn't it?"

"That's right."

"With the British Second Army. We couldn't have done it without you Yanks. Your crew opened up Germany. Where were you?"

"We liberated Camp Dora. Ever heard of it?"

He shook his head. "Can't say that I have. There were so many. That must have been terrible for you."

By the time Mittelbau-Dora was liberated, the world had already heard about Auschwitz and Buchenwald and become inured to the news. Mittelbau-Dora was considered too gruesome for the public and little of its story made it stateside. No one wanted to talk about it. It was a private grief you could never share. But seeing Panks's burned body, his tattoo, brought all of it flooding back.

"You know, Panks was a Nazi," I said.

He looked at me like I'd peed in the punchbowl. Then his face became jovial once again. "They were all Nazis, every single one of them."

"He was a major in the SS."

"That was a long time ago. Surely—"

"He was there at Dora. I saw him."

Asheton slipped off his eyeglasses and polished the lenses with the back of his tie. When he finished, he put them back on and looked at me. "How can you be sure it was the same person?"

"When an SS Major tries to kill you, it makes an impression."

He leaned back, assessing the situation. "Well, well. Maybe there's more here than Hugo let on. I could see a different kind of story around this." He brought his hand to his chin. "One for the *Times* and something else for the *Mirror*. I have a friend there, always willing to pay for something on the side." He paused in his scheming. "You, my friend, might be very valuable. Who else knows about this?"

"This is an active investigation," I said. He was starting to annoy me. "It's not a county fair."

"Good, good. So no other reporters."

I gave him a cold look.

He raised his hands to acquiesce. "Just wanted to be clear. Don't worry, I won't file anything until I get home."

"He have any enemies?"

"Who?"

"Panks," I said a little too loud. I was exasperated. No wonder he'd had a desk assignment in the war. No one would have put up with him in a foxhole.

"Well, what SS Major doesn't?" His fingers splayed his mustache. "I only met him once, at dinner this evening. There was a bit of a kerfuffle between him and Schuler."

"What happened?"

"It took me by surprise. At some point, Hugo made a toast. I wasn't really paying much attention. But it was a toast to Panks. And I gather Schuler was a bit put out. He said something in German and then Panks blew his cool. They were like an old married couple."

"Then what?"

"It was rather awkward. Hugo had presented this rosy story of collaboration across his team, and then it all went pear-shaped. Panks knocked down his glass and stormed out. Said he was going to the Brass Lantern."

"What's that?"

"Local pub, by the train station."

"And then?"

He pursed his lips and shrugged. "I had another glass of wine."

"And where were you when the explosion occurred?"

"That was some time later. I had another interview with Dr. Hugo after dinner. I was trying to get a bit more color on the team, something that might be relatable to the layman reader."

"Anything seem odd?"

"Mr. Hugo was obviously uncomfortable about what had happened. He said Schuler had always been jealous of Panks. Do you think that has any bearing on your case?"

I stood up. "All right, Asheton, that's it for now. Thanks for your help. And if you don't mind—"

"I won't say a word to your sergeant."

I turned to leave.

He called after me. "Do keep me posted if you pick up any more details on our German friends."

I nodded. Asheton was running some kind of play here. I just didn't know what it was.

CHAPTER 13
Solid with a Browning

I had just walked into the hallway toward the living room when Duffy blocked my path. "I need to talk to you." He stood there, hands on his hips, loud and large. A brick wall on two legs.

"What is it, Sergeant?"

"The way you handled Schuler. I can't have you intimidating the guests here at Blakely Lab."

"What guest? Schuler's a suspect, like everybody else."

"Don't tell me my job. He's on Hugo's payroll and that's what matters."

"Like you?"

"Whatzat supposed to mean?" Duffy's face flushed.

I didn't know where this was going, but I didn't like it.

"You think 'cuz you're some ex-cop from Detroit you're better than everyone else? He planted himself two steps closer to me, his shoulders back. "Well, this is my case. You're here only as long as I permit it. You got that?"

"All right," I said. "I was out of line."

"Damn right. Hugo is an important man. I don't want anyone raising a ruckus about how they been treated. Don't look good for me or anyone."

I tried another angle. "What do you make of Schuler?"

"He's a harmless egghead. He's just shook up. Panks was his friend, right?"

"You're not buying that story, are you?"

"You know what your problem is? You don't trust people."

"Schuler's as Swiss as the Chinese ballet."

"How would you know?"

"You saw Panks's tattoo. He was a Nazi, so was Schuler."

"I saw a burnt-up body. Don't you get it? The war is over. Nobody cares anymore."

"They were both there at Mittelwerk. They ran experiments at a secret facility. Panks was a major in the SS and they escaped."

"Yeah, what makes you so sure?"

"Because I let them."

Duffy let out a snort. "You're nuts, Waters. No wonder you blue ticketed out of the war."

That was it. I'd paid for that blue ticket too many times over the last five years. I put my hand on his chest to stop him from leaving. He flung it away.

"You get away from me before I knock you one."

"You gotta listen. It's the truth."

"I don't gotta do nothin'. I was willing to give you a break, 'cuz you were a GI. But you're . . . crazy. You know that?"

"I know what I saw."

"This is a small town and I can't have you going off half-cocked bad-mouthing Alan Hugo."

"I didn't say anything about Hugo."

"You're off the case, sport."

"What?"

"You heard me. You go park yourself in the front room. When the rain lets up, I'll have an officer take you home."

I was outside in the rain, feeling sorry for myself. This was a set-up from the get-go. Duffy was covering for Alan Hugo, and I'd ruffled enough of their feathers to stuff a mattress. It was not yet 10:30 p.m. and I could still catch the Del-Fi's at the San Moreno Inn.

My spirits brightened when I saw the dim headlights of Faith's old car as she pulled up the driveway. Then I thought about how I had to explain that she drove out for nothing, and I felt like I'd lose her all over again.

She bounced out of the car, files under her arm, sharp and bright like a lighthouse beam. My eyes stayed low, watching the rain splash into the puddles.

"What gives?" she asked. Her lips were full, lipsticked, and making a statement.

"Change of plans, sweetheart." I looked up, not quite meeting her gaze. "I'm off the case."

She sniffed the air. Then she looked into my eyes. "You're high as a kite."

I couldn't lie. I took a deep breath.

She grabbed me by my jacket. "You swore to me. You told me over and over, never on a case. All we had together—"

"Honey, it's not like that."

"Jesus Christ, what were you thinking?"

"No, that's not the—"

"How can I trust you to have my back when you're halfway to the moon?" There was a catch in her voice and she turned away.

"It was exceptional circumstances," I said.

"Like what? Is Mick here? You guys are gonna play some jazz for Alan Hugo?"

"The DB is from Mittelwerk. I knew him."

"What?"

"He ran the experiments in the tunnels. *Sturmbannführer* Panzinger. He was working here under another name, Kurt Panks. He was SS."

"Oh my God." She turned back around and put her arms around me. "Jack, I'm sorry."

She squeezed me for a moment and I just held on.

"Look, I'm okay," I said. "Just a little buzzed."

She looked into my eyes, pulling them upward. Her lips pursed. She stretched her shoulders back, raised her chin. "This is our last case, right?"

"Yeah."

"So let's do it right." Her eyes scanned the courtyard. "What's the scene?"

"Forget it. I was fired."

"They hired Robner & Waters." Her head vibrated side to side. "Waters is cut, but Robner is still on the file." She looked over at the back of the house with the lights blazing and then back at me. "Besides, who's gonna know? They're all inside, right?"

Faith plowed ahead to the barracks, walking briskly despite the dark. "Come on. I drove all the way out here. I'm at least going to look around." She swung open the door. "Maybe we can find out what's really going on."

I told her what I'd found, and she kept going, through the empty rooms, flipping mattresses, opening footlockers and wardrobes. I didn't know what she was looking for, but when she was on the hunt, she kept at it and apologized to no one.

Eventually we came to Panks's quarters, a room still occupied, and did a thorough search, poking, prodding, opening, upending, and overturning everything. She pulled out a thick olive-green duffel bag from the wardrobe and read the letters stenciled on the side: K PANKS 0427 OMGUS, BERLIN.

"Bingo." Unhooking the closure, she reached in and pulled out a tight packet of C-notes secured with a rubber band. "Interesting." She rummaged with both hands inside and counted nine more. "Lot of money for a dead guy." She did a quick count. "That's twenty grand." She put the money on the desk.

"Actually, I'm guessing it'll be nineteen thousand nine hundred."

"Why's that?"

"He had half a torn one-hundred-dollar bill on him."

She nodded, filing away the information, letting it steep.

"There's more." I told her about Panks's tattoo, and the train tickets to Mexico.

"So he was on the lam," she said.

"Maybe his past caught up with him."

"It's a lot of money."

"Enough to get him killed."

"But the money's still here."

She looked at the pile on the desk and I looked at her.

It was more than either of us had ever seen.

She looked up and our eyes locked. We were both thinking it.

"I mean, he's dead, right?" I asked

"And you're off the case."

"We could just . . . " I fluttered my fingers.

"Jack, I'll break your hand." And she meant it.

Stealing from a dead Nazi wasn't a crime in my book, but I'd never convince Faith of that. Anyway, money wasn't going to bridge the gap between us.

"Where'd the money come from?" she asked.

I could think of a few sources, none of them legal. If Blakely Lab was working on new technology, Panks might have been selling secrets to a rival. We'd helped Northrop Aircraft run down an industrial espionage case last year. A draftsman was selling blueprints on the side to pay a bookie. That was chump change compared to what Faith had found.

I shrugged. "Embezzlement? Black market? If what they're doing here is so valuable, why are they out of money?"

"But what *are* they doing here?" Faith asked.

That was the sixty-four-dollar question.

"The experiments back at Mittelwerk—"

"You said everyone died."

"They got out just before the tunnel blew."

"They?"

"There's another guy here. Schuler."

"What is this, a Nazi convention?"

"Now you know how I feel. Look, if they made it out—" She froze. "Jack, no."

"—then why not Jordan? You gotta admit, it's possible." I slapped my hands together.

"Leave it. It's the past."

"I can't!" I raised my voice, despite myself. "Don't you understand? This is proof. He's still out there. I can feel it."

She let me stew for a moment. Then she spoke slowly. "Jack, you barely survived the explosion. They dug out that tunnel and they didn't find a thing."

"Just one more chance is all I'm asking."

She picked up the duffel bag, scooped the money into it, and slung it over her shoulder. "This ends tonight."

"Check this out." I swung the open duffel bag toward Duffy, then yanked it back once he saw the cash inside. "Twenty grand," I said.

We were standing in the rain next to the cruiser, Faith by my side. Duffy's face flashed a three-act play in about a second and a half. Shock. Greed. Fear. He bent his neck and rubbed it as he tried to work it out.

I fastened the bag and tossed it underhand to Faith. She caught it with her right hand and cinched it back over her shoulder in one continuous motion.

"Who's the skirt?" he said, turning his back to Faith.

"Sergeant Duffy, let me introduce you to my partner, Faith Robner. She found the bag."

"That right?" He turned back to Faith. "And what's the story?"

"This is Panks's bag," she said. She turned it so the stenciled letters showed. "He was leaving town with twenty grand."

Duffy crossed his arms. "No, *your* story."

"I was a war correspondent," she said.

"Scribbler," he said, stretching the word out an extra syllable.

"Got shot at."

He spat on the ground.

"Shot back."

He stepped back an inch.

"And I'm still pretty good with a Browning. In case you were wondering."

Duffy turned toward me. "I told you, Waters, you're off the case. Both of you. So why don't you and your girlfriend get outta here."

"Not so fast," Faith said. "We want to enter the bag into evidence."

She walked toward Duffy, removing the bag from her back and shooting it out in front of her. Duffy caught it this time.

"Yeah, so?"

"I need to write it up."

"What?"

"It's official evidence. I've got to notarize it with your signature as the presiding officer, along with Alan Hugo's."

Duffy turned to me. "What's she talking about?"

"It's not a simple accident investigation anymore. There's something else going on here."

Faith jumped in for the close. "Now we have to file a 514 Asset Valuation Form with the insurance claim."

"I don't know nothing about that."

"That's fine," Faith said. "We'll tell them in Sacramento you can do it in person."

Duffy's head swiveled from me to Faith and then back again. "What is this nonsense?"

Faith continued. "If I don't notarize the documents now, Alan Hugo, you, and the rest will have to convene before the insurance board in Sac to have it done there. I'm sure the captain will give you time off to travel."

"You trying to pull some kind of stunt here, Waters?"

"It's no stunt, sport," I said. "When we're in Sacramento, I'll testify that Panks was here under a false identity. His real name was Conrad Panzinger of the SS. And I know five reporters who'd love to pick up a story on Alan Hugo harboring Nazi scientists."

Duffy's face flushed. "No. That ain't right. That ain't how Mr. Hugo operates."

"It's all a matter of public record once the testimony gets filed."

Duffy thought about this for a few seconds, then shook his head. "Okay, what is it you two birds want?"

Faith chimed in. "Jack got called to work the insurance case and we want to finish it."

"All right, all right. You can continue with the case, but you're both under my control. You don't do nothing without checking with me. No reporters, nothing. I don't want any blowback on Alan Hugo. Got that?" He loaded the duffel bag into the trunk of the squad car.

"Understood," I said.

He heaved a sigh. "You two are made for each other."

Faith suppressed a smile, and I hoped Duffy was right.

Duffy leaned in and put his thick arm around my shoulder. His eyes were within inches of mine and I could feel his hot breath. "I suppose you and me should take a look around and see what else we can find."

He gave my shoulder a squeeze. "Don't be getting too smart about all this. Once we wrap things up here, I've got some other business to tend to. I've had my eye on the San Moreno Inn for a few weeks. I think they're running a dope ring out there." His mouth was wide open and smelled of onions. "Can't tell who might get pulled in, right, Waters? You saw the place. A hive of criminal activity."

"All right, Duffy. You made your point."

"Faith," I said. "Bring the paperwork to Hugo and keep him busy in the living room."

Duffy looked at Faith. "You got lucky with that find." He put his big hand on her shoulder. "But now you leave it to the professionals."

It was the wrong thing to say.

CHAPTER 14
Dynasty or Destiny?

I didn't like Duffy, but I needed him on my side. I'd worked with lots of people I didn't like over the years, from cops to DAs, informants, and army chaplains. The trick was to find a connection and figure out what they needed.

We were walking along the driveway, toward the barracks. From what I'd seen of Duffy, it was just a matter of time before he'd reveal what *he* needed. As we got on the stone path and out of earshot of anyone, he let it out.

"Where do you think that twenty grand came from?"

"No idea," I said.

"Never seen so much money in my entire life."

It's like he played a melody line on a sax and all I had to do was play it back on the piano. Call and answer.

"There's only one source for that much money."

He squinted. "You think he robbed a bank?"

This was going to be harder than I thought. "No, I mean, around here."

He thought for a minute. "You think it's Hugo money?"

"You said it yourself. The guy's loaded."

"That's what I always thought."

"But?"

"Well . . . "

I was getting ready for my solo. "Come on, Sergeant, I know you're looking out for Hugo. What's he got you on, a weekly retainer?"

"Monthly. Just so I keep an eye on the place. I do a couple of extra patrols, and I run security when he has, like, a social function."

"Good for you. Copper's wages aren't what they used to be."

"You're telling me." His mouth hung open. He wasn't done yet. "Only . . . "

You had to take your time, hear what the other guy played. I bowed my head a fraction of an inch to let him know I was listening. I let him come to me.

"Only, I haven't been paid in a while." He looked away.

"A week or two? I mean, how bad could it be? He's good for it, right?"

"I ain't been paid since Easter." He threw his hands in the air. "Three months, mister."

I let out a low whistle.

"I worked all day Easter Sunday when Hugo invited a bunch of local businessmen he was trying to get funding from."

"And?"

"So how come Panks has twenty Gs and I'm still out more than a hundred?"

"It's not right," I said.

"My wife is still angry about me missing Easter with her family. I got no leverage."

Time for some improv. "We could look around his office."

"Yeah, but what are we looking for?"

"You never know." I smiled as if there was some secret meaning.

"Oh, I get it. We find some way to rattle his cage." He rocked his head back and forth. "You ain't as dumb as you look, Waters."

We turned around and went back to the main house. Duffy led the way down an open corridor. There was a large oil painting of a tall man in a white shirt and khaki shorts, crouched down, working with a woman and a young boy. The boy and mother were looking at each other with soft, bright eyes. The mother had a Mona Lisa smile. The boy's mouth was round with a look of awe, as if in wonder. The old mission of Loma Vista was visible in the distance. Beyond that was a large, dark meadow to one side and a lighter meadow to the other. It was like the cover of an old *Doc Savage* magazine. A small brass plaque below read, "Blakely Hugo and the Mission."

"Tough act to follow," I said. "Your old man is a millionaire businessman *and* an explorer."

"He rebuilt the mission. And I bet he paid his bills on time."

We stepped into the office. With just the two of us, the room seemed larger than before. Alan Hugo was everywhere, eyeing us from the photos around the room, a shrine to his ego.

We got busy with our search. I looked at some of the personal items in the office. There were the assorted knick-knacks of government service, a commendation from the Army Intelligence division for his work in the war. I found a binder with press clippings, yellowed with age. I blew off a thin film of dust and started reading.

Loma Vista Courier—April 28, 1927
Hugo Family Dynasty Extends Its Reach

Today Alan Hugo, the son of prominent Loma Vista resident Blake Hugo, married Amy Gold of Philadelphia.

Alan Hugo is a recent graduate of Miskatonic University in Massachusetts and met Miss Gold when he was delivering a lecture on theoretical physics at a conference at Columbia University in New York where Miss Gold was studying.

The couple plans to live in Arkham, Massachusetts, where Mr. Hugo can continue his research into the new field of fusion at Miskatonic University.

Another clipping from May 1939 said Hugo was to attend a physics conference in Copenhagen. A scientific paper, written jointly by Hugo and his wife, was to be presented on the topic of "Crossing Beyond Multi-Dimensional Boundaries."

And in April 1941, a few sentences appeared in the *Arkham Gazette* beneath a vague headline announcing, "New Government Joint Research Program." The story said that Hugo, now described as "head of the controversial fusion lab at Miskatonic," had been dispatched to the army. But there was no indication what was being researched or why the army was involved. We weren't at war at that point, and no one knew when things might heat up.

I looked around at the pictures on the bookcase. There was a sepia-toned bridal photo of Amy Hugo. She had dark eyes and was wearing a cream-colored silk wedding dress with lace trim. Her wedding veil framed her face, and she wore a silver necklace and pendant that shone brightly. There was another, more casual, picture of the bride and groom with two men. One of the men had an olive complexion, and the other was lighter skinned, both wore suits.

I called over Duffy.

"Do you know the people in this picture?" I asked. "It's from Hugo's wedding."

He looked it over. "That Mrs. Hugo was quite a looker."

"Never mind that. What about the men?"

"The one on the left, that's Charlie Cordero, Hugo's handyman. Been with him a while. I don't know the other. You put a guy in a monkey suit and he looks just like everyone else."

"You find anything?"

"Well, I ain't the only one Hugo stiffed." Duffy held up a letter. "From his old college, Miskatonic. Says he's behind on Beverley's tuition." He rifled through a few more papers. "Oh, wait." He read another letter from a correspondence file and looked up. "Take a look."

He handed me a letter on Miskatonic letterhead from the Dean of Science. Beverley had been suspended from Miskatonic. But it wasn't the usual skiver case. "Never in my career have I had faculty and staff afraid for their lives," the Dean wrote.

"This is getting stranger all the time," I said.

"Oh, it gets better, Jack." He handed me another paper. It was an invoice from Arkham Psychiatric Hospital. "Girl's a nut job. Three months of electro shock treatment this past April for a total of $250. But that includes room and board," Duffy added. "Might be the thing for you and your lady friend."

I reached over and slapped his chest, more for the noise than the impact. "Knock it off, Duffy."

"What's the matter? Can't you take a joke?"

I turned away from Duffy. But he went on talking.

"I've seen it before with rich kids. Don't let Beverley fool you with her private-school charm. She's spoiled and thinks she can do whatever she wants."

"I want to understand what they're doing with this Z-machine."

"What do you care about all that? All you gotta do is write up your insurance report and get paid."

"It's what Panks was working on at Mittelwerk."

"So what?"

"Someone killed him to put a stop to it."

Through the window, I could see someone walking from the lab wing toward the residential side of the compound. It was dark and they were barely visible. It wasn't Hugo and it wasn't one of Duffy's patrolmen.

I stiffened and nodded toward the figure, alert. Before I was sure Duffy had understood, he'd sprung into action.

"Move," he yelled.

And I did.

CHAPTER 15
A Transcendent Man

We ran through the garage and Duffy opened the side door so we could intercept our shadowy figure. Duffy darted outside. I followed. It took a moment for my eyes to adjust to the darkness, but soon I could see him, lit by moonlight from behind the clouds. He was a mountain. He had something under his arm and looked around before turning toward the garage.

"Stop," Duffy said, raising his gun. I braced myself as the figure stumbled back half a step. He was only eight feet away and still a clear shot. I shone my penlight on him. He raised a large hand to cover his eyes.

"What is this?" He held a pile of books under his right arm. I kept my light on them and stepped forward.

"Where you going with those lab books, chief?" Duffy called out. "I ordered everyone to stay in the house." It was Charlie, the handyman, whose photo I'd seen earlier. He was a tall, heavyset man with black hair that flowed down past his shoulders.

Duffy lowered his weapon for the second time that evening, seemingly unperturbed, while my heart rate slowly dropped back to normal. Charlie looked calm considering how things might have unfolded. I lowered the light to the ground, and Charlie brought his hand down from his eyes.

"I'm sorry, Sergeant Duff." Charlie's languid eyes softened. "Alan asked me to pick up some of his lab books."

"This way, Cordero." Duffy laid his hand on Charlie's shoulder with a heavy slap and steered him inside. "Mr. Waters here wants to ask you a few questions for the insurance company."

"Sure, no problem." He narrowed his eyes, but his expression stayed neutral. "I'll help any way I can."

We walked back through the garage in silence. I pocketed my penlight. We entered the house and turned toward the kitchen.

Sitting down in the confined space of the kitchen table, Charlie loomed even larger. It was hard to tell his age, but his hands were weathered and there was a touch of gray at his temples. I figured he was in his early forties.

Charlie wedged himself farther into the bench seat beneath the window. Duffy and I sat on curved steel chairs with gray cushions on the other side of the square wood table.

"You're in the insurance business?" Charlie asked, as if this were a cocktail party.

"What were you doing in the lab?"

He must have heard me, but he gave no indication. He sat there, coolly assessing me.

Duffy leaned in. "What's the matter, Charlie?"

Charlie eased back half an inch. I knew what it was like to feel Duffy's hot breath up close.

Charlie turned his whole body toward me. "You police always push for the answer, the quick fix, but you don't know what questions to ask." He took a deep, silent breath and let it out slowly. Duffy and I both watched his chest as it expanded and collapsed over and again. I could have baked a pie, waiting.

"The fool is quick to answer," he said. "In my studies, I have learned to answer only after contemplation." He put his arms on the table, letting each hand rest in the opposite elbow. He looked up. His face was calm and untroubled, like it was carved in stone.

Duffy started to drum his fingers on the table.

"Okay," I said. I looked at Duffy and he shrugged. "Why don't we start with a few basic questions." I took out my notebook and pencil. "How long have you worked for Mr. Hugo?"

"I've worked for Mr. Hugo since I was a boy."

I looked up from my notebook.

"Mr. Blake Hugo," he said. His voice was deep, full, and relaxed. "I was an assistant, helping with his research." I flashed back to the oil painting in the corridor. I wondered about the woman and made a note in my book. I waited for him to continue, but nothing came.

"Mr. Hugo must have thought highly of you. That's you as a kid in that painting at the mission, right?" I asked.

"Where we going with this?" Duffy interrupted.

Charlie's jaw stiffened for a half second, then his shoulders let down.

Duffy continued. "This is an investigation, not art appreciation."

"Sergeant, why don't you let me handle this?"

"Suit yourself. I'm gonna check in with the captain."

I could see Charlie wasn't impressed with me or Duffy. And why would he be, working so many years for the late great Blake Hugo? We were a couple of mooks by comparison.

I counted silently.

One, two, three, four. Charlie's belly rose and collapsed, like he was meditating.

Five, six, seven. He carried himself with pride. Eight, nine, ten, eleven.

He wanted respect. Twelve, thirteen, fourteen.

Fifteen, sixteen, seventeen, eighteen, nineteen . . .

"Mr. Blake saw that I was special and that I could help him," Charlie said.

I waited a beat. "I've heard a lot about Blake Hugo," I said. "Tell me about him."

"He was a pioneer, a great man. He understood both the Chumash and the Christian worlds."

"How did he do that?"

"He had the gift of vision."

"And you?"

"I have lived and studied both. My people, the Chumash, believe that the gods come from separate worlds. There's an upper world and a lower world." He pointed to the ceiling and then the floor as he spoke, then he held his large hand flat just above the table. "We inhabit the middle. It's possible to pass between these worlds, but it is not easy. I've seen these worlds."

I'd seen my share of cons as a cop and the best ones played the supernatural angle to win over their marks.

He frowned. His eyes searched mine. "Mr. Waters, there are things and people you see which exist and others you see that do not seem to exist, isn't it so?"

I had no idea what he was talking about, but I nodded to keep him talking.

"You understand lightning and thunder as one thing, even though your senses perceive them separately." He paused. "You doubt me, but you let me speak, which is more than most men would allow. These worlds exist. They are separate from us, the same as the sun, the sky, the land." He spread his hands as if to say look around.

He had charisma all right. It wasn't an act. This was what Charlie believed deep in his heart. He had more faith in the world than I'd ever had.

"Mr. Blake asked me to help him understand Chumash culture. When Alan went east to college, I went with him. I studied the science of theology at Miskatonic. And what I learned was that all religions are bound by common beliefs. Christians, Jews, Muslims, my people, the Chumash, or the Cree. It is one world we inhabit, all of us. We're all equal, no matter your birth, your job, the color of your skin.

"I was with Alan when he was assigned to the army. And now I am a gardener and I protect the land. It is all connected." He brought his hands back together.

"I see." I scribbled some words in my notebook to buy time. "Let me get back to some of the more routine questions. Where were you earlier this evening?" I asked.

"I was in my room, in the barracks. Listening to the baseball game."

I could go along with that for now. "Anyone else there?"

"Yes, Dr. Dietrich was there. Reading."

"He said he went out," I bluffed.

"No, he was reading his German poetry. All evening." He placed one of his hands on the table.

"And how was the game?" I asked.

"The game? It was slow. I fell asleep. I only woke up when I heard the explosion."

"That good, eh?"

"You know the Angels." He smiled but didn't mean it. "Better luck next year."

"Let's get back to the accident. You were in your room, you fell asleep, then you heard the explosion. What happened?"

"I heard the noise. I woke up and I ran to the lab."

"Where was Schuler?"

"Dr. Schuler was in the barracks, but I ran ahead of him."

"You didn't say anything about what you heard? Ask what he thought it was?"

"No—no time to think. You hear a bomb go off, you react."

"What happened when you got there?"

"I could see Dr. Panks was on the ground and smoke was blowing through the room. His body was badly burned, there were papers on fire. Mr. Asheton, the Englishman, was there. He was crouched near the body. He arrived ahead of me. He told me that Dr. Panks was dead."

"How did Asheton get there so quickly?" I asked.

"I don't know. He just did. And then Dr. Schuler came a moment later, he fell to his knees, sobbing. He seems so lost now. Finally, Alan and Miss Beverley came in. Alan made me take Miss Beverley away. He didn't want to upset her, seeing an accident like that." He paused, considering his words. "I led her back to the house and she had a drink."

More than one. More than several, if I had to guess. "And you and Dr. Panks, did you work together closely?"

"I worked with Alan on this project for five years. Since before he brought Dr. Panks and Dr. Schuler over from Germany. I was at Los Alamos with them and now we're together at Blakely Lab. They are Alan's partners." He tugged at his fingers. "But I'm part of the family."

"Answer the question, Charlie."

Charlie said nothing. He didn't even shrug. But his look said it all.

"Panks wasn't like Blake Hugo, was he?"

His face darkened. "Dr. Panks trampled this area, the sacred grounds," said Charlie. "He destroyed the meadows."

He pressed his hands together in prayer and his eyes moved up and to the left as he contemplated. Then, as if he had worked out a complex calculation, his face beamed with satisfaction.

He began reciting, slowly from memory: "The soul which cannot endure fire and smoke won't find the secret." He paused. "That is from Rumi, the Sufi poet."

I nodded.

"Now you know all you need." He slid sideways on the bench, preparing to stand.

"Not yet. Charlie, the lab books."

"There is nothing here for you," he said.

"If you don't let them go, Sergeant Duffy will pursue it higher up."

"There's no basis here for the seizure of private property." Charlie's voice was steady, matter-of-fact. "I also studied law at Miskatonic. If there is a warrant, that's different."

"You're correct, Mr. Cordero," I said. "But a policeman with a grudge is a bad thing in a town like this. Why not lend the books to me for a few hours while we look into the accident? I promise their return."

His eyes scanned mine.

"Your Sergeant Duffy is of no concern to me," he said.

"I'll make the case to the captain that you did right by us."

No reaction.

"I owe you one," I said.

He sighed and shook his head. "All right," he said, to my surprise. He held the notebooks in his large hands, spreading them out like a kid playing Old Maid.

After Charlie left, I examined the lab books. The last two pages of the most recent book were torn out.

Every step forward on the case confounded me. It was like Manny and his three-card Monte. You could pick any card, but you only got what he wanted you to have.

CHAPTER 16
Hogwashing

Faith and Sergeant Duffy were standing beneath the portico outside the back door. The rain was heavy, the temperature had dropped, and each had their hands deep in their pockets. Faith held her file folder tucked under her arm. They were huddled together, heads bowed to the ground, the way people stiffen in the rain.

They were both smoking, which was unusual because Faith doesn't smoke. I could hear them laughing as I approached. Was she joking around? Faith hated all that tough guy cop stuff. I thought it was more likely I'd have to talk her out of slapping him after what he'd said.

"Have another on me, Sergeant. I'm celebrating." Faith held out a silver flask.

Duffy's mitts surrounded it and he knocked back a big slug.

"That hits the spot all right," Duffy said. "With the rain, it's colder than a—"

"Than a witch's tit," said Faith, jabbing him lightly.

Duffy laughed like one of Jack Benny's radio sidekicks. "I wasn't gonna say that in front of a lady, but that's exactly what I was meaning."

"What's to celebrate?" I stepped lightly under the portico.

"Jack, I was about to tell the sergeant—"

"Call me Duffy," he said.

"I was about to tell Sergeant Duffy about how we finally got paid on the Sanford case."

"Oh yeah, that was something," I said. Faith was on stage and I had to give her a wide runway.

"We made a killing today. You know Sanford at Claire Elegance in LA?

"Sanford? You collected from that deadbeat?"

"Yes, sir. I did, sir." Faith was beaming 500 watts of sunshine for Duffy.

"You two got more going on than I thought." Duffy took another swig from the flask. "He still owes me fifty for a security detail last year. How'd you do it?"

"I can be pretty sweet, when I have to." She inhaled on her cigarette and then blew a smoke ring directly at Duffy.

His eyes were transfixed. "That's what I need. A partner." Duffy shook the flask. "What is this stuff?"

"B and B, I told you, Sergeant, Benedictine and—"

"And Brandy, oh yeah. Goes down well. Where did you come across this stuff?"

"I took to B and B in France, in the war, but this I got inside."

"Inside?" said Duffy.

"Stevie gave it to me, when he signed the forms." She wiggled her arm to indicate the file folder.

"Stevie?"

"Alan Steven Hugo." She did a false baritone. "Call me Stevie." Then she cackled.

Duffy laughed for an instant. Then he tensed. "Dr. Hugo?"

She leaned up on her toes and did her full impression. "'Pretty girl like you, you need to keep warm if you're going to be outside on a night like this.'"

"You're hogwashing me," Duffy said.

"Look at the flask."

Duffy turned the flask in his hand and read aloud the engraved letters. "A.S.H."

"Alan Steven Hugo," she said. "He asked for my personal follow-up on the case."

Duffy took a breath and then a deep drink from the flask. "Ha, that's nothing. I got a story for you. Only you gotta promise me, you don't say nothing. Dr. Hugo doesn't like the hired help gossiping."

Faith leaned forward and nodded.

"You know Dr. Hugo runs a tight ship. Well, let's just say Schuler's been missing his curfew lately. Seen his car out three times in the past two weeks, well after midnight. I don't know if he's seeing a lady friend or if it's some shady business, but I plan to keep an eye on him. You never know how that might pay off."

He took another swig from the flask. "I asked Charlie about Schuler's late-night prowling. He played dumb with me, saying Schuler has been tucked in early every night, so I know he's in on it, too."

He handed the flask to me. "I gotta go check the radio. Meet me inside."

As Duffy walked away, I smelled the flask. Wild Turkey. I looked at the engraving, then passed the flask to Faith. "A.S.H?"

Faith whispered, "Alpha Sorority House." She was off-stage now, serious. "That's not all. I spoke to Beverley, the daughter. She said her mother was running an experiment the night she died. A storm hit and then a fire broke out in the lab. And after her mother died, they changed the design of the Z-machine to make it safer. It has a two-man power switch. The machine can't be operated alone."

"Somebody else was there."

"And there's more." She flipped open her file and handed me a worn, leather-bound diary with gilt edging. "This was her mother's. I want you to read it."

"Faith, we're in the middle of a case; can't this wait?"

She put her hands on her hips. She wasn't going anywhere until I gave in. I moved under the light so I could see.

June 20, 1939

I've been having terrible dreams. This must be a side-effect from the work on the Z-machine. I've not mentioned it to Alan.

The other day, I took Beverley for a walk. There were crows in the trees nearby. I was gripped in panic. The whole flock was squawking and then suddenly they all flew toward us to prevent us from leaving. The skies darkened, not with clouds, but with hundreds, thousands of crows, screeching at us.

I was frozen with fear but I was powerless to move. Then Beverley tugged at my hand calling "mummy" and I was back in the moment. A mere handful of crows scattered from the trees. The vision vanished but my heart continued racing.

"Faith, I don't see that this has any bearing. It's just the rambling nightmare of a woman going through a difficult time."

"Just keep going. There's more to it, you'll see."

I sat down and flipped to the next section. Below the text was a sketch of birds in flight over a meadow, with lines emanating in a pattern of waves, with more sketches of waves in the margin and on subsequent pages. Some were crossed out and replaced with darker, rougher patterns as if drawn in anger.

June 25, 1939
    Last night I had a dream with more of those dreaded birds. There were large crows, flying in pairs over a dark, moonlit sky. They flew to an ancient stone tower set in a large meadow. To one side was light and the other darkness. The tower represented the knowledge of the ancients and the birds were there to protect it.
    As the moon rose, the birds started flying in intricate patterns. Now the pairs joined others, and there were dozens and then hundreds of crows flocking together and then separating in a rhythmic pattern. I knew that the pattern was important and they were communicating with me. They were calling out, saying, here is how it's done.
    When I awoke, I realized I could create a design that would allow me to raise the Z-machine's voltage by having multiple paths of energy. I could create a web of energy that fans out, enabling us to increase the voltage safely.
    Finally, I had a solution to the most vexing design problem we'd ever faced. But where did it come from? Was it a product of my subconscious mind? Or something darker?

June 29, 1939
    Tonight, I was able to drive the Z-machine further than ever before. It started off as usual. I had the tingling feeling of energy flowing through my body. That is always exciting, like a blast of cold air, but from the inside. Then I burst through a dark fog. There were gray shapes of bizarre proportions and angles. It all seemed wrong. I could feel the gaze of a thousand eyes upon me, judging me. Then I was transfixed, as if on an examining table. I could hear the voices of the elders. I could hear them talking in some

*strange tongue that sounded like machinery with grinding
gears and scraping metal.*

*I could see myself, distinct from the world. It was a
bird's-eye view from a higher perch, and then another,
and another, expanding like a hall of mirrors. Our world
here on earth was just a speck to them. I was no more
significant than an earthworm on a tractor wheel. But
then everything began collapsing, like doors slamming shut
from a strong wind.*

*Shapes approached, all moving in shades of gray. I was
panicked. They were circling, communicating. Strange
words reverberated inside my skull, beckoning me to their
world.*

June 30, 1939

*I woke up in a start, gasping for air, my heart racing.
I must have blacked out but for how long I couldn't tell.*

*This will be my journey alone. I don't know if it will
work, but I must give it my best shot. I've reviewed my
calculations over and over and checked everything. Every
piece must fall into place at the right time.*

*I've removed the formula and all my notes on the new
design from the lab. I need to make sure they are safe in
case anything happens.*

At the right time, all will be unveiled.

I closed the diary. Faith was leaning forward, waiting for
my reaction.

"Look, I appreciate you getting Beverley to open up and
share this. But I don't see what this has to do with Panks's
death." I said.

Faith crossed her arms tight. "It's not about Amy or Panks.
It's about the Z-machine. What is it, Jack? What does it do?"

CHAPTER 17
Beverley Remembers

"Jack, I want you to talk with Beverley."

"About what?"

"About her mother."

"Why?"

"I don't know. But I think Amy Hugo's death has something to do with what happened here tonight."

Faith wasn't taking "no" for an answer. I could see that from her expression. I was hoping to get her back on my side, but this made no sense. I was focused on Schuler and what he might be able to tell me about Jordan.

Faith was adamant.

"It was the same thing," she said. "There was a fire in Amy Hugo's lab. Don't you think that's strange?"

"It's a coincidence. It's a lab. Things go wrong."

"What about the diary? She was onto something."

"The ravings of a mad woman."

"She was a scientist. Whatever may have happened, she wasn't mad."

"Well, Beverley certainly is."

"I'm what?" Beverley asked, strolling toward us from the direction of the lab. How had she gotten back there without us noticing her? She looked from Faith to me as she took a drag on her cigarette.

I tightened my face as I wondered how badly I'd stepped in it.

"I was telling Jack how helpful you've been," Faith turned to me without missing a beat.

"Yes, thank you, Beverley," I said. I could never stop Faith when she had an idea.

"For what?" she asked.

"For sharing your mother's diary with us," Faith said.

"She was something else, wasn't she?"

"She sure was. Let's go inside and sit down." Faith pulled the door open and we trooped into the foyer. Faith gestured at the table.

"Why don't you tell Jack what you told me?" Faith said.

"About Mother?"

"About what happened that night."

"Like I said, there was a big storm, same as tonight. I was in my room next to the kitchen and the shutters were banging from the wind. I was reading a Tom Swift book Father had given me for my birthday. It was silly, about a photo-telephone, of all things. At some point, Charlie came by and said we should visit Mother in the lab. That was odd because Mother's work was a bit of a secret."

"What do you mean?" I asked.

"Mother wasn't supposed to be working on the Z-machine while Father was away. My parents fought over that. I think she squared it somehow that with Charlie nearby, it would be all right. But it was our little secret."

Beverley revered her mother, that was clear. Losing her at such a young age must have knocked her for a loop. No wonder she was a mess.

"Mother liked having the run of the lab. She would spend hours working on the equipment, losing all track of time. I was intimidated by it, but she was completely in command of it.

"That night, she said she had to run a test. I knew she would be working for several hours. The mornings after she worked late, she'd be exhausted, sometimes giddy, sometimes stumped by the results. I found that very exciting. It was one thing to have a father as a scientist, but to have a mother who might have a breakthrough in quantum physics, that was a storybook."

"What does that mean?"

"Mother was friends with Professor Schrödinger. Ever heard of him?"

"Can't say that I have."

"Okay. Well, he invented the quantum theory, how particles change dynamically over time, moving in and out of stability. She heard him lecture once at Columbia, and then they exchanged letters. She built on his theory of wave mechanics and began extrapolating even further. He was very encouraging to her. Her big leap was to ask if particles can be unstable, what does that mean for time? You could have different worlds, and they would all exist at the same time, sort of in parallel." She was excited as she told the story and waited for my reaction.

"Uh-huh," I said. She was obviously gaga. "Very interesting, but we need to get down to business. Tell me, did Charlie know how to operate the Z-machine?"

"He didn't have to. Mother designed the controls and they were all within reach. I'm told the original Z-machine was much simpler than what we have now."

She leaned in, quieter. "Charlie knows more than most people give him credit for."

"Tell us what Charlie did," Faith said.

"Charlie insisted we had to visit Mother. I was miffed because I wanted to finish my book, so he told me to bring it with me.

"A vacant lot separated our house and the lab. We had to walk outside, behind the house. That's when the rain had started. There was lightning. So we ran quickly. When we got there, Mother was in the middle of an experiment. She had her headgear on, so she wouldn't have noticed us.

"There wasn't that much to see, so I probably just sat down somewhere." Beverley closed her eyes, as if she was trying to remember what had happened. "That's right, I started reading my book. Charlie said he wanted to make sure everything was operating properly." She opened her eyes and paused. She breathed in at the top of her chest with a stutter.

"At some point, I heard a loud crack. I jumped. I thought it was lightning. But it was much closer. Something had shorted. There were sparks flying and then suddenly . . . "

Her voice quavered and became a whisper. "There was an explosion, a bright ball of fire shot from the console and bitter smoke poured out of the Z-machine." She shook her head. A lock of hair fell across her right eye, but she didn't blink or brush it away.

"Charlie grabbed me and we ran outside. He kneeled down, put his hands on my shoulders. I can still feel how heavy they were. He told me to run to the house and call the fire department. He ran back to save Mother, but . . . " She started to sob. A minute later, I was holding her against my chest while she cried. I gave Faith an awkward glance, but she signaled me to go with it.

"The whole lab burned down," Beverley said in a choked voice.

"It's okay." I didn't know what to say. A moment or two passed.

"All this time, I never wanted to face how Mother died. I kept thinking it was my fault. That's why I decided to study physics, so I could try to make sense out of what happened to her."

Faith said, "Tell him about the Z-machine."

"Father was against it, but I talked Dr. Panks into letting me use the Z-machine in one of his experiments this spring. I thought I could retrace her steps, see what she saw. But it was a nightmare. I ended up in some kind of shock. When I came to, I was in the Arkham General." She swayed at her waist slightly, like a buoy at sea.

"Sometimes, I . . . I speak to Mother. I know that sounds strange. She told me everything would be okay. I hope you don't think I'm a spinner."

"No," I said. "Strange things are possible." She was a kid starved for attention with a father who treated her like a lack-luster employee instead of a daughter.

"Do you think so?"

Before we could learn anything else, Alan Hugo stormed into the room. He looked at me like a dog that had soiled his living room carpet.

"Just what is going on in here?" His voice boomed in the way only a father's could. His hands balled into fists. "Waters, help me to God, I am going to report you to the California Department of Insurance."

"It's not what you think, Mr. Hugo," I stammered, stepping away from Beverley's grasp.

"Daddy, I think it's time that I told you. Mr. Waters and I are going to be married," Beverley said, smiling. Faith barely suppressed a snort of laughter at my awkwardness. I felt like a class-A idiot.

"Oh, Beverley, please. Stop acting the fool," Hugo said.

"Mr. Hugo, your daughter was very upset this evening and I was just trying to comfort her."

"Get away from me, Waters. I need to prepare for my interview and this is the last thing I need."

"Mr. Hugo, we'll take care of this, don't you worry," Faith said. Hugo waved his hand in dismissal as she pulled me into the other room.

She spoke quietly. "There's some connection between Panks's death and Amy Hugo's. I know there is."

"Forget it," I said. "We don't know anything about her or whether any of what she wrote was even true. Her death was an accident and it's got nothing to do with Panks. How could it?"

She crossed her arms. "So then what's your theory?"

"I think the Z-machine creates some kind of psychosis in people. Maybe that's what it's intended to do. Brainwash people, induce hallucinations." I lowered my voice. "That would explain . . . " I nodded toward Beverley in the other room.

"This is particle physics, fusion energy. You don't know what you're talking about."

"I saw it with Jordan!"

She pulled on the hem of my jacket. "Jack, we've been over this. Please stop this rumination over Jordan. You have to accept that he's gone." Her face reddened.

"Whatever kind of research they were doing in the tunnels, it had an effect on Jordan. It was like he was in a trance, having some kind of psychotic episode. If there's a link between these two cases, that's what it is."

"You're not listening."

"Look, I can't give up on Jordan. If it was the other way around, and he came out of the tunnels instead of me, he would never stop looking."

"You're not thinking straight."

"I get it. You found the diary, you talked to Beverley. I have to follow up with Schuler first."

She shook her head slowly. "That's not it. I'm worried."

"I know how to take care of myself."

"Jack, what they're doing here is dangerous. Amy died on the Z-machine eleven years ago. Now Panks. If it's tied to what happened at Mittelwerk, then who knows how deep this goes?"

CHAPTER 18
On the Air

"We take you now to the site of Blakely Labs in America, where some of the world's top scientists are working to harness new energies for the world," Edmond Asheton said in the earnest tones of British radio. He had rounded shoulders and sat with a slouch in a dining room chair in front of a chrome, slotted microphone on a metal tripod. His sandy-blond hair was like an overgrown field. His wristwatch was on the table next to a pad and pencil. He had set it ahead more than an hour to 12:00 to track the recording and pushed in the crown as he started speaking. He'd hiked up the sleeves of his jacket and his tie was loosened.

I watched the needle of the sound meter on a tabletop reel-to-reel recorder swing back and forth as he spoke into the mic. He marked the start time on the pad as *00* and wrote *Intro*.

Asheton had converted the front dining room into an impromptu radio studio. He was to file a story to the *Times* and also record a radio interview for later broadcast back home, he'd said. Alan Hugo was at the center of the table with his own microphone, no notes, his cane leaning against his chair. He was beaming.

Duffy and I sat to the side, invited to listen. Hugo couldn't resist having an audience. In fact, he demanded it. Behind the glass doors in the next room, Beverley, Charlie, and Faith sat on a line of dining room chairs. Beverley looked at the floor. Charlie contemplated other worlds. Faith sat in the center chair with a file folder over her knees. She caught my eye and nodded her head toward Beverley.

I thought the whole episode was bizarre. We were in the middle of a murder investigation. What the hell was this midnight radio show about? To Hugo's entourage, it was just another quirk of their eccentric boss who loved attention.

Asheton had the old boy so stoked that Hugo wouldn't have missed his chance for fame overseas if he had to record it on the roof in the rain. And Duffy? He was like the dog by the phonograph, mesmerized by his master's voice.

Asheton put a hand to his right ear as he leaned his mustache within kissing range of the microphone. "Tell our listeners, please, Dr. Hugo, were you really the youngest physics professor at Oxford?" Asheton projected the cool confidence of English radio and it made him sound more competent than he was. His head bobbed left to right and back again, hunting for the wisdom that Hugo would share with his radio audience.

"Well, thank you, sir, it's my special privilege to speak to the world today about my many experiences," Hugo said. And this coming from a guy who was born into an easy life. He glided through it like a Cadillac banking the curves of the coastal highway.

Asheton marked on the pad and silently clapped his hands together as if he were Moses having completed his transcription of the word of God. "Righto," he mouthed to nobody. He dipped his head close to the mic again.

Beverley stretched as she yawned and then covered her mouth. She'd heard a lifetime's worth of Hugo's victory speeches.

Asheton continued with a series of open-ended questions. He stumbled through them with an occasional stutter, like the fawning college-age music fans who went backstage after a show, asking questions to convey their awe.

"And, Dr. Hugo, you were inspired, I think by your father, also a scientist and an explorer," said Asheton.

"I learned all I needed about exploration at the knee of my father, the great Blake Hugo. But I set my sights quite a bit higher than the old man ever did. I went off to university at just sixteen. And that was just the start. I was teaching at Oxford at twenty, and I got to meet Professor Lindemann and many of the famous physicists I'd studied. But, you know, they were like Blake Hugo. They'd made one great discovery early in their career." He ground his hands together. "They just stayed with that one thing the rest of their lives." He looked up and pointed his thumb back at his chest. "Me, I wanted to keep on exploring. I wanted to make new discoveries, develop new scientific methods, identify new worlds. Blake Hugo, he just . . . settled."

Hugo's eyes filled with disappointment, but it was all a show. I wondered what the old man would have made of it. The prodigal son, as ungrateful as ever.

Asheton brought us back to the present. "Ah, how did you meet Panks?" he asked. "Were you familiar with Panks's work before you met? Oh, where was that conference, again? And which government agency sponsored you? Yes, yes, I see, and what were Panks's politics at the time?"

He had a radio voice, but he wasn't much of a newsman.

Hugo was unruffled. He loved talking. "Panks's politics?" he repeated. "Panks had no politics." He wagged his index finger, bumping the microphone. A squawk of feedback came through the speaker. Hugo was thrown off his script for a moment. He tapped his chest. "He was loyal to me. And, anyway, the key was the multi-field energy convergence."

I didn't think the radio audience was going to be enlightened by this claptrap.

"Loyal?" Asheton asked.

"I saved them from the Russians," Hugo said. "We cut them off minutes before they would have stumbled into a Russian advance team. I should have gotten a medal for that."

"You saved *them*, you say," said Asheton. "Panks and?"

"Schuler," said Hugo. "Panks was the main man, but Schuler came along for the ride."

So that was it. I should have realized. Hugo had been there. He was the one who had brought these Nazi bastards to the States.

"What were you doing in Europe?" Asheton asked.

"In the war, I was part of U.S. Army Joint Intelligence. We identified technologies in which the Germans were ahead, what they called their *Miracle Weapons*. But the real value was the scientists who built them. That's what we were after.

"The Army had gotten to Mittelwerk and locked everything down. We were just a few miles away, going through an area the Russians had occupied. It was a race.

"The Russians were camped on the far edge of the forest, and I scooped Dr. Panks and Dr. Schuler before anyone could figure out who they were. I had to get them out of there. So we dressed them up in our army jackets, and then Charlie and I, freezing our keisters, pardon me, we drove right past the Russians honking and waving. The Russians had no idea how close they'd been."

Asheton glanced at his watch on the table, but Hugo was undeterred.

"We drove all night, and when we got to Spandau, we toasted them with the best champagne we could find. It was quite a coup. I knew Panks's work from before the war. Panks was the only person in the world who knew more about fusion than me."

Hugo sat back, clearly pleased with himself.

Asheton was looking at him sideways, stroking his mustache. "So, driving off with a couple of enemy scientists . . . how was that considered?"

"It was against protocol, but no one cared about that. It was every man for himself, and I got what the U.S. needed. The Brits were pretty pissed about it, I can tell you that. Well, no offense, Asheton. All's fair in love and war, right? You would have done the same, given the chance. Anyone would have.

"Of course, I was working with the Osenberg list," Hugo added. "It was part of what we called Operation Paperclip. Don't look too closely if there's one attached, you know what I mean?" He laughed.

I clenched my fists at my side. How could he joke about it?

Asheton raised a finger in an attempt to ask a question, but Hugo galloped along without pause, milking the story for all it was worth.

"They were as pure as the driven snow, as far as the State Department was concerned. We got every scientist who mattered. Every single one."

"Who decided who got what?"

"It was all me," Hugo said. "The rest of the senior guys were West Point. They didn't know a V-2 from a V8. It had to be a scientist in charge. So I divvied it up. Without what I gave them, the Russians would be nowhere today. They were lucky. We gave Britain access to the rocket technology, too. We were all allies, so it was only fair."

A pained look crossed Asheton's face.

Hugo continued, "Truman's man, Admiral Leahy, told me to keep everyone happy in preparation for Potsdam. These were just scraps, but it was enough to keep the Russians in line. They got quite a bit further than I would have expected."

"Mittelwerk was in the Russian zone, was it?" Asheton asked. His voice was chirpy, like a bird that had found a worm.

Every time they mentioned Mittelwerk, Faith looked over at me to see if I was okay. And every time, I tensed a little more, feeling nearer to bursting. I couldn't take much more of Hugo's sanctimonious nonsense.

"Well, sure, but that didn't mean anything." He scratched his forehead. "It was just a concept at that point. The last thing in the world German scientists wanted was to end up in a Russian DP camp. I saved them."

"And what's the relationship between Panks's research during the war and your own?"

Hugo's face froze. He blinked twice. "What kind of reporter are you?" He turned so he was face-to-face with Asheton. It was obvious he was angry but trying to control himself. "You should focus on the future, not the past. It's all behind us and we won."

"Yes, you did, sir," Asheton said. "Thank you, Doctor Hugo, and that is it for Science Week on the Home Service. Signing off for now, from sunny California in America." He checked the watch and wrote on the pad. The room was silent. Hugo passed his hand through his hair.

I couldn't stand it any longer. I stood up and opened the glass doors to let in some air. "I was there, too," I said. I had hoped my voice would be strong, but it was shakier than I would have liked.

"You were where?" Hugo brushed lint from his suit jacket.

"Mittelwerk."

Hugo's head swiveled. He squinted, frowned, and then broke out a sneering smile. "You're the . . . the coma kid?"

"Yeah."

"I read about that. Your brother went missing."

"That, too."

Hugo's head swiveled back and he laughed. "Well, then you're a hero, too," he said. "Panks was worth all of it and more." He clapped his hands. "You know, just today, Panks got us the breakthrough on energy that we've been working toward."

"I've got news for you. There is no breakthrough," I said. "It's gone." I bent down to retrieve the top lab book from the pile under my chair.

"What are you talking about?"

I handed the notebook to Hugo. He sighed, seemingly exasperated by my intrusion on his moment of glory.

He flipped through the book, head down, pacing around, tapping at the pages as he read. He muttered the headings, each one a confirmation of his accomplishments. "Derivation of the Tillinghast constant, resonance cascade effects, the Ranke method for calculating dosage, it's all there."

But then, when he came to the end of the book, he stopped. He flipped back and forth between the last few pages, like a record player stuck on a scratch. His lips puckered, then froze. He puffed. "What the hell is going on? Where are today's notes? Someone has torn pages out of here!"

He flung the lab book across the table at my head. I ducked as it flew across the room, through the doors.

"Gentlemen," said Asheton, "I'll get coffee." He slunk out of the room, head down like a nervous rabbit.

"You find those pages," said Hugo. His face was red. He looked at Duffy, then at me. "Or you'll wish you'd never heard of Blakely Lab."

I was about to say I wished that already, but Faith had her eyes on me and I thought better of it.

Charlie and Beverley stood awkwardly in the silence, presumably used to Hugo's outbursts. Charlie looked over at me, but if there was something to be gleaned, I wasn't picking up on it. Hugo walked out and the two of them followed a moment later.

I passed through the door and stood beside Faith. Her eyes were down and she scanned the room. "Jack," she whispered, "where's the lab book?"

CHAPTER 19
Black Sun

I pulled Duffy aside to get his attention. We climbed the stairs quietly and were standing outside the doorway of the second-floor bedroom.

I heard a sharp click followed by the sound of fitted metal sliding in a groove from behind the door. It wasn't a pistol, but I recognized the sound and it meant only one thing. I pulled my revolver out and Duffy did the same. He didn't hesitate.

Duffy was on the right side of the door. I flanked the left. He nodded for me to take the lead. I shouldered the door. It sprung easily, wood chips flying from the doorframe. We blew in, guns up, cocked, and pointed at our man.

"Gentlemen?" Asheton was standing in his undershirt. A cigarette hung at thirty degrees from his mouth and bounced slightly as he spoke. There was a white shirt with soiled cuffs lying on the bed. He straightened up, uncoiling his spine, standing a half-inch taller than before. An open suitcase was in front of him on the bed. "I was looking for something in a blue-striped Oxford, size 42."

"Shut up," said Duffy. He looked at me and raised an eyebrow. Then his eyes scanned the room.

I held my gaze and aimed steady for a count of three. A half-inch of ash stayed in place on Asheton's cigarette. I looked past him, to the wardrobe and dresser. A portable typewriter case sat closed on the dresser top. A small black wire peeped out.

"Who're you working for?" I circled around him, approaching the case, my revolver locked on his chest.

"Has the *LA Times* hired you to steal my story?" He was full of bluster, assessing his options. Alarm bells were sounding. Asheton was a harder man than he let on.

"Hands high," I said.

Asheton tucked his elbows and brought his hands up a few inches. Judging by the roll of his shoulders and his stance, legs apart, weight back on his right foot, this could go either way. He sucked in a puff of tobacco. The faint crackle of the cigarette burning was the only sound. The ash grew longer. This guy didn't ruffle.

With my eyes on Asheton, I opened the case. It was a high-frequency radio transmitter. I'd seen them in France and Belgium. The stray wire was the antenna lead. The radio was good for hundreds of miles, maybe even thousands in clear weather. Nearby on the dresser was a pocket Minox camera. That explained the sound I'd heard.

"What the hell?" Duffy said.

"If you'll allow me, Sergeant." Ignoring our weapons, Asheton removed the cigarette from his mouth. His voice was deeper now. The slight stammer and meandering style were gone. His words were taut, clipped. "I have some . . . official business. With your government. Before either of you get too jumpy with your handguns, why don't I show you my identification?"

Duffy stepped closer.

"My credentials are in the shaving kit."

Duffy reached into the suitcase with one hand and drew out a small leather pouch. He holstered his gun, opened the pouch, and pulled out two passports and a stack of white calling cards.

"E. F. Asheton, Ministry of Defense, Assistant Deputy Naval Attaché, International Affairs Coordination Unit, London," Duffy read.

"Naval Attaché, my aunt," I said.

Asheton raised a palm in placation. "You understand my position."

Duffy looked at me.

"Military Intelligence." I lowered my revolver. "MI5."

Asheton shrugged. "There's a government issue Webley & Scott police revolver inside the false bottom, so there are no surprises," he said.

"What are you doing here?" I said.

"National security," said Asheton. "I'm working with your Federal Bureau. My contact there has full knowledge of my role."

"He's got British and Canadian passports under two other names," said Duffy, "and there's a card for FBI special agent Robert Lamphere in DC."

"Gentlemen, this can go one of two ways." Asheton flicked his cigarette on the wood floor and stepped on it. "I can let you continue your investigation into this little accident—"

"What the hell—" Duffy said.

"Or I can call Lamphere, and you'll be removed from the case within the hour. I understand Mr. Hoover's men lack some of the social graces so helpful in a joint investigation."

"Joint investigation?" I asked.

"With your cooperation."

"Meaning what?"

"I'll share what I can, but everything we discuss here is confidential. None of it goes beyond the three of us, and none of it goes in any of your reports." He reached under the suitcase, and Duffy lurched for his revolver. "Sergeant, please," said Asheton. "I believe you were looking for this?" He nudged the barrel of Duffy's weapon away with the edge of the lab book. "With Panks's accident, there's nothing else here for me. I thought some of this might make its way into the background file for HQ, but the science would be wasted on me, even if the book were intact. Maybe it'll be useful in your arson investigation."

"Is that what you think this is?"

"It's not my concern. That's for you local Johnnies."

"Why *are* you here?" I asked.

"Panks's name came up in a security flag on our side." Asheton reached into his suitcase and swung out a folded, pressed white shirt. He put his arms in the sleeves and began buttoning up, eyes on me.

"You mean Panzinger?"

For a moment, Asheton hesitated on a button. "Panzinger?" He looked down, passed the button into the hole and then smoothed down the front of the shirt. "I see nothing slides by you."

"Why were you investigating him?"

"I'm tying up some loose ends after the war."

"Killing Nazis? Is that what you mean?"

"No, no." He shook his head. "That's simply not how the game is played. Lamphere would have me in Fort Leavenworth before I could wire London to say I'd be late for dinner."

"What then?"

He looked down, took a deep breath, then looked up. "The Thule Society."

"Hitler outlawed those quacks in '35."

"You know your history, Mr. Waters. The Thules were disbanded and branded as occultists. But all that did was push the work underground, which suited Himmler, just fine. He wanted to control the research and use it for his own ends in the SS."

"Which was what?"

"The Thules believed the way to achieve a thousand-year Reich was to harness forces that had been rumored for centuries among ancient cultures. No research was too exotic for Himmler's taste."

He looked to the door, then dropped his voice. "We have a list of Thule scientists who scattered as the war ended. Herr Doktor Panzinger's name was at the top. Heinrich Himmler personally funded Panzinger, almost from the start, at Berlin Technical. When the work started to show promise, Himmler christened it the Black Sun project and moved the lab under his direct control.

"But wasn't it all just Ouija boards and digging up ancient ruins?" I asked.

"That, too. But I assure you, the Nazis took this work very seriously," said Asheton. "And we take *that* seriously. With his money and influence, Himmler had quite a few devoted followers in the scientific community. '*Machtwerk aller Zeiten*' was their slogan: a power weapon for all time."

At that, I was jolted back to a vision of the burnt body. Duffy's mouth fell open.

Asheton frowned. "Does that mean something to you?"

"The tattoo on the vic," said Duffy. "Panks had that—what you said—tattooed under his arm."

Asheton turned to me. "You saw it?"

I nodded.

"I've been hunting Panzinger since '44. I thought we had him when Mittelwerk was seized. But then he ended up in the

U.S., out of our reach. Your side brought over hundreds of Nazi scientists, and the worst were given clean identities. I've followed a dozen leads, all dead ends. I wasn't sure until right now, but with that tattoo . . . "

"Fanatics, all of them," I said.

"Too right,"Asheton agreed.

"What was this Black Sun?" I asked.

"We don't know," said Asheton. "Some kind of energy work, possibly nuclear. It was a highly secretive project being conducted at the same site as Mittelwerk where Von Braun built his V-2 rockets. We had a report of another set of tunnels, Dunkelwerk.

"It wasn't on any of the blueprints," he said. "We knew damned little about it. The name suggests that's where the heavy science was undertaken. A secret lab for Panzinger to ponder the imponderable." His eyes narrowed. "It was a bad business. It sounds crazy but they were trying to find a way to alter time, to go back and change the course of the war.

"As the Allies advanced, Hitler issued orders to destroy it all in the event of capture. Soldiers burned records. Scientists fled and the *Technische Truppen* was sent in to obliterate everything. You Yanks managed to liberate Camp Dora and capture Mittelwerk. Unfortunately, there was an explosion that destroyed the lab at Dunkelwerk." He looked at me coolly. "Who knows what really happened?"

I stared at Asheton as I tried to put it all together. Suddenly he knew an awful lot more about Mittelwerk and secret Nazi projects than he had let on during his interview with Hugo. What else did he know?

"It was supposed to be a joint operation, sharing all scientific findings, but by the time I got there, the U.S. Army had cleaned out everything down to the soup pots." Asheton looked in the mirror by the window as he tied his tie. "What do you make of this Z-machine they're working on?"

"That's what caused the fire," Duffy said.

Asheton looked at him like he was a slow schoolchild. "Schuler says all their work was destroyed. Could take years to rebuild."

Duffy gave me a confused look, but Asheton had his eyes on me. Asheton was a pro. He was digging for something. I had to play it cool.

"Years," I repeated. "If ever."

"Lucky they got that crackerjack insurance policy," Duffy said.

Asheton ignored him. "What was it Panks was working on?"

I shook my head. "I'm just a detective. But whatever it was, it's finished."

"Couldn't Schuler rebuild it?"

Duffy chimed in, "Schuler's just—"

"Schuler's just a technician," I said. "Hugo has to talk him up. But Panks was the genius behind all this. Without Panks? My guess is Hugo will burn through his insurance and by year end, shut it all down."

"All right then." Asheton pocketed the Minox, smoothed down his shirtfront, and put on his suit coat. "To everyone else here, I'm just a journo from the *Times*. But you two remember this." He held his finger up within an inch of my face. "You hold anything back from me, I will have the FBI here, escorting you to court-martial."

Duffy and I left. I waited until we were outside and out of earshot.

"What do you think, Sergeant?"

"He had me fooled. So, he's some kind of Nazi hunter?"

"That's one way of putting it."

"At least we got the lab book back."

"Sure. After he photographed what was left of it. He's looking for those missing pages, same as Hugo."

He thought about it. "You were right about Panks being a Nazi."

"He's not the only one."

"You don't think Schuler's behind the accident?"

"I told you, he's dangerous."

"But you didn't say that to Asheton."

"You know how those intelligence guys are. They don't care about the men on the ground. They just want to submit a report that makes them look good."

Asheton was a spook. And I didn't want Duffy thinking too much about the reason he was here. Now I knew Schuler was up to something.

I stopped and turned to him. "Duffy, I need your help."

"Forget it. Whatever you're up to, I don't want any part of it."

"Look. It's easy. I need to see Schuler, but I don't want you saying anything to anyone, got it?"

Duffy looked down at the floor. "I don't know. I don't want any trouble."

"Look, if anyone asks, just say I'm walking the perimeter, okay?"

"What's this all about?"

"Schuler's the only person that really understands the Z-machine. If I'm not back in half an hour, burn the lab books."

CHAPTER 20
Vanishing Point

"For now, we walk without the light, you understand?" said Schuler.

"So no one sees us," I said.

I'd found Schuler in the barracks, where we'd left him. Once I'd hinted at Asheton's interest in missing Nazis, he became surprisingly cooperative.

"*Ja*. We need not attract any attention from Mr. Hugo. He might not appreciate what I am going to show you."

I didn't know how to interpret that, but I figured I'd won Schuler's confidence by not ratting him out to Asheton. So for now, I'd stay *shtum* and see what I could learn about the Z-machine, about Jordan, about any of it. I lit up when we stepped outside and inhaled deeply, but Schuler shook his head, so I put it out. It was a bad habit.

The rain had died down to a fine mist that cooled the air. We walked on the far side of the barracks through some shrubs and down a small incline that opened up onto a meadow. He turned on his flashlight at that point, but the moon was bright now and it was easier to follow the path without the flashlight messing with my night vision. I could see the building a few hundred feet ahead: old and rundown. But who was I to talk? The painted wood had faded, making it look like an old farm-house, shabby and angry, long since abandoned to nature.

Schuler stopped about fifty feet from the entrance. "This was the original building," Schuler said. "In recent years, it was abandoned."

"I can understand why," I said.

"We have sometimes stored old equipment here, when we have no more room in the lab. That's what I will show you." Then he held the palm of his left hand out. "And it is raining a bit, yes?" He waved his flashlight toward the workshop. "Over this way," he said as he headed left.

We walked a bit farther. He turned right and then he shone his light on the building. "Watch for the birds."

Suddenly there was a loud flapping noise and cawing as two very large crows launched from the roof of the storage building. They rose up and glided toward us. "Pay them no mind. They won't harm you," he said.

I couldn't help reacting, ducking my head as they flew past us, emitting ever-louder screeches. "What the hell?" I said.

"They can be very protective."

We walked the remaining distance to the storage building in silence. He stopped again about ten feet from the building. "Now look up. What do you see?"

"Nothing."

"That's right." He held out his hand. "And the rain?"

"The rain stopped," I said, not understanding what he was getting at.

"We turn off our lights," he said.

He turned off his flashlight.

"Now where are the moon, the stars, the clouds?"

I looked up and there was nothing but blackness. I couldn't see Schuler. The sound was strange, but then I realized it wasn't a sound at all—it was silence. The wind had died to nothing, the crickets were gone, so were the birds. There was nothing. The silence rang in my ears. I felt a chill. It was like when I entered the tunnels at Mittelwerk. It was strange how silence could transport me back.

I clicked my penlight but no light came. The click sounded muted and delayed, water hitting the bottom of a well.

"What are you playing at, Schuler?"

He answered, but his voice was strange, as if it were coming through a pipe. "It is a very special place."

"What is this, a haunted house tour?"

"It is no joke. I do not fully understand it and I have studied it for some years. I believe that we have stepped into a convergence area."

"What do you mean?"

"There are some strange phenomena here. I believe that the Chumash discovered this area and then made it *verboten*, as sacred land. But when Mr. Blake Hugo closed it off, it was not because it was a burial ground. That was a story he told. I think it was because the Chumash told him about this place; he knew it was dangerous."

"You sound like Charlie with his spiritualism," I said. I started to step back a few feet, to try to understand what was going on.

"Yes, that's good. Walk back. You see that the sky, the rain, they are all as normal?" Schuler said.

I walked back another three steps. I could see the moon, clouds, and stars once again.

"And all is come back," Schuler nodded like a conjuror finishing a favorite parlor trick.

A fine mist floated in the air. As I stepped forward, it became black again, as if the moon had set and the stars were extinguished.

"I did the same thing myself," he said. "Making observations, trying to determine the exact location and what caused these phenomena. I thought I could study this, write an interesting paper for my colleagues at *Annalen der Physik*."

"And?"

"Alan Hugo decided it was better to not call attention to the work we were doing here. And anyway, I didn't have the time to pursue it." There was an awkward silence. "Charlie doesn't like that we have a workshop here. So please don't mention to him our exploration."

I stepped back again, and the birds took another swoop at us and I covered my head with my free hand.

"And please remember about the birds."

I followed Schuler toward the storage building. It was larger than I first thought and built on a solid concrete foundation that seemed more suitable for an industrial facility than for storage. A few small trees nearby seemed to be dead or dying. A large concrete square was embedded in the ground adjacent to the building. I wasn't sure what it was for, but whoever built it wasn't fooling around.

Schuler reached into his pocket, futzed with the keys, and eventually unlocked a padlock and opened the wide door. It slid noisily on its track.

"Come. I show you," Schuler said. As I followed, in the corner of my eye, I thought I saw something move behind the trees. I turned quickly, but there was nothing to see. The place made me jumpy.

Schuler flicked on a few lights. I was surprised the building had electricity given how it looked from the outside. Inside was a different story though. The room was vast, orderly, and mostly empty. There was a large wooden chair with ropes of wire hanging off it next to a desk loaded with electronic equipment full of switches, dials, and multi-colored cables. The hairs on the back of my neck stood up. It wasn't as elegant or tidy as what I'd seen, but I knew at once what it was. It was another goddamn Z-Machine.

An image of Jordan strapped to a gurney flashed across my mind. I saw Jordan screaming silently just before the explosion. I gripped myself and clenched my eyes shut until it passed. I needed to know what Schuler had done to Jordan. But I had to play it on his terms and wait for the right moment.

"You see, I have my own workshop." Schuler pointed with pride. "We have had many different designs over the years. Sometimes we try a new approach and it does not fully work. Here I build the new parts."

"You've got a third shift going on here, don't you?"

He blinked at me.

"Running experiments off the books."

"Dr. Panks authorized me in this work," he said. "It was a way for me to stay productive. This is where I made my discovery, the idea to parallelize the resonators. This is the breakthrough I told Panks about." He looked upward as he remembered. "It is strange because I was walking down the trail to the workshop when I had the idea."

Schuler went on talking. "I was studying the birds as I made my way. I saw that they flew in interesting patterns, and I wondered how they did this. We know birdsong is a language and calls have different meanings. Could the patterns of their flight also be a form of communication? Then it struck me: if you thought about the flight of a single bird, you could not see the pattern. It was the behavior of the entire flock that was interesting, not the single bird. It was the entire sequence that mattered. Do you follow?"

It sounded like what Amy Hugo had written. Could two scientists come up with the same invention independently?

"Go on," I said.

"What do you think?" he said, looking at me curiously. "Could two birds come up with the same sequence independently?"

I felt like I was going to pass out. The light flickered and all the color drained from the room. It was a strange sensation, like I had been here many times before.

"It's a strange sensation, isn't it?" Schuler said, watching my face. "Sometimes I have the feeling I've been here so many times before. Do you ever have that feeling?"

I ran my hand through my hair. "What did you say?"

"Sorry, I don't mean to bore you with my theories."

"You said it was a strange sensation?"

"Did I? I was explaining how I came up with what I call my fan-out design. It's much more complex than we had built previously. We are controlling dozens of small resonators in parallel. Each component part is quite simple, but put together, it's like—"

"Jazz," I said.

Schuler frowned. "I would have said a symphony. But I suppose jazz is equally true."

He looked across the makeshift lab like a farmer eying his storehouse in October. "But so far the machinery here has been used strictly for measurements. It has never run at full potential."

"What's the matter?" I asked. "No more volunteers?"

"You have such a hard nature." Schuler stiffened. "You believe in nothing. I want you to understand what the Z-machine is capable of. Perhaps, Mr. Waters, you can pass the test that I cannot. Only a small number of people are able to benefit from the Z-machine."

He tapped his forehead. "I believe it is related to the genet-
ics of the pineal gland, but so far, we do not know the full
reason. Your brother, Jordan, had the ability, and so I believe
you will have it also."

At that moment, I saw him as the monster he was, clipboard in hand, licking his lips, prepping one more for the stack
of cadavers. My blood was boiling over; I couldn't hold back
anymore.

"Because of you, my brother never returned from the war.
I don't know if he's dead or missing," I shouted.

"As you say, it was war," Schuler said flatly. "And yes, scientists like me, like Fermi, like Oppenheimer, we supported
our leaders. They do not ask us to kill. They think we are too
refined for that. They ask us to think. To create equations. To
invent. To push beyond the limits of physics."

He leaned his head back, distancing himself from his words.

"I do not know what happened to Jordan, but, yes, what
you condemn me for is true. My experiments killed. Exactly
so. Dozens of twins. Believe me, I know the price paid. We
had such hope for them all. With each experiment we learned
more. But it was only your brother who fully recovered each
time. The others, they were blinded or suffered from such brain
damage they were not human anymore. We had no choice but
to destroy them." He shrugged. "And then, when we were
finally on the cusp, we released you. So we never performed
the last experiment."

So the deaths of dozens were justified in the name of science. I shook my head. "You're a cruel sonofabitch, Schuler."

"It was not cruelty. Tragedy, perhaps. Your President
Truman pushed science to the furthest limits at Hiroshima.
One hundred thousand dead. And after three days, Nagasaki,
another fifty thousand. Truman wept, but he did it. To prove

what was possible, so that all would see. The Japanese, the Germans, the Russians."

"My brother was lost. For what?"

"What do you mean, lost? Did they not search?"

"Yes, they searched the wreckage of the tunnels, but he was never found."

"But others were found?" he asked.

"Yes, of course."

Schuler scratched his chin. "We learned so much at Dunkelwerk. I am still learning. Others would have taken five years to achieve what we did in six months."

"And how many died for your Z-machine?"

"We worked on a hundred and thirty-nine twins. One hundred and thirty-eight died. I suppose, you may count Jordan dead, making it one hundred and thirty-nine." He looked directly into my eyes and I held his gaze. He paused, then his voice softened. "I see that in a different way."

He removed his glasses and polished them on his sleeve. "I knew all of them. I picked them out at the platform when they arrived at Mittelbau-Dora. And when we needed more, I went to Buchenwald. Or Auschwitz, Ravensbrück, Dachau. I went everywhere. It was hard to find so many twins during the war. I saved them. I gave them a chance to help us with science. And then it turned out your brother was our best test subject. An American spy. Ironic, isn't it?"

"You killed them all," I said.

Schuler nodded. He blinked and put his glasses back in place.

"You're a monster."

Schuler didn't flinch. "My experiments were a rounding error compared to how many died of starvation digging the tunnels to make rockets. Twenty thousand, at least. Maybe more.

"My twins, we fed them. We clothed them. I am sorry that they died. But believe me, they would have died much worse otherwise. They were willing to risk it all to advance science."

"Then they all died in vain."

"No, you're wrong. Because now we have succeeded."

How deluded could he be? I felt my face growing hot, and when I spoke I realized I was shouting. "All you do is destroy! Even Panzinger."

"No. I do this for him. To continue our research."

"This is finished."

"Not at all. It is a lucky accident you are here, isn't it? You have come to understand this place. You know what we are working on. You are no insurance investigator."

"I am."

"But that is not why you came here with me, to see this place. It is not the insurance, the fire, all of that. A routine death. You must have seen hundreds in the war. What would it matter to you?"

"I recognized Panzinger. I knew that whatever is going on here is connected to the past."

"Yes, it is all connected. And the strange phenomena we have witnessed outside? The crows, the silence, the darkness?"

"What about it?"

"Do you think it is a mere coincidence? Some trick of the light?"

"Don't play your games with me, Schuler."

"What do you want from me? Tell me."

"I need to find Jordan." I whispered it like a confession. He had me.

I had stumbled around in the dark for five years. Drunk. Stoned. Getting nowhere. Faith was right. I was wasting my life away.

And then a door had opened. The door happened to be held open by Nazis, one of whom was dead and the other a killer, a scientist who would tally as many deaths as required to further his research. It was madness.

Could I risk it? How could I not?

"Where is Jordan?" I asked.

"Now you are beginning to understand." He nodded. "You see, Jordan had not fully returned from the experiment."

"What?"

"His body, yes. But his mind, his being, was still under the control of the Z-machine. The explosion interrupted our experiment. That was a situation we had not anticipated. In effect, the experiment never ended. I have been working on it these five years. Your brother's location is complex. It is not just a question of *where*. But also of *when*."

Could it really be true?

"Your brother is a hero," Schuler said. "The first to make it to the vanishing point. And as a result, I am able to make my breakthrough discovery after all these years. Doctor Panzinger trained me well. I recorded the results from every experiment. And so we have a way to resolve the issue." He pointed to the Z-machine.

"You're out of your mind," I said.

"You, too, would become a hero."

"Shut up!" I yelled.

"Forgive me, Captain Waters, for my English is not so perfect." He looked at the floor and his head swayed. He peered up at me. "What I mean is that you will have fulfilled your role . . . your destiny.

"I remember when we started the experiments with your twin brother. He was very bold. Argumentative, like you. It took some time to crack him. It was necessary. I think he understood that, even from the beginning. And do you know what kept him going?"

I stared at him, not moving a muscle.

"Your brother said you would come for him." He looked at me, hawk-like, unblinking. I could see my reflection in his glasses. His mouth congealed into a thin smile. "So my only question is, will you?"

That was it. I could continue pissing away my life with no hope of finding Jordan or I could take a wild shot with a sociopath scientist claiming to reveal some new world behind his curtain.

I wasn't afraid of dying. I had seen death up close during the war. And I'd come close to taking a swan dive off the Ambassador Bridge in Detroit. My fear, my real crushing fear, was that I would never see Jordan again. And that I would continue to wonder every day what I could have done differently in the tunnels to save him.

It was preposterous.

So how could I say no? This was my last chance to make amends. I couldn't trust Schuler. He'd ruined my life by taking Jordan from me. But he was right. I had a duty.

"There is only one way for you to understand what happened to your brother. I will re-calibrate the Z-machine to take you to him."

"This is quackery." Even as I said the words, I knew I had to do it. What was I risking? I had nothing. A flimsy business. A girlfriend ready to skip town. A bunch of ne'er-do-well musicians and flannel merchants as friends. It was nothing compared to Jordan. I would do anything for him. Anything to bring him back or to even know, after all that had happened, that he was dead.

I would put an end to it.

I walked forward and sat in the chair attached to the Z-machine.

I bowed my head and I thought of how Jordan must have felt.

"All right, Schuler. How does this work?"

Schuler gave me a damp smile. "It has taken many years of research to perfect what we started at Mittelwerk. You will have an easier time of it than your brother."

He reached over and strapped my arms to the chair.

"And how do I get back from wherever it is I'm going?"

He shrugged. "It is an experiment, not a bus excursion. I have set the machine to take you to the vanishing point."

"You're not helping."

"It's where our dimensions join with other dimensions, beyond our world, like when you look out in the distance. Remember outside, when the crows, the rain, the moon receded from perception? It is like that, augmented by the power of the machine, a place at the edge of infinity."

"Jesus, Schuler, I don't even know what that means."

"Your brother has seen it many times. My calculations show he is still there. As you saw from the demonstration outside, one can be only a few feet away and seem to inhabit another dimension. This is why your involvement in the experiment is so important. Your body should react identically to Jordan's. And so it should be easy for me to replicate the original experiment."

I tugged at the restraints. I wanted to show the tough guy again. But it was too late to change my mind.

"We have three stages to transcend," Schuler said. "The first stage requires an injection of Pervitin. It helps the pineal gland become more receptive to the waves we create with the resonators. Dr. Panzinger's method was to add a dose of

Dolantin near the brain, to ease the shivers. I will give you that same courtesy."

I nodded.

He drew a large syringe, filling it with a translucent, light brown liquid. When he finished, he held my head tightly and shot the syringe right into my right eye socket. Christ, I screamed. It burned into me. He pushed my head forward until my chin touched my chest. A second sharp jab in my neck, just below my skull. No burning this time.

I wondered how many times Jordan had been shot up with narcotics. When I found him in the tunnels, he seemed terrified, a lunatic. What had he seen?

I may have passed out momentarily, until Schuler grabbed my face and shook it. He whispered into my ear. His voice was distorted and welded directly into my brain: "When you get to the stasis zone, you will see some strange, translucent images. They won't cause you any harm. But whatever you do, do not move suddenly. It is quite dangerous if you should get stuck there. Time will seem to move at a different rate for you. So you must count to seven and then pull the switch at your right hand."

I thought of all the time I'd spent searching for Jordan. I would have paid any price just to learn what happened to him. Could this really work? It was insane. I regretted my decision already. Schuler had me strapped down tight. What did he care if he killed one more twin?

Schuler pulled a large power lever. The lights dimmed momentarily. There was a low electric hum and static electricity filled the air. "I have calibrated the machine as best I can. We will see if you have the ability that I do not."

"And if not?"

He pointed down on the ground. "Please to use the bucket," he said.

The noise of the machinery was as loud as an aircraft.

His voice was louder now. "Waters, you are a good man, but you understand so little about science. Dr. Panzinger was truly a visionary and his work must continue."

"He betrayed us. He blew up the tunnel," I shouted.

"Of course not. Dr. Panzinger was a man of his word. When you return, I will tell you my theory and answer any questions you have."

He slipped a pair of goggles over my eyes. "Try to relax your mind," he shouted over the noise.

"But if it wasn't Panzinger—"

"Three . . . two . . . "

"—then who was it?"

" . . . one."

I became aware of the low thrum of the electric machinery pulsing through my legs, then my arms and fingertips. Then a deep rumbling that got louder until it sounded like a Panzer Brigade charging through my head, blocking my mind and any capacity for thought. I felt a surge through my body, an explosion from the inside followed by a deafening noise. The air danced like the heat rising from asphalt on a summer day.

In the blur, I saw Schuler mouth something as he pointed to his wristwatch. His face was enlarged and distorted, as if in a giant curved mirror an inch from my face.

In the corner of my eye, a tiny figure emerged from the shadows. He seemed to be a mile away, but he was in the same room. I thought for a moment it was Jordan come to rescue me.

Then I heard the distinct metallic sound, amplified like a crash cymbal. It was Asheton with his Minox.

PART II

CHAPTER 21
The Color of Dreams

There was no sound. No light. Nothing. I wondered whether I was anywhere at all, whether I even existed.

I've been kyboshed before. That happens when you're deep into the wrong kind of case against the wrong kind of people. But this was different. My head didn't throb. I had no sensation at all. I was a speck of dust floating in air, slowly, slowly falling to ground.

I had to give it to Schuler; his Z-machine put me out beyond the far edge. You could kick the gong around on a three-day bender and end up in a place you might not want to come back from, and I was way past there now. I was staring into a deep dark mirror with nothing reflecting back. It scared the hell out of me.

I heard a cough. It was Sergeant Major Kolchak, my drill instructor from Camp Adair, *ahem-ing* to get my attention. Then there were three or four of him coughing. Then a whole platoon. The coughs were getting faster and higher pitched until they became the cawing of crows.

The air rippled and I was back. The room was the same as before, but everything felt hopped-up, like a movie set. That was it. It was a set-up. A bunch of Hollywood razzmatazz to spook the defective detective. But when I looked up, there were no klieg lights. Just a 40-watt Edison hanging from a wire.

I could see more detail than before. I saw the wood grain in the wall down to hair-sized lines. In a corner, across the room, I saw an ant walking up a beam. It was carrying a white particle the size of a pencil tip. I could smell it. It was a breadcrumb. But it had mold. I could smell that, too. *Be careful there, Mr. Ant*, I thought. I shook my head. I shouldn't be talking to ants. That was a bad sign.

I looked around again. I didn't notice before, but the room was familiar. I'd seen it dozens of times in my dreams. I looked to the corner again and the ant was gnawing on his bread. His fuzzy antennae were vibrating in sync with the clenching of his jaw. Only now he was looking at me with his black oval eyes, as if I were the ant.

I closed my eyes and tried to shake myself out of it. My eyes felt scratchy and sharp.

I felt pretty stupid falling for Schuler's theatrics about Jordan and the Z-machine. It was a bunco job. The room was cold and silent with a thin ray of moonlight shining in from the windows. At least the rain had stopped.

Good that Schuler had untied me and left my gun on the table. I suppose he didn't want to stick around and risk my wrath when I came to. I got up slowly, but my head swayed. My legs wouldn't hold and I fell back into the chair. I took a deep breath. I held my weight on my arms and then gradually stood up until I regained control. I walked toward the table to get my gun, weaving like a drunk on a Sunday morning. I checked the gun and it was loaded. I put it in my pocket. It'd be a helluva thing to explain to Duffy.

I looked at my wristwatch again but couldn't make out the hands. I could hardly blame Longines for that.

"Schuler," I called out. "Your experiment didn't work." The sound was muffled and flat, as if after a snowstorm. Nothing sounded right.

"Schuler's not here," a woman's voice answered. "It's just me."

It was a voice I thought I recognized. A light fog rolled into the room obscuring everything. I tried to take a few paces forward, though I wasn't sure if I was actually walking or just standing in place thinking about it. Whatever he had dosed me with, it was working overtime. Everything seemed off.

She had her back to me. She wore a long, black dress that rippled as she moved; it seemed to glow, lit from above.

"Beverley?" I proffered. She shouldn't be messing around here. Maybe Schuler had put her up to this, part of their elaborate theatrics to throw me off. That's when she turned around and I saw the face from the oil painting staring back at me. "Not Beverley," she said. "I'm Amy Hugo."

Amy Hugo. Beverley's dead mother. But that wasn't possible. It had to be Beverley, dressed up like Amy. "Yeah, sure you are. And I'm Roy Rogers. Look, I've seen every grift you can imagine, so I'm not buying this back-from-the-dead act."

She had a calm look, as if she knew every objection I could offer but was undeterred at the prospect. She had dark blue eyes that stared, the same as Beverley's.

"I've been waiting a long time to meet you, Mr. Waters. Such a long time."

"Whose lunatic pantomime is this?" I asked. I was trying to call her out on her act. But something was wrong. The fog was everywhere now, engulfing me. I couldn't see. I slashed through the air to try to clear it, but to no avail.

She came forward then. Rising like a ghost as she reached out a hand, as if to stroke my face. "Jack Waters... *five for waters, six for thee*," she said in a lilting voice. And then she touched my cheek. It was real. It wasn't a vision or a hallucination. That's what sent me over the edge.

"What the bloody hell!" I cried. I looked around at the swirling mist but I could see nothing. No ceiling, no sky, no objects, nothing. And then I realized my feet weren't touching the ground. I was suspended in air, weightless, standing on nothing. In school we were taught physics. Things like gravity and the idea that the world was an actual place. But now reality itself was a gaping void with no end.

"I know it's a lot to take in," she smiled. She seemed amused as though she'd expected my reaction. "Everything is going to be okay."

And then as if a soft summer breeze had blown in, I felt calm.

"We're here in a kind of temporal limbo."

Even that didn't bother me as much because it gave me some hope. If there was a rational explanation for what was happening, it meant I wasn't mad and I could get back from whatever this place was.

She seemed eager to explain it all to me. I could see thoughts beaming through her eyes. Maybe it was all part of some strange experiment.

I frantically eyed the void around me. Initially it seemed to be a medium-sized room, but now it was as big as a carnival midway. There was nothing I could grab hold of in my defense. Defense from *what* exactly? I didn't know, but wherever this was going couldn't be good. My head had begun pounding from the strangeness of it all.

Bright lights were emanating from behind her and I had to cover my eyes.

"I'm in hell!" I cried. The pain in my head was too much. I tried to block it, but it was crushing me.

"There is no such thing as hell," she said. "What you are in, right now, is a parallel dimension. A kind of in-between place where travelers such as you and I can meet safely for a little while."

"I'm not interested, sister."

"Listen to me, Mr. Waters. This is serious business. Lives are at stake."

"Are you threatening me?"

"This isn't about you, me, or even Faith."

"How do you know about Faith? Leave her out of it." I felt a surge of anger and I reached into my pocket in case I'd need to play the heavy, but I came up empty.

"Faith will very much be part of this." She looked across the expanse. "Your gun is back on the table."

"No, it's . . . "

I had come undone. I'd had my gun. I had felt it. And now it was gone. My whole body turned heavy. This was some sort of twisted world. She was in charge, making things happen or vanish or suspend in mid-air, any way she wanted.

"There's a reality in which you picked up your gun. But there's another in which you left it on the table. There's a world where you save your brother and one where he saves you. There's a life in which you and Faith never meet and another where you lose her. Do you understand what I'm saying?"

"Okay, Amy Hugo." I stepped forward. I leaned right into her gaze, the most intimidating cop-stance I could take, so she could smell my breath. Her brow wrinkled for a moment but she remained calm. "I need you to understand something," I said slowly and emphatically. I drew an X in the air. "I am ex-ing myself out of this. I'm not sticking around for this ballyhoo. It can't be true."

"It is not a question of truth. It is about possibility and consequence. Every path is its own discrete story. Some are better, most are worse. But at any given moment, only one path comes to life, though many more can spring from it. The only reason I'm here with you now is because of the breakthrough I had with the original Z-machine."

"That's got nothing to do with me."

"I wish that were true. Unfortunately, it has everything to do with you and Jordan."

Every time I was ready to turn and walk away, she pulled me back in.

"How do I know I'm not just a pawn in all of this?"

"You *are* a pawn." She laughed. "You captured a factory during the war." She looked deep into my eyes.

"Mittelwerk? What of it?" I felt dizzy. Images of the prison camp flashed in my mind. My failure. The cold, damp smell of the tunnels filled my nostrils. I was there living it all over again.

"That's the reason for your dreams, Mr. Waters. That's why you ended up in Loma Vista. It's not by chance. It's connected. So that you can do what you should have done."

"I don't understand."

"You didn't know about Panks and Schuler. How could you? But your actions at Mittelwerk changed the course of history."

"How do you know about any of this?"

"I have seen every path you have gone down and every path you didn't. I know your past better than you do. Now it's up to you."

"And what happens with the other paths?"

"They are like shadows. They fade over time."

"So they're not real?"

"That is the wrong question. They are as real as you or I. But they are of no long-term consequence."

"And are we?"

"That remains to be seen. Panks discovered the access point to other dimensions during the war, as part of the Black Sun project. It should have been destroyed, but you killed those two German soldiers. All of Mittelwerk, including the early Z-machines, should have been buried in rubble. Instead, Panks and Schuler escaped, and five years later we are on the brink of disaster. Scientists will use that technology to create weapons more powerful than you can imagine. How do you think that plays out?"

I turned my back and walked into the mist. Sooner or later, whatever this was would vanish. I'd be back to normal. I'd get the gun I'd left on the table and never let it go. To hell with Amy, Panks, Schuler, and the whole lot of them.

"Let me show you what happens to your world if you don't."

I turned back and followed her gaze. I knew where we were headed. It was my nightmare.

The walls rippled. Suddenly, they blew past me like a freight train at a hundred miles an hour. The ground ripped apart and I was seeing all of the Blakely Estate from a perch high in the hills. I saw the meadows off in the distance, but as I got closer, I could see there was nothing left. They were barren, full of rock and ash. The farms were gone, burned down and abandoned. Then I was overlooking the town. Buildings were boarded, store windows smashed, cars set on fire.

I'd seen this in my dreams, hundreds of times before. But there was something new. I saw Faith on the street, begging. She was old, her hair was gray, her skin burned and covered in festering sores.

A flash burst on the horizon and I was blinded for a moment. I saw only whiteness and then gradually a shape took form. A cloud emerged from the ground and shot up to the heavens and spread out, blocking out the sky, the sun, and all light. A blast of heat came with the force of a hurricane and knocked me to the ground.

I stared up at the sky, my face caked with dust and dirt. The clouds became twisted faces. Skulls, bones, and bodies piled up in front of me to reveal a massive tomb that became a skyscraper, then a city of horrors. Wild dogs feasted on the carcasses. It was an obscene vision with tortured voices calling out, begging me, urging me to end their existence. I saw myself from a distance, frozen on the spot, unable to get up, unable to draw a breath.

I was hallucinating something wild. I'd seen hop-heads get the heebie-jeebies, and now I understood what they went through.

"Waters!" Amy commanded. She raised her hand and, suddenly, everything was quiet.

She drew me back in. The light she cast drowned out the dark vision like a sunrise in a desert. "It doesn't have to end that way."

"I don't believe any of this!"

"It doesn't matter what you believe. You know what you did at Mittelwerk. You've seen this world before. Eleven years ago, I designed a new mechanism that enabled the Z-machine to break through to higher dimensions beyond our world. But once I understood its power, I destroyed it. Now Schuler has made the same discovery, which is what brought you here. You need to finish what was started. You need to destroy it all. That's the only way to shut the door on this dark world."

She bit her lip and then slowly let out her breath.

"The Z-machine will show you things you might not want to see. What happened in the tunnels has created memories. These will be triggers when you go back. Or maybe waypoints is a better way to think of them. That can lead to side effects."

"Like what?"

"Different dimensions start to compete in your brain. It might appear as a form of psychosis. You may have a sense of déjà vu, confusion, synesthesia," she said.

"Syntha-what?"

"It's when your senses become blurred. You can see music. Colors become associated with words or sounds."

See music? I'd been doing that for years, when I was in the groove. I assumed it was just part of being a musician. "I'll deal with it," I said.

"These are signs that you are in a gray area, that multiple dimensions are in conflict. You can't ignore these warnings. Things can go badly wrong."

What did I care? I'd already lost everything.

"Why should I even listen to you?"

"Because there's a parallel universe where Jordan doesn't die," Amy said.

That did it. "You know nothing about Jordan," I said. "Don't even say his name."

I walked back to where she was. I had nothing at hand, so I ripped my watch off my wrist and threw it at her. She moved aside, effortlessly. Then I reached into my pocket and pulled out a tin of mints. "You can take your stories, take your parallel universes, and get out of my head," I said. I clenched the bottle of mints.

"Jordan asked me to tell you something: Code Boxer." She smiled, unblinking.

I dropped the tin. It clattered to the ground. The little green mints rolled around on the floor. They reminded me of tiny crabs in a frenzy, trying to find their mother crab, going in circles, giving up and then falling to the side on the ground.

Code Boxer.

That was a phrase only Jordan and I knew. It wasn't military. It was a private lingo we used, in homage to the dog he made me put down. It signaled a grave situation where the normal rules didn't apply.

Jordan had used it on our eighteenth birthday. I'd gotten drunk with some friends and we'd busted some windows at the train depot. Someone must have heard the noise and a patrol car pulled up. He whispered *Boxer* to me and then ran to the cops, waving his arms excitedly. In that case it meant, *I'll take the rap. Get out of here.*

Boxer could mean a lot of things, but mostly it meant *do the hard thing, no matter what your instincts tell you.*

"How do you know about Boxer?" I asked. It wasn't something either of us would have told another person. That meant Jordan had betrayed a secret. But it also meant something else. The seed of an idea sat in my mind, growing larger.

"Jordan's alive," I said.

"Yes."

I heard a *whoomph* that sounded like a gas stove igniting.

Her dress started to quiver in the light, rippling green and then some other colors I'd never seen before. Her skin became translucent and she started to fade. She bowed her head but her face was impassive.

I hesitated to even blink, trying to hold on to her image and her "yes" as she faded into the darkness.

CHAPTER 22

Into the Night

Antwerp, Belgium
November 23, 1944

The waitress slammed the heavy beer chalices down on the table. Foam poured over the sides, as it always did. It melted into a puddle on the table and caught my eye, the way the light reflected orange and blue from the Christmas ornaments that had been hung along the window. I had seen it before. We were at Quinten Matsys, one of our favorite places.

It was Thanksgiving and I made the best of it. Holidays in the war reminded me how far I was from home. If you were lucky, you got a letter or maybe a package. But I'd won the grand prize: a visit from my brother.

"I brought you some turkey," I said, handing him a small package wrapped in pink butcher's paper.

Jordan laughed, buoyant as always. "You guys had turkey? I'm impressed."

"It might be chicken. It's hard to say. But it's better than K-rations."

It had been too long. Opportunities to meet during the war were rare. We clanked our glasses in celebration.

The bar was located down a narrow cobblestone street and looked like it hadn't changed in two hundred years. It hadn't suffered any damage in the war and the German officers used it as their own private refuge. Since liberation, it had become an informal gathering place for Allied officers. The people of Antwerp were generous and kind, and they left you alone when you wanted a quiet conversation. This wasn't a place for GIs. If a soldier peeked his head in looking for excitement, he'd see enough brass to start a bell factory and would back out discreetly.

An upright piano stood at the back, and maybe a dozen small round wooden tables. A couple of Brits smoked Woodbines and huddled with men who had been part of the resistance.

I was in my army fatigues with a three-day stubble. Jordan was wearing a dark civilian suit, looking like a Swiss bank clerk. Every now and then we'd get a double take when someone noticed our resemblance.

"*Tweeling*," they would say, pointing to each of us in turn.

We were used to it, not that we wanted the attention. We'd nod politely, not smiling, not engaging. Better to keep a low profile.

I was grateful that we had a break from the front, before we'd make our push through the wetlands of Belgium and across the Roer river into Germany. The fighting had been hard, and we did a lot of it at night to keep the casualties low.

Allied troops had been advancing at a rapid rate in the last month. Unfortunately, they were moving faster than supplies were arriving. The British Second Army captured Antwerp in September and my division, the 104th, was attached to the Canadian First Army.

I recounted our landing in France and how we cleared the port, which would enable the supply lines to catch up.

"That must have been something," Jordan said. "This is the real war, right here. It won't be long before the Germans are fenced in." He took a gulp of beer and wiped his mouth with the back of his hand. "I miss this."

"Come on. It's just a grunt operation. Tell me what you've been up to."

Jordan had studied languages so he started in the war as a radio operator and translator. In a few months he'd mastered all the regional dialects and accents. One night there was an urgent call to translate communications with Swiss agents reporting on German rocket production. That got the attention of Allen Dulles, who pulled Jordan on a temporary assignment to Bern that would last the rest of the war.

"Well, it's a bit complicated." He scanned the room, but no one was paying any attention. He lowered his voice. "The OSS has assigned me a job at Dehomag. It's IBM's business in Berlin."

"Congratulations," I said, and we clinked glasses. "Don't tell me you're running the show."

"Believe me, nothing so glamorous. *Ich bin Dehomag Mechaniker.*" He shrugged. "I'm a repairman."

"Did you do something wrong? Did you write mom?" I laughed. Jordan lit a cigarette and leaned in with his lighter to light mine.

"You know those punch cards?"

I shrugged. Everyone had heard of IBM.

Jordan drew on the cigarette with his right hand, then leaned back and reached into his jacket with his other hand. He raised the cigarette above his head and then fanned the cards with his left hand. They were wide cardboard strips emblazoned with the word *Rassenamt* and twin-lightning bolts. Like a magician, he held them out for just a second and then they disappeared back into his jacket in one swift motion.

I had a vague premonition. People lined up. Stripes. Rotting food.

"The German government has been using IBM punch cards and sorting machines to run their census since '33. They encode all the information about people on the cards by punching holes in different columns for age, height, religion, and so on."

The image faded. My mind reshuffled like a deck of cards.

"Jack, pay attention. This is serious. *Rassenamt* is the racial settlement department of the SS. The Nazis have been using this information to route Jews to the ghettoes and put them on trains to prison camps."

I'd read a few stories in the newspapers but I was doubtful. It was hard to know what to believe in the middle of a war.

"It's all true. I've seen the tabulations. The Nazis are shipping thousands of Jews, Slavs, Poles by train every day to slave labor camps. They track everything on these machines. I'm like the guy at the circus, following behind the elephants with a broom and dustpan. They've got IBM machines at every train station, every prison camp, every factory. And they have to be cleaned and serviced regularly."

"So you put some gremlins into the machines, is that it?"

"Jack, that's not how it works. The German government is IBM's second biggest customer. We're learning everything we can about V-2 rocket production and new weapons. The German army is way ahead of us.

"We've got Allied scientists following troops into every city where there's a university, a research center, or a lab. As soon as we control an area, we're going in and stripping everything we can find to give us a leg up for the rest of the war." Jordan's leg was bouncing with energy.

"I thought this was going to come to a close by the summer."

"In Europe, maybe. But who knows how long we'll be fighting in the Pacific?"

I took a sip of my beer, feeling outmatched. Jordan was operating at a different level. He always had.

"So, IBM knows you're . . . ?" I didn't want to say anything out loud.

"No, of course not. I'm just 'Swiss repairman,'" he said it with a sing-song accent. "I have a boss in Germany at Dehomag, and then I have my other boss in Bern." He looked upward for a moment. "There are only three people who know my cover. Plus you." He paused. "Strictly speaking, that's one too many."

"Got it."

"One of the biggest sites for Dehomag is a factory called Mittelwerk. It's outside Nordhausen in central Germany. They've dug into an old gypsum mine in the mountainside. They moved all the V-2 rocket manufacturing there."

"Underground?" I had a feeling he'd told me this already, but I hadn't seen him in months. A few more officers entered the bar and the small room was getting crowded.

"They moved everything underground so they can't be bombed. Luckily, they're nowhere near full production. It's a slow process to build these things. So, like everything else, they just throw thousands of laborers at it."

"In a small town? How's that even possible?"

"Jack, are you listening? They've got a slave labor camp there called Mittelbau-Dora. There are forty thousand prisoners in the area. They use slave labor for everything. Military, civilian, every factory in Germany is running slave labor from occupied territories. Siemens, Krupp, Ford, they all do it." He shrugged. "That's one of the reasons the SS rounds up all these people. They hire them out to factories to fund the war."

I shook my head. "I had no idea." One of the Englishmen puffed heavily on his pipe, giving off an overwhelming peppery smell. The warm air and smoke were making me hazy.

"How could you? That's why you have to keep pushing on the Western front. We need to get to Germany before they ramp up production. Meanwhile, they're expanding Mittelwerk, opening up more tunnels for a new lab. They've ordered dozens of new IBM machines, and they want more frequent maintenance. We think they're building other types of *Wunderwaffen*, what they call their super weapons. And they're going even deeper underground."

"With all the air force bombing, is it safe for you to be behind the lines?"

"Probably not," Jordan laughed. He brushed a lock of hair from his forehead. "They wouldn't put me someplace I couldn't get out of. I've got papers, some cash, gold coins."

A wave of nausea came over me. I stood up and knocked the table, upending my beer glass. It rolled and smashed on the stone floor. Conversations stopped as all eyes turned to us, and then, like a scene change in a theater, the conversations resumed. An older man in an apron tut-tutted his way from behind the bar. He had a wet rag in one hand and wiped down the table. Then he bent down to pick up the glass with a piece of newspaper in his other hand.

"Let's get out of here," I said. I pulled out some coins and left them on the table. More than enough to cover our drinks, the glass, and another round. Jordan pulled a face and downed the rest of his beer with a shrug. We stepped through the stone archway of the Quinten and onto the street. It was dusk and the light was fading.

"Sorry, I just—" I waved my hand. "I needed to get some air."

"It's fine." He put his hand on my shoulder. "You okay?"

"All that smoke was getting to me." I stretched my shoulders and made a show of breathing in the cool, damp air. "Let's take a walk." We headed west toward the river, walking for a few minutes. There was a quarter moon rising in the horizon.

We stood for a few moments at the Het Steen castle and looked out at the ships in the water. I asked him, "What if you get caught?"

"Come on, Jack. It's no different from what you do. You focus on the mission. If we can get their technology, we can bring the war to an end. That's why we're *all* doing this."

"Yeah, but I've got a whole division with me. You're out there on your own."

He stuck his hands in his pockets. "I've got what I need. Anyway, it's like shooting a river. It's kind of exciting." He arched his back. "And if it works, think of the stories we'll tell."

"Goddamn, Jordan," I said softly and shook my head. "Hey, remember this?" I pulled out a picture we'd taken at boot camp. We'd just had our buzz cuts.

He held it in his hand for a moment. "A couple of farm boys," he said.

I thought it was a black-and-white snap, but for a moment, it was in color. I saw the blue sky and orange sunshine as I remembered it, the start of a great adventure.

He looked at me and then reached to hand it back.

"No, keep it." I stiffened and then tried to soften my words. "Dad sent it to me." He nodded and put it in his coat pocket. "I'll tell them *hi* from you."

Jordan looked at his watch. "It's getting late. I gotta go, Jack." He turned and tucked the paper-wrapped parcel under his arm and walked into the night.

It always ended that way. Jordan considered it bad luck to say goodbye. Our goodbyes were always too short for me, too long for Jordan.

I watched him wander off and then took a seat on a nearby bench. The nausea was doing a number on my balance. This made no sense. I'd drank less than a beer.

I tried to prop my head up with my right hand and I missed, brushing the top of my ear. I rolled my shoulders back and then stood up. Too fast. I sank, falling onto my back on the ground. My head rolled under the bench. I looked up through the wooden slats at the night sky and I heard crows. Dozens of them. They were circling nearby, swooping, cawing. Getting louder, closer still.

I closed my eyes to make it stop.

CHAPTER 23
The Cathedral

Köln, Germany
March 16, 1945

I don't know how I got to Köln.

I had memories from Antwerp—broken glass, the slats of a bench, Jordan. And I knew how our battles had gone for the past four months. We had been moving ten to twelve miles a day across the marshes of Belgium and into Germany, earning every mile. But there were gaps in my recall.

It was like when I was in the coma at the evac hospital. I was in a different world and things were happening around me, not to me. But how is it I could remember the coma when we were still two hundred miles from Nordhausen? This wasn't battle fatigue. I was skipping through time and I couldn't control it.

Köln was deserted. There was hardly a building left standing other than the cathedral. Whether it was fate or the Royal Air Force's need for a navigational marker was anyone's guess, and there was no one to ask. It was like traveling back to a prehistoric time. The few remaining buildings looked like they'd come down if a mortar was pointed in their direction.

I gazed across the sky toward the cathedral. It stood alone, a mile in the distance. The sun was starting to rise, struggling to break through the clouds casting the landscape in black and white. The war had knocked out the last of my small-town Catholicism, but the sight of the cathedral standing amid ruin was too strong to ignore. The feeling haunted me more than it beckoned, but after so much death and destruction, I felt a need for solace. I remained on guard as we stepped through the rubble of the city toward its twin ancient spires. If I could get to the cathedral, everything would be jake.

I set out at dawn with Sergeant Baldwin from Atlanta and two riflemen from Texas. The Texans had been out a few hours earlier and spotted signs of life along the river, including the remnants of a campfire. The German army was running thin. Their only objective was to slow us down. If there were any stragglers, we expected them to be in the central area of town between the river and the cathedral. I moved steadily up the street, eyes scanning the alleys, doorways, and piles of brick-work, looking for a sign.

"Mickey Mouse," a hoarse voice whispered. The words echoed in my mind but I saw nothing. I signaled for my men to stop. I wondered whether I had imagined the voice, but the look on the face of Sergeant Baldwin, behind me, told me I hadn't.

"Mickey Mouse," it repeated, like a passcode. The voice was coming from behind a crumbled brick wall ahead of me on the left. I waited for it. "*Amerikaner?*"

"*Ja, Amerikaner. Zeige dich!*" I shouted.

My rifle was out and aimed toward the opening in the wall. Everyone followed suit. A young soldier stumbled out from behind the wall, nearly falling to the ground.

"*Arschloch!*" he said, but it was clear he'd meant it for some-one still behind the wall. He straightened himself quickly and threw his hands in the air. He had blue eyes and curly hair and looked like a kid I knew back home in Michigan. I did a double take. He was about thirteen and couldn't have weighed more than a hundred pounds, including his oversized coat and the hat that hung too low over his ears. I put my rifle down and stepped slowly forward.

"Cap, you sure?" Baldwin asked. But I waved him off. This was a kid. I knew it would be okay.

"Where's your friend?" I said, pointing to where he'd come from. His eyes looked furtively at the three men with rifles aimed at him. "*Bitte*," he croaked. "*Wir geben auf.*"

"It's okay," I said as calmly as I could, walking slowly forward. "You want a smoke?" I reached into my pocket, and I thought the kid was going to faint.

"*Zigarreten*," I called out.

He nodded vigorously, trying to keep it together. "*Ja, ja,*" he said.

I threw my pack of Luckies at him. It bounced lightly off his chest, and he just barely caught it with both hands.

His mouth opened in surprise. "*Ja, danke,*" he said. "*Gunter,*" he hissed to his friend behind the wall. "*Komm schon.*" He opened up the cigarette pack, plucked one out and stuck it in his mouth, and then put his hands up again.

A head popped out from behind the wall. It was a taller version of the kid, with the same deep blue eyes. He couldn't have been more than a year older. His face was dirty and hollowed out and he was shivering. He held a gun in his hand and it was shaking.

All eyes turned to Gunter. And then I heard the faint click, click, click as the men cocked their weapons.

"Captain," Baldwin called out. "Get out of there. I got a clean shot."

"Stand down, Sergeant." I said quietly. I stretched open my arms, palms out, and took another step. "I don't have any more cigarettes," I said. "I've got some sausage . . . *Landjaeger*." I reached into my jacket and pulled out a piece of dried sausage wrapped in paper. It was supposed to be my breakfast.

"*Du hast Wurst?*" he pointed to me with his gun.

"Yeah, we have *Wurst*. We have soup, coffee, *Zigaretten*," I nodded with my head toward the kid.

Gunter looked over at his brother, who nodded eagerly.

"You gotta drop the pistol," I said, still holding out the sausage.

"*Gunter . . . die Pistole,*" the kid said.

"Listen to your brother. Drop the gun, we can all have breakfast. You, me, Mickey Mouse . . . "

At that, he ran toward me, his pistol out, and I wondered whose gun would go off first, Gunter's or Sergeant Baldwin's. It wasn't what I expected. I took a half step back. I braced for the impact of a bullet and then Gunter plowed into me and grabbed the bratwurst. He dropped his gun and took hold of the slim sausage with both hands. The younger kid ran toward him, hoping to get his share. The two were arguing over a piece of meat and didn't seem to notice how close they'd come to getting killed.

I picked up the pistol from the ground and rechecked it. Sergeant Baldwin came forward, shook his head, and swatted the kids up by their jackets. They were smiling now, more excited than scared.

"Get them cleaned up and fed," I told Baldwin. "Mickey Mouse," I said to them. They said it back to me, laughing like they'd pulled off a great stunt.

The sun gave off a light glow against the sky and I figured with Gunter and his brother, we'd dispatched the last of the German soldiers in the area. I picked up my Springfield and started toward the cathedral alone. This was how it was supposed to go. I felt sure of it.

From the square in front of the church, there was a clear view to the Rhine river. The bridges had been knocked out months earlier, but the river kept flowing, its motion in contrast to the lifeless landscape.

I removed my helmet, made a silent cross, and entered. A hole in the ceiling bled sky and a chunk of wall had come down. Sandbags crowded the exterior wall. But there was no denying the gothic beauty. The cathedral was a massive, ornate building, with ceilings more than a hundred feet tall. It was more train station than church, with its many connected chambers laid out in a Latin cross. My instincts guided me past the massive black marble high altar, down the stone-tiled ambulatory, east toward a smaller chapel.

I put my helmet and rifle down in a pew and kneeled. What else could I do?

After a moment, I felt cool air on the back of my neck and I realized a side door had opened behind me. I made a quick silent plea to God and reached quietly for my Colt 45 just in case. I stayed kneeling, but turned my body slowly, so I could look behind without making noise.

Behind me was a man in a dark overcoat, silhouetted in the dim light.

"Jesus Christ, you scared me," I said. I stepped out of the pew and walked toward him, raising my arms to give him a hug. He stood stiffly, a kid meeting an unwelcome aunt. "I knew it. You son of a bitch, you. You look great."

Jordan wore a black suit under his coat, and his gray tie matched his haggard face. He must have had the only pressed suit within two hundred miles. I felt embarrassed, with a week-long stubble and dirty combat fatigues.

"How did you get here?" I asked.

"Between my Dehomag credentials and the OSS, you'd be surprised." His eyes didn't move and his face looked ready to crack. "I had to pull a few strings. It's not easy catching up with you. You got the orders."

"What orders?" I asked.

"To meet here. The joint mission."

"No, I just . . . I saw the cathedral and came in."

He shook his head. "Well, it worked out." He paused. "I don't have a lot of time. I'll brief you."

"We can head back to the camp if you're hungry. It's just a couple miles," I said.

"My driver gets nervous when we're in a city."

"We cleared the area. It's safe. Pretty safe."

"*Pretty* safe?" He clenched his right hand and scratched it against his coat.

"We took down a couple of kids. Young soldiers, but tough. It took four of us. So, ah, what kind of reports are you getting on the Germans?"

"It's all bad. When the Russians liberated Auschwitz, we didn't know what to make of the initial reports. They were too strange. We assumed they were fabrications. You know, Hitler kills babies, that type of thing." His body tensed and I could tell he was holding back. He let out his breath. "The Nazis have been running experiments in these camps. Horrific." His voice cracked. "It was worse than I ever imagined."

"You were there?" Even as I asked the question, the images came to me. Prisoners in bunks. Smoke from pits in the ground. The smell. My stomach turned.

"Wherever they have the IBM machines, that's where I go. They have them in every KZ." His expression was blank, like he was reading a news report.

"Yeah, I remember. I can't imagine."

Jordan gave me a look. "You don't want to. Mittelbau-Dora is the worst. No one survives."

I had never noticed how red the rims were around Jordan's eyes. The muscles around his mouth twitched before he spoke.

"They work them until they die and then they send for more. It never stops." He stared, then blinked twice. "The way the U.S. and Russian troops are advancing, the Germans are going to be surrounded. And when Berlin falls, it's all over but the shouting."

"That's great." I raised a fist, but Jordan didn't respond.

"Unfortunately, the Russians are going to get to Berlin before we do."

"We're allies, though, right?"

"For today. For as long as it takes to bring down Germany. But after that? A lot of complicated backroom negotiations have to take place before we get a peace treaty. And there's some German technology that we need to get hold of." He pointed at my chest. "You're being seconded to work with the Secret Intelligence Service."

"The Brits?"

"I'm running a joint op. I told you about the expansion at Mittelwerk, right? I've managed to get a few snaps. Nobody in Washington or London has seen anything like it. The Germans refer to it as Zeus."

"It's a weapon system," I said. I could picture it. The wires and tubes. Broken glass everywhere.

"It's some kind of scientific project. But it's not clear what they're using it for."

I shook my head. "Jordan, you don't need to do this. There's always another mission. Tell them you're finished."

"We have to get there, ahead of the Russians. It's tight." Jordan looked at his watch and started to walk to the back of the cathedral. There was a volley of distant gunfire and he ducked his head.

"What do you mean?"

"Conrad Panzinger, the lead scientist, wants to run one last experiment. But they need the latest IBM machines from New

York to tabulate everything. The machines are in Switzerland and we're slowing the delivery. When they get the equipment, it's not going to work. Then I'll go in and stall for time. The idea is to keep the scientists there as long as I can. Once the 104th has the perimeter, everything changes."

"How do you know it'll be us?"

"I pulled some strings. You're going to get new orders. I've already cleared it with your C.O. You're to meet a British contact inside the tunnels. You get me out, and he takes the scientists.

"Who's my contact?"

"SIS. Operating under the name Frederic. Captain Frederic."

Jordan looked at his watch. We heard the booming of artillery several miles away.

"Christ, are you sure about this?" We tentatively opened the door to the street and Jordan peered around for his jeep. We stepped out cautiously.

"We have to grab what we can before the Nazis destroy it or the Russians take it for themselves. The timing is tight, but the rest is easy. You get within thirty miles of Nordhausen, the guards are going to flee and it'll just be Panzinger and his scientists. He pulled out a piece of paper from his jacket pocket and unfolded it. "This is a map of the tunnels." He drew a path with his finger. You have to go through a lower cross-tunnel at the south end. That's the rendezvous with Frederic."

I looked at the map. I saw the tunnels. Cold, damp. The silence. Everything seemed wrong.

"Jordan, don't do this. Tell them you're finished."

"Tell *them*? This is *my* mission. I recruited Frederic myself. He's as hard-edged as they come."

"Look out," Jordan shouted and he pushed me to the ground.

A machine gun fired and the bullets flew over our heads. Jordan crouched down, turned, and pulled out a pistol. He aimed it toward a blown-out window across the street where the flash had come from. Jordan squeezed off two shots and then ducked down. He counted to three and then fired two more shots at each of the windows on either side. Hopefully it was enough to send them on their way.

Jordan's jeep pulled up, his driver honking madly. A block away, a Panzer tank came out of an alley and fired a shell in our direction. "Jack, get out of here," he shouted as he ran toward his vehicle.

"You can't trust Panzinger," I shouted. But it was lost to the noise of a mortar shell that landed just thirty feet from us. There was a bright flash, then an explosion, and I couldn't hear anything except the ringing in my ears. Jordan's driver hit the gas and the jeep spit up a cloud of dust and exhaust, fish-tailing as it accelerated.

One of the new low-slung Sherman tanks came from a side street and fired at the Panzer, scoring a direct hit. The Panzer started belching smoke, clouding everything in a haze as American soldiers surrounded it.

A German officer in a gray uniform with a black high-collar climbed out coughing and spitting. A couple of GIs grabbed him and threw him on the ground. They checked him for weapons and then frog marched him roughly. His face was skeletal, caked in blood and dirt. He looked up at me and grinned. He said something in German that I couldn't hear. Then he cocked his hand like a pistol, pointed it to his head, and laughed, jerking his head back. The laughter turned into a hysterical scream. I looked away. But it never stopped.

CHAPTER 24
Return to Mittelwerk

Nordhausen, Germany
April 11, 1945

We received orders to take the Mittelbau-Dora concentration camp at Nordhausen, just as Jordan had said we would. Captain Frederic of London briefed me by coded wire for the covert part of my mission concerning Mittelwerk.

My time lapses, as I thought of them, had passed and life was proceeding normally, or as normally as war would allow. I slept poorly and dreamed of explosions and screams. And Jordan.

We moved and fought mainly at night, often marching for ten or twelve hours. I'd see men asleep, walking in formation. Their eyes were open but glazed. I spoke to them and occasionally I'd get a grunt as a reply, or some fragment of a dream would pass from their lips. *We'll stop at the Texaco. Get ice cream*, that sort of thing. We were all marching in a trance.

During those long hours of marching, when I actually had some time to think, I became aware I was reliving events. I remembered things sometimes before they happened, a snatch of conversation, an image of a map, or just a feeling. Some things were different, but there was an echo of familiarity. I'd been here before.

Most of the time, I thought I was half insane and half stoned to the eyeballs, but that didn't make me any different than the men I was marching with. We were all filthy. I hadn't bathed properly in weeks, and I had battle fatigue. We all did. Going mad hardly mattered. As long as I could read a map and shave regularly, I was the captain in charge of my company.

I experienced memories in flashes, like signal flags. When our unit approached Eschweiler, about a week after we left Köln, I looked at the pink morning sky and I knew then exactly where the enemy snipers were perched, down to which roof and behind which chimney, and I was able to protect my men.

This morning, my company of eighty men were among fifteen hundred soldiers of the 104th Infantry Division tasked to secure and liberate the Mittelbau-Dora concentration camp. Our assignment was to take the nearby little town of Nordhausen at zero seven hundred hours.

I didn't like the place from the start. Nordhausen was a mean industrial town. The sky was roiled and gray and it was pissing rain. The side streets were littered with cast-off metal parts from ancient steam engines and a collapsed grain mill. A 1920s milk truck was sunk into a potato field; its rear doors flung open, rusting away. The main street was cobbled and could have been pretty, but it was short and narrow and lined with tiny, unwelcoming houses jammed up right against the road, lacking any individual decoration. Street signs and house numbers had been removed.

And unlike, say, the towns that surround Detroit, where small shops supply car parts to GM or Packard, in Nordhausen, the trade went the other way. The small workshops here rented slave labor from the factory down the road that was also a concentration camp.

Once we marched into Nordhausen, the few town folks out at that hour ran inside their houses. I heard heavy wood doors slam, followed by the clink of metal bolts sliding into place. I saw lace curtains being drawn. The locals were separating themselves from whatever we were to discover at Mittelbau-Dora.

We secured the town without much incident. An old woman who was missing a few teeth, maybe more, and with a pale-yellow kerchief tied over her head called at us from an upper window. At first, we thought she was cheering us on. But she was spitting and yelling. *"Juden"* was the only word I recognized. I heard a man behind her shout, followed by the sound of breaking glass, and then she disappeared from sight.

I kept forty of my men in place to hold the town until the 3rd Armored Division arrived.

A few hours later, the rest of us were the mop-up crew at the camp. The rain had let up and the sky was clearing. Abandoned meadows straddled the road as we walked up the hill to the camp. A breeze signaled that spring had finally come.

I scoped the tunnel entrance as we made our way in. Two American MPs sat guard beneath a camo net. They were surrounded by sandbags and backed by a tripod-mounted .50 caliber machine gun. They could stop a train.

Word was there had been almost no fighting. Someone said a couple of grandpas were guarding the place. We saw one lone sniper in a guard tower, somehow overlooked. We took care of that.

I pulled my men to the side of the gatehouse and issued orders. We'd take the barracks up the road.

The place looked like an abandoned logging camp. But this camp had a parade square with a six-man gallows front and center. A crow hopped up the three wooden steps of the gallows, then flew off.

We marched ahead in column formation, arms ready. I knew there were no more enemy soldiers, but we still followed protocol.

I scanned the horizon and saw a large fire smoldering in a ditch beside the road. As we approached, what had looked like a woodpile was a stack of emaciated corpses. Bones stuck out from the smoking ashes of the fire.

Nobody spoke.

We'd heard stories about Nazi camps, but we hadn't believed them. It was propaganda, wasn't it? Just like Axis Sally on the radio. Now we knew evil. It was all around us.

My eyes fixed on a small metal pole farther up the ditch and, through the smoke, I saw some kind of skirmish erupt between two American soldiers. I heard a shot and a sharp animal yelp.

One of the GIs was now bent over at the waist. "You didn't have to," he wailed.

The other held a pistol by his side. The shooter's mouth was open, his jaw tight, and there was no light in his eyes. I kept my company out of it and we gave them our broad side.

As we passed, I saw a German shepherd splayed in the ditch, a chain running to the pole. If this was what we did to a German dog, what would become of enemy soldiers?

It was a short run to the barracks, so I called out double time to get us away from the scene.

Sergeant Baldwin opened the flimsy wood door of the barracks and from within the darkened room, the horror greeted us. It took a few seconds for my eyes to adjust and much, much longer for my heart.

More than a hundred prisoners were packed tight in straw-lined bunks and on the floor. They wore caps, but I could see that most had little to no hair. Their faces were so thin that their ears stuck out wildly. They wore ragged striped uniforms. The smell was overwhelming, I had to step back, closer to the door.

One old man was sitting upright on a lower bunk. He looked about seventy and had a wisp of gray hair above each ear. He reached out his bony hand. "*Les Américains sont arrivés,*" he said. He fished out a harmonica from his pocket, but his grasp was so slight, it fell to the floor. His eyes followed it, but he hadn't the strength to pick it up. The man behind him patted his shoulders in consolation.

I stepped forward and shook his hand delicately. It was cold and damp and weighed nothing. It was like meeting a ghost.

I had a flash. "Seventeen dead," I said to Baldwin. It just slipped out. He looked at me and squinted. "I counted them," I said.

I checked my watch. Eleven-forty. "Sergeant, we're secure here. I need to get to the tunnels. JIC business." Joint Intelligence Committee meant don't ask.

"Cap, twenty more buildings." He hit me with his rapid fire. "Could be more Krauts."

"It's secure." I stared him down. "Above ground, it's secure." I nodded slowly. "Below ground, not so much." I looked at my watch and then toward the door. "Thirty minutes, code Tarzan."

One of the corporals pulled something from his ditty bag and handed it to the old man on the bunk. It was a hunk of bread or some kind of food. Two prisoners on the ground were stuffing cigarettes into their mouths and chewing them.

"No food," I barked. "Jesus, get those cigarettes. You can't feed them." I softened. "Their stomachs can't handle it. The medics will be here shortly. For now, liquids only. If they can sit up, move them outside." I stepped out the door and turned back. "If not, tag 'em."

I ran to the tunnel. Stones flew from my boots. More memory flashes were coming. Just like my nightmares, fireballs, a piercing scream. Black silence. My arms and legs moved like pistons. I swallowed hard and thought of Jordan.

I was to rendezvous with Captain Frederic, if that was his real name, at eleven hundred hours inside the tunnels. It was a tight schedule. A four-minute window to meet. He would exfiltrate the German scientists and equipment for the Allies and I would get Jordan. We had to get in and get out before either the Nazis blew up the tunnels or the Soviets caught wind of the equipment.

It was part of a joint intelligence operation called T-Force. I didn't give a rat castle about the scientists or whatever they had built. I was there to rescue my brother. From what, I didn't know. But judging from the atrocities we saw at the camp, things were bound to be worse underground.

I tried to fire up a memory of Jordan, but nothing came, except screams. The screams were familiar but everything else was shrouded in fog. Was there any clue to help me get to him in time? I had no answers.

Thoughts of the .50 caliber caused me to skid and slow to a rapid walk as I approached the tunnel entrance. I couldn't afford to be mistaken for an enemy soldier. One MP saluted, the other kept both hands on the machine gun and then, without moving an inch, he said, "State your business."

"T-Force." I gave the target code word.

"That there's your open sesame," said the first one. His open palm pointed to the entrance. His expression was that of a ticket-taker at the movies. He didn't care if I went in, came back, or died inside, as long as I had the code word.

The tunnel entrance was fifty feet high and big enough to move freight trains. Two sets of railroad tracks led from the loading station across the meadow into the tunnel. I started toward the tunnel and the MP called me back.

"Sir," he said. He held up a small cardboard folder. It had bound black edges on three sides and was wax-sealed on the other. "Secret" was printed in big red letters at the top, next to a purple ink-stamp with a date and signatures.

I broke the wax, opened the folder, and pulled out a map. Two large snake-like tunnels were marked A and B and there was a series of numbered, perpendicular side-tunnels running between them. A path was drawn in green grease pencil, but there were no other markings. There were no titles, no legend, nor any printers' marks to identify the map as American, German, or even British, for that matter. Then it dawned on me that I didn't need the map; I knew it already. I'd been here before.

I put the map in the folder and handed it back to the MP and then headed into the darkness. I heard him mutter to his pal: "Shitbird doesn't know what he's doing."

Now I was moving from the evil of the camps to the void of the tunnels.

Within a few steps inside, every sign of life had disappeared. Overhead lights every few hundred yards shone a pale, yellow glow. I saw no birds, no rats, no vegetation. Only concrete. The air was cold and smelled of iron. Apart from my footsteps, which echoed far and wide like a squad of marching soldiers, there wasn't a sound. This place was dim, cold, and heartless.

I ran as fast as I could just to feel something. My eyes stung as salty sweat dripped from my brow. I knew what to do.

I followed the path down a massive tunnel, passing by dozens of numbered, smaller side-tunnels. The place was as big as a Ford factory, loaded with heavy equipment like winches, loaders, and railway cars. I saw workshop cubicles for the more delicate work: electrical harness wiring, the welding of fins, and propulsion tanks. It didn't take long to figure it out. This was where the Nazis built the V-2 rockets that terrorized London and Antwerp. I'd seen the destruction firsthand in Antwerp. Massive four-story holes blasted into the city. The rocket workers had left in a hurry, that much was clear. Tools and even the occasional tin water cup were left on worktables. Someone had dropped their striped cap on the floor under a table.

So this was what happened to the prisoners of Mittelbau-Dora. They built the tunnels and then they worked on the death machines until they, too, died.

I was so mesmerized when I finally saw a fully assembled V-2 about a hundred yards ahead that I kept running toward it and missed my turn. It was as big as a city bus, maybe a bus and a half, standing on its end with fins at the base and a nose cone pointing to the sky. When I checked the side tunnel number, I had overshot bay 47. I checked my watch. I had two minutes to go.

I ran hard. I pleaded, *God don't let me miss again.*

As if in reply, a memory surfaced. I knew exactly where bay 47 was. Aim for the two-story storage room, the one with the pile of gyroscopes below and the paint buckets above. Turn left. I saw a dim 47 painted on the wall. The carbide lamp overhead had burned out. No wonder I missed it.

I went down the passageway and then saw something I didn't expect. Instead of Captain Frederic, two U.S. privates stood in the dark, guarding bay 47.

They saluted and one of the men said, "It ain't been secured yet, sir." I returned the salute and told them I was there to meet a British rep. "No contact," the other said.

"You need to clear away any personnel," I said. "Gas leak. Listen." I let the eerie silence of the tunnels make my case. "Smell that?" I hissed. They scrambled.

After they left, I waited one minute in silence to be sure there were no enemy guards. I didn't move and I barely breathed. I checked my watch. Three minutes past rendezvous. Christ. Get in, get out.

I knew where to look. In a dark corner to the right, two little metal hooks extended above the floor line, and a steel ladder descended down a concealed shaft to the secret floor below. I climbed down, but still, there was no sign of Frederic. Only a black steel door.

My army training told me to abandon the mission. But this was never about the army or about training. Jordan was my brother and I had to save him. I waited two more minutes, which was all T-Force would allow, and I plunged ahead.

I pulled out my Colt and opened the door softly with my left hand.

I was in a narrow corridor that opened up into a well-lit chamber. Two other doorways were visible. The air smelled of carbolic soap, like a sick ward. Papers were scattered on the floor. It was a laboratory of some kind. I saw filing cabinets with the drawers pulled out and racks of wiring, similar to the wiring harnesses in the rocket workshops above.

A wood and steel chair stood at the center of the room, with a mess of wires flowing up its back. At one time, there had been a dozen of these chairs. I could tell by the little post stumps in the tiled floor. Now there was just one, under a bare bulb. Around the edges of the room, a dozen gurneys were pushed here and there, each one with two identical, naked corpses.

That cut close. They had been experimenting on twins. My guts liquefied.

I heard the loud slam of a door and I jumped behind one of the filing cabinets.

Two German guards waddled in. They looked like teenagers. Their hands were full and weapons were slung on their backs. They were here to burn the place. They had kerosene and dynamite. I kept my calm this time. It was like watching a movie for the second time. I knew every angle, every line.

"Halt," I shouted. I pointed my Colt at the closer of the two. It felt heavy and cold in my hand. "*Amerikaner*. Army." He dropped half his load of dynamite out of fright. The other pissed himself.

Everyone knew what was supposed to happen. But this time I had my own script. "Arms down," I called, and I pointed to the floor with my left hand.

The dynamite kid shuddered, then got to his knees. The kerosene kid looked back and forth between his pal and my Colt, unsure what I wanted. Christ, nothing was easy.

"Mausers," I said.

"*Wir geben auf.*" They were giving up. Yeah, I knew that.

"Mausers," I repeated. I felt like I was in a Vaudeville cross-talk act.

They looked at each other and then slowly placed their weapons on the ground, a Mauser rifle and a Schmeisser machine gun.

"Go." I pointed to the door that they'd come through.

They didn't move. It's not like I had a lot of time to explain. I looked at my watch and I shouted my command to go, followed by obscenities in English and German. When they went through the door, I exhaled.

As if on cue, *Sturmbannführer* Conrad Panzinger walked in from the other door. He had a skier's tan and wavy blond hair. He did a double take when he saw me, and he started to retreat back toward his office. Behind him, I could see a wooden desk with a large book on the corner. I followed him.

"Well, you're not going to shoot me, are you?" he said.

I approached closer. "Where's my brother?"

He stopped. "You are American." He lit a cigarette. "We have no Americans here." The bastard smirked. Some people never change.

I pressed my Colt against his chest.

"Forgive me, please," he said. "Your brother was posing as a Swiss, interfering with our tabulation machines while purporting to repair them." His eyes flicked past me for a split second.

I jumped back, swung around, and fired a wide shot overhead. Schuler, who had been sneaking up behind me, startled and dropped his pistol. It clattered on the tiles. As he dove down to retrieve his weapon, his glasses fell off. I kicked his gun away. Alarmed, Schuler looked every which way, but without his glasses, he was lost. I bent my knees and snatched the Schmeisser from the ground with my left hand. I held it waist high, cocked it, and flipped the thumb switch to full auto. As blind as Schuler was, the sounds of the Schmeisser made my position clear. The threat of five hundred rounds a minute put an end to any nonsense.

Schuler gulped, slowly got to his knees, and patted the ground until he found his glasses. He put them on and stood back up, tottering.

Panzinger stood like a statue through it all. "Come now. We each want something," said Panzinger. "It's Captain Waters, is it?"

I gave no reply.

He shook his head. "You Americans, usually you work in groups, like the turkey vulture who feeds in groups, for protection. But today you are on your own."

"Where's Jordan?"

"Your brother is fine, naturally." He studied me. "We have done a lot of research on twins." He started to say something in German to Schuler.

"English," I commanded.

"My assistant will bring Jordan."

I pointed the Schmeisser directly at Schuler. "If your blood starts to rise, remember the machine gun," I said. He stifled a whimper.

Schuler walked to my left and pulled back a heavy white curtain. Jordan was strapped to a gurney. I tried to speak, but I couldn't say anything. Jordan looked thin and pale. His once crisp business shirt had dark stains on it. His face was bruised and vacant, then he saw me. His eyes lit up. He shook and struggled against his leather straps before giving in to exhaustion.

Schuler beckoned me toward Jordan. "It'll be okay," I told him.

His eyes were frantic, searching. "The mission," he whispered. "Burn it all."

"So, you are the brother in the photograph, yes?" Panzinger asked me. "*Zwillingsbruder*," he said in German. "Twin brothers. We don't have so many good ones anymore. We wanted to run one more experiment, you see."

"It's over. You've got American troops above you and the Red Army approaching." At the mention of the Russians, Panzinger twitched.

"In a few minutes, there's going to be some cracks in the ceiling. Dust will fall, then pieces of the ceiling. There's rocket fuel stored in these tunnels—within minutes, the whole place is going to blow up."

"How do you know this?"

"I've seen it before."

"*Gott im Himmel*," Schuler said under his breath.

"We can wait; we can all die under here. We can go through this as many times as you like."

"What do you want?"

"Bring Jordan back into this dimension and let us leave on our own."

Panzinger narrowed his eyes. "How do you know about the other dimensions?"

"I know everything about your work."

Panzinger looked down at Jordan. "He will be fine in an hour."

"We don't have an hour. Do it now."

"And what is our portion of the deal?" Panzinger asked.

"You don't want to come to my side and face a war crimes trial."

"Naturally."

"I can guide you to a safer place across the forest. You'll be able to meet an old friend there. He'll get you away from the Russians and put you in contact with a more receptive group of Americans. People who value science."

Panzinger narrowed his eyes.

"Alan Hugo," I said. "He's with Joint Intelligence and he's shopping for *Wunderwaffen*."

Panzinger's mouth opened briefly, then closed. I had dealt him aces and he knew it.

"*Gut*." Panzinger clapped his hands together. He turned to Schuler. "You see, better than we hoped." He flicked his head.

The younger scientist went to the table and selected a syringe. He filled it carefully and then tapped it twice with his finger. "This will bring him out of the stasis zone more quickly." Schuler approached the gurney with caution. "But it will take some minutes for him to become awake." He held the needle aloft, waiting.

I nodded and he plunged the needle into Jordan's arm. Jordan's eyes rolled, and then he sank into the gurney.

There was a crunching sound of a tank overhead. Dust and dirt sprinkled down from the ceiling like filthy snow.

I heard a noise behind me. A metallic click at the door to the tunnel. I smelled tobacco smoke. I turned and saw Baldwin.

He seemed reluctant for a moment, then he smiled. He had the waxed mission folder in his pocket and a Johnny gun in his hands. He kept the weapon trained on Panzinger as he walked forward. "Thirty minutes, code Tarzan," he said.

We were home free. Baldwin had used the code word and the MP had given him the map.

Panzinger blinked and shook his head. He was stunned. Schuler looked from Panzinger to me, then back to Panzinger.

"Captain, we're about to seal the area." Baldwin kept his muzzle on Panzinger. "What you want me to do?"

I looked to Jordan. He stirred and shook his head slightly, his eyes almost closed. I was off script, but I could make it work. I had to.

I nodded toward Panzinger and Schuler. "Get these two back to Divisional HQ. I'll help Jordan and we'll follow you in about two minutes."

"You lied!" Panzinger shouted.

"*Auf Wiedersehen*, Panzinger," I said.

Baldwin escorted the two German scientists out while I untied Jordan's restraints. I tapped his face gently. His breathing was labored. His head tossed side to side. "Jordan, wake up," I said. I clapped my hands loudly right in front of his face. "We gotta get out of here. Jordan!"

He opened his eyes wide. His face was covered in sweat. "Jack, what have you done?" he asked.

"We've got to get out of the tunnel."

He raised himself onto one elbow and looked around in confusion.

"There's no time. Just follow me," I said.

I grabbed him by the shoulder and pulled him up off the gurney. He was moving slowly on unsteady legs, his knees nearly buckling. I put my arm around his waist to steady him as we went through the door into the tunnel. I pushed Jordan into the tunnel and yelled, "Go."

We were halfway up the metal ladder when I smelled the kerosene. I heard a splash below, then a deep rumble. From somewhere in the tunnels above, I heard Baldwin call out. I bolted to the top of the ladder, pushing Jordan ahead faster. Just as I reached the top, I heard a single crack in the distance. Echoes of the gunshot reverberated through the tunnels.

Before I could figure out what had happened, a steel girder and one of the lab walls below us collapsed. I felt a rush of hot air and saw a tide of blue flame roll up from the lab. My eyeballs felt the heat. As I turned away, my feet lifted, and I saw Jordan rise into the air, too, screaming. For just a moment, we flew and I saw everything from above. I fell hard on the ground and then a shower of brick and rubble and metal pipes rained down. I covered my head and glanced up. The air above turned into an orange ball of fire and then everything went dark.

It was supposed to be different this time.

PART III

CHAPTER 25
Thin as Smoke

Loma Vista, California
June 27, 1950

I regained consciousness in Schuler's make-shift workshop a few moments later. It had all been a dream. A nasty, dirty trick of a dream. There was no sign of Schuler, and as in the dream, he'd left my gun on the table. I lifted myself unsteadily out of the Z-machine. My ears were ringing. I had been through the wringer. I took a few tentative steps. All this machinery for what? Some kind of experiment in mind control?

Still, the images stuck in my mind like a fever. Seeing Jordan felt so real that it almost seemed worth it. But then I lost Jordan all over again.

I couldn't tell what was real anymore. The veil was thin as smoke. But it didn't change anything. Jordan was gone and I was on the other side, alone. Jordan wasn't missing; he really was dead. And it was my fault.

I shook myself and stepped outside. The rain had slowed, leaving the air heavy. I pulled my jacket collar tight and walked the trail back to the main house. I had to pull myself together and find Faith.

As I made my way, I recognized the thick shape of Sergeant Duffy outside. "Hey, Duffy," I said. "Am I glad to see you." I slapped him on the shoulder.

"No one calls me that anymore," he said stiffly. "It's Sergeant Duff, okay? You look like hell. Where were you?"

"I told you, I was meeting Schuler."

He eyed me suspiciously. "Doctor Schuler's in his office."

"I heard something near the gulley," I said. "I must have gotten turned around."

He gave a snort. "Well, let me take you back to your partner. I oughta pin you two together so you don't get lost." Duffy grabbed my forearm and before I could protest, he was walking me into the kitchen.

As I entered the room, I froze.

Was I still dreaming?

He had his back to me, but it was enough for me to recognize him.

It didn't seem possible. And yet . . .

The height, the build, the hair. He turned around to face me.

It was Jordan.

Was this real? Or some manipulation. But there he was, not twenty feet in front of me.

"Holy Christ," I stammered. I rushed toward him and put my arms out, tears in my eyes, ready to give him a big hug. But he just stood, arms by his sides, and stared.

"What is with you?" Then in a hushed voice, "I told you, you can't mess around when we're on the job."

Wasn't he glad to see me? The room shimmered in tune with a thrumming that seemed to be circling around me. I couldn't believe it worked. Schuler was a genius.

I was in a different dimension.

"Jordan, I swear." I held up my right hand. "I was out at the old storage building and I was a little worried, that's all."

"Find anything?"

"It's hard to explain." Did he know about the Z-machine? About what they did here?

"Jesus Christ, you either found something or you didn't."

"It was nothing important."

"In case you've forgotten, I've got an investigation to run."

I needed to get the lay of the land. "What's your take on all this?"

He looked up at me surprised. "You really want to know?"

"Yeah, you've always been better at this than me."

Jordan shrugged and his face tightened. "How is it some Nazi scientist from Mittelwerk ends up here in Loma Vista? How did Schuler even get into the country?"

"I think it was all Panks's doing."

"Who?"

"Panzinger," I said. "The dead body."

Jordan tensed. "What are you talking about? Did something happen?"

I put a hand against the wall to steady myself.

"Forget it," I said. "I . . . I don't know what I was thinking of."

"Panzinger . . . that was the major in the tunnels, wasn't it? He's not involved in this, is he?"

I shook my head.

"You okay?" he asked.

"I'll be fine. I just need a minute."

He rubbed his chin. "You ever get this feeling, like you've seen something before?"

"You mean like déjà vu?" I asked.

"Yeah. You believe in that?"

"Things are connected in ways we don't always understand."

He looked around. "There's something about this place, gives me the creeps. You know, I still have dreams of being in the tunnels, trying to get out. And then Schuler. And when you walked in here, you looked like a ghost. I thought maybe . . . "

"Maybe what?"

"You were back on the stuff."

"What?"

"I know," he raised his hand in protest. "I know you're clean. But your eyes had that look. Like that time, when I dragged you out of that opium den in Detroit. I saved your ass, didn't I?"

Had I sunk that low? "We'll call it even," I said.

"Of course."

"I didn't mean it that way."

I was ashamed of a past I hadn't lived. The Z-machine had put me in a different world. The whole thing was making my head spin. Was this my new life? How was it connected to my past?

"Hey, where's Faith? I want to check in with her."

"Miss Robner? She's in the comms room."

I didn't even know there was a communications room, let alone where it was. But I didn't think I could ask Jordan without getting an earful.

There was a narrow corridor off to the back that I hadn't noticed before. It looked like more recent construction than the rest of the house.

I heard the faint clicking and whirring of a switchboard and so I followed the sound around a corner.

I entered the room. And there she was, Faith Robner. It was like I was seeing her for the first time. She was wearing a white silk blouse. Her hair was different, pinned up in the back. And her lips were a lighter shade. But there was no mistaking the shape of her mouth, the light in her eyes.

She turned to look at me.

"Can I help you, Mr. Waters?"

"You know me?"

"We met earlier. You're Jordan, the detective, right?"

"No, that's my brother." I held out my hand. "My name's Jack." I was back to square one. I could fall in love with Faith all over again. Maybe this time I wouldn't ruin it.

"Well, you two certainly do look alike. What's that like, having a twin brother?"

"It's like living with the person you always knew you should be."

"That doesn't sound good."

"It's better than the alternative."

"And what can I do for you, Jack? I've already spoken to your brother and Sergeant Duff."

"Well, I was hoping to learn more about what happened here."

"I've gone through all that. Look, I'm just the communications manager."

"What does that entail?"

"It's nothing too exciting. Blakely Labs has an affiliate network—"

"A what?"

"We work with a group of scientists and mathematicians around the world." She pointed to some clocks on the wall behind her. They were labeled Loma Vista, New York, London, Moscow, Sydney.

"No kidding."

"Mm-hmmm," she said. "And every day, I receive teletypes from the scientists. Depending on the subject, some I relay to the whole group or to working committees, others are private, for Dr. Schuler only."

One of the machines made some squawking noises and started printing. She glanced at the clocks. "Early morning in Europe." She walked to the machine and pulled out a couple of pages that had curled up in its basket.

"What about Mr. Hugo?"

"He doesn't get involved with the technical details." She pushed the hair off the side of her face. "But he stops by to see how I'm getting on."

"And how are you getting on?"

"I do all right," she said. She blushed a little. She smoothed out the pages and placed them in an in-box on the desk.

As she looked down, I stole a glance at the material. There were dozens of equations followed by a diagram I recognized.

"And then Dr. Schuler has me send out his own messages, after he's reviewed things. Once you've learned how to do it, it doesn't take more than a couple of hours. Sometimes the tele-type machine jams and that creates a little excitement."

"You can stretch it out if you have to."

"When absolutely necessary."

"And the rest of the time?"

"I keep busy."

"Let me guess. You're a writer."

Her mouth opened and her smile was on full display. She always loved the banter. "What makes you say that?"

"Well, you've got a typewriter by the side of the desk with half a sheaf of paper. Four crumpled pages are sitting in the trash can and you have ink stains on your hands. Looks like you do more than babysit the teletypewriter."

She gave me the top-to-bottom look. "I'm working on a book."

"A detective story?"

"Hardly. This is a serious book about —"

"Women war correspondents."

"Yes, how did you know?"

"You wrote that story about Jordan and me." I nodded over to the framed newspaper on the wall with the headline: SOLDIERS RESCUED FROM DEATH CAMP TUNNEL.

"I'd almost forgotten."

"Your first front-page story?"

Her head wobbled slightly. "I didn't connect you with that story."

"My picture's right there."

"Below the fold."

"We spoke."

"I spoke to you and a hundred other soldiers that day. She raised her palms and shook her head. "It was five years ago."

"So just a face in the crowd? I thought we had something."

She crossed her arms. "You're something else, aren't you?"

This was going to take time. But I could fix this. I could win her back.

"So, how is it you ended up here?"

"My family's from San Moreno."

"I mean working at Blakely Lab."

"I met Alan at the end of the war and . . . "

"Another front-page story?"

"It got buried on page five. It was a good story until Army Intelligence got hold of it."

"That's an oxymoron," I said. "Like jumbo shrimp."

"Well, that's old news," she said, in on the joke. "They didn't want to say what Hugo was doing in Germany and that took the wind out of it."

"What was he doing?"

"Recruiting German scientists. I thought you knew all this? What's with you, anyway? You're like some jealous schoolboy. I hardly know you."

"But you were there."

"Where?"

"Mittelwerk."

"Of course I was there. I was on assignment in Germany and I was filing stories."

"Don't you think it's strange that you, me, Jordan, Alan Hugo, and Schuler were all there?"

"What about Charlie? And that Mr. Asheton? Maybe the cook and cleaner, too, though they've gone for the weekend."

"You're not taking this very seriously."

"Did I bat my eyelashes at you in the hospital and you've been looking for me ever since?"

I took in a deep breath. "Yeah, me and a hundred other soldiers."

She took a step forward and slapped my face.

It took me by surprise, but I deserved it. I was glad that Faith hadn't changed. "I didn't mean it that way." I rubbed my cheek. "Sorry."

"Was there anything else?" she asked.

"What can you tell me about the work Schuler and Panks—" I corrected myself. "I mean, the work Schuler and his team are doing here?"

"I don't know anyone by the name of Panks. But Dr. Schuler has contacts around the world."

"And the Z-machine?"

"Well, that's not something we really talk about with strangers. Loose lips and all that."

"Does it work?"

"This is . . . how do I put it? It's a long-term research project. It's not like writing a book." She looked down at her papers. "Besides, I've handed in my notice. Today is my last day."

"Off to San Francisco then?"

"You do take in a lot. Anyway, it wasn't fair to Alan."

"Not your type?"

"He's a good man. Raised his daughter on his own." She looked directly at me, and for a moment, it was as if she were lying next to me, whispering in my ear. "No. Not at all."

"You don't strike me as the lab type. I picture you having cocktails at the Mark Hopkins, looking out on the city."

"I used to listen to Marjorie Trumbull's show from the Top of the Mark." The rain had started up again, tapping heavily against the window. She looked out in the distance. "It seemed so classy. That's why I became a reporter."

"I didn't know that."

"How could you?" She bit the inside of her cheek. "And anyway, my old editor from the *Chronicle* asked me to fill in on some assignments."

"I do some work up the coast once in a while. Maybe we'll meet there some time."

Her face lit up. "You're quite different from your brother, aren't you?"

"Jordan's okay. He's like me but more intense."

"I can't imagine."

She busied herself with her papers, and I was all right if she spent an hour shuffling the same files over and over. I was falling in love again.

"I need to speak with Dr. Schuler, if you don't mind."

Once she turned, I was back to business. I snatched the teletype paper from the pile, rolled it into a tube, and slid it inside my coat.

Filching paperwork wasn't any harder than reading upside down. Anyone could do it with enough practice.

CHAPTER 26
Repeating Waves

I found Beverley at her desk in the office, reading a letter. Dressed in a tailored jacket and pants, she looked like a junior executive on the rise. There wasn't a trace of the awkward young woman I had met before. "Must I go over this again?" she asked. Her tone was exasperated.

"I'm afraid so," I said. "The insurance company requires every interview to be verified and confirmed." I had my notebook and pencil out, trying to look official.

"I already spoke to your brother."

"That's what I mean; now I have to verify it."

"It doesn't seem very efficient."

"We've been brothers a long time."

"You ever get a laugh with that?"

"Not lately." I doodled a line of repeating waves in the notebook. "Tell me about the communications room."

"You've seen it, haven't you?"

"Faith, ah, Miss Robner gave me a tour."

"We operate a switchboard, a bank of teletypewriters, and so on."

"And what's it all for?"

"We work with scientists from all around the world."

"Don't you have a team here?"

"Of course we do. But sometimes we need to tap into more specialized expertise."

"And what's your role here? I take it you're not just working here for the summer.

She laughed. "Well, it wasn't that long ago that that was true . . . Now I run the lab operations. I work for Dietrich—Dr. Schuler, that is." She patted her fingers, showing the ring. "He's also my fiancé."

I didn't see that coming. But people find happiness in the strangest of places.

"Family business then, is it?"

"No different from Waters & Waters."

"And these scientists, how long has that been going on?"

"My father and Dietrich had been working together for years and they kept hitting roadblocks. We could never figure out how to increase the voltage sufficiently without blowing out the Tillinghast resonator. In May, Dietrich went to the Symposium on Theoretical Physics."

"In Copenhagen?"

"Helsinki. He got help from an old colleague."

"Panzinger?"

Beverley's expression registered surprise. "How do you know him?"

"I'm acquainted with Dr. Schuler's work in fusion. The insurance company keeps us up-to-date with their clients' research."

"Well, that . . . that must keep you very busy." She drummed her fingers.

"That's why there's two of us," I said. "So, Dr. Schuler was at the conference . . . "

"Afterward, he thought, why do we need a conference in order to collaborate? Why not work with the best scientists all the time? Dr. Panzinger is developing some new formulas to calibrate the resonators, and Dietrich was hoping it would come through on the telex this morning. Well, maybe Monday."

"When's the wedding?"

"Oh, not until September. I think that's a nice time of year."

"And your parents?"

"My father couldn't be more excited." She paused. "My mother passed away when I was a girl." She bit her lip and I caught a glimpse of the fragile young woman I had met before.

"I like to think she's looking down and she's happy for me, proud that I'm a scientist."

"That's a good way to look at it," I said.

"You think so?"

"Yes, I do." I glanced down at my notebook. "So, what happens next, when you get this new formula?"

"We'll start on human trials."

"What do you mean?"

"Until now, we've only tested the Z-machine with animals, because we can't calibrate it reliably. But once we get the new calibration formulas, it should be safe enough for people, which is the whole point anyway."

"Is that so?"

She straightened. "I'm going to be the first."

"You can't be serious."

Her face flushed. "And why not? We need more women in science."

"It's not safe."

She threw her hands in the air. "And how would you know?"

"Schuler's been working on this since before the war."

"Yeah, so?"

"For the Germans."

"How's that?"

"It was part of Hitler's Black Sun project."

"What, now you're the FBI?" She crossed her arms.

"No."

"Then what?"

"I—"

"What?"

"Your mother taught you a nursery rhyme—"

"Yes, she also walked me to school. So what?"

"—about counting crows."

"It's-it's common enough. One for sorrow, two for mirth—"

"Only she got it wrong. That's not how it goes."

"Three for death, four for birth," she spoke loudly.

"Five for waters, six for thee," I said.

We said the final line together: "Seven for my mother who watches over me."

"It was a message," I said.

Her mouth opened without words and her eyes bulged.

"Your mother sent me to protect you."

She stood up, leaning back against the desk.

She started to ask, "How is that even—?" She looked at me as if I'd appeared in a puff of smoke. "Oh, my goodness. It really works."

CHAPTER 27
Something's Not Right

I walked back from Beverley's office to look for Jordan. He was at Alan Hugo's desk, filling out the Standardized Workplace Accident report.

"Hey, I got something."

"Yeah, what?"

I pulled out the rolled-up teletype message from my pocket and spread it out in front of him.

He glanced down. "What's this?"

"It's our friend Panzinger."

"What are you talking about?"

"He's alive and living in Russia. And he's working with Schuler."

"So what?"

"Jordan, don't you get it? This is what they were doing at Mittelwerk."

He turned back to his papers. "Forget it."

"What?" I kicked the foot of the desk. "I don't believe this. After what we went through? We were supposed to put an end to their work."

"No, the goal was to bring it stateside. The mission failed but we won the war anyway. We won, they lost, and now they work for us."

"What do you mean?"

"Who do you think is funding Blakely Lab?"

"Tell me."

"This whole thing is paid for by U.S. Government contracts."

"But . . . "

"Nobody cares about Panzinger, Schuler, or any of them. You shouldn't be poking around in this."

"But the teletype printout shows—"

"Listen to me. Whatever is going on here is a dangerous business. If this is connected to Mittelwerk, I don't want anything to do with it. We're just a couple of detectives, and not even good ones. So put it back, and pretend you're actually working for the insurance company, because that's the only way we're gonna make next month's rent."

"Look, maybe you don't care anymore, but I've got to stop this."

"Jack, forget it." He looked spent. "I'm not fighting anymore. I'm done with that."

The wind was rattling the windows now. Lightning flashed in the sky.

"Hey, Jordan . . . "

"What now?"

"Why did we move out here?"

He looked up. "What?"

"I took up running, right?"

"Yeah, running with the wrong crowd."

"I don't understand."

"Jesus Christ, you were a junkie! Did you somehow forget all the crap you put me through back east?"

I had to hear it. I wanted to know what my life had been in this world.

"Okay, but the specifics of that day."

"I dragged you out of that shooting gallery, and we left that night."

"September fifteenth, right?"

"Yeah. You can remember the date, but you don't remember what happened?"

"Humor me."

"You'd run up some debts, and I wasn't gonna stick around when they came collecting. These guys weren't the usual hoods. I don't know what they were. They wore dark suits and they were cold as ice."

His face tightened and he braced himself with his arms. "I thought you were a goner."

"How did you find me there?"

"Manny called me. He said that old guy had come into the bar. What was his name? Tilman?"

"Tillinghast?" I asked. This was getting strange. There was a Tillinghast resonator in the Z-Machine. That was another strange connection.

"Yeah. Manny said he had a bad feeling, like something wasn't right. He thought the old guy had paid you off; he was worried you were going to end up back at that flop house."

"I don't remember any of this."

"Yeah, why would you? We took you down, cold turkey for the week it took to drive to California. You were a mess. We kept throwing blankets and hot water bottles back there. You shivered and slept through a lot of it. Okay by OK City. That was our motto, remember?" He started to sing. "Gonna ride, gonna ride, gonna ride to Okla—"

"You and Manny?"

"We were worried it looked like a kidnapping." He was dejected because I cut off his story. "I guess it was."

"I'm sorry for what I put you through."

"Yeah. Me, too, Jack. Me, too."

I couldn't reconcile what was going on. I was in a strange world without a past, or at least nothing I could understand. Was this my fate?

I walked down the hall, back toward the comms room, about to light up a Lucky. I listened for a moment to the clicking and whirring of the switchboard equipment. Something about it seemed odd. Then I smelled smoke. I ran the length of the corridor. The doorknob was hot and I opened it quickly.

Blue smoke lingered in the air. An electrical fire, but something else as well. The room was in chaos. The clocks had been knocked off the wall, equipment scattered, the teletypes smashed to the floor. Ashes swirled in the air. I stepped farther into the room. One of the heavy black desk phones had been smashed into the corner of the desk, the handset dangling from the spiral cord inches above the floor.

Above my head, a loose electric cable swung from the ceiling. It sparked against the metal curtain rod. I pulled my jacket over my hand and knocked it away.

Then I saw it. A pair of feet lying on the ground by the desk. I recognized the shoes at once. Patent black leather, the ones with the delicate buckle that I had kidded her about.

It made no sense.

I ran toward the crumpled body. It was like a doll. It couldn't be.

My heart fell through the floor. I froze. I had stopped breathing and the world had stopped, too. I had seen hundreds of deaths in Germany. Soldiers, prisoners, old men, widows, even children. I couldn't understand it, but I accepted it. That was war. This was so much worse.

It was Faith.

I got down on one knee. Her skin was pale blue. I checked her pulse. Nothing. I reached my arm out to cradle her head and held her. My hand came back damp and sticky with blood. For a moment, I stared at my hand, frozen, as if I were trapped in time. How could I live without her?

A scream shot through the room. I turned around and raised my bloodied hand as I stood up. It was Beverley Hugo.

"What have you done?" she shouted. "Don't take another step or I'll scream again."

"Take it easy," I said. "I didn't kill her."

I thought she might fall into my arms sobbing, but this new, improved Beverley was made of sterner stuff. I was glad it was Beverley who found me and not Duffy. I didn't want to think how it might have looked to him.

"What are you doing back here, anyway? This area's off limits. We told you that already."

"I heard a noise and came to investigate." I pulled out a handkerchief and wiped the mess off my hand.

"What happened?" she asked.

"Electrical accident," I said. "There was a live wire back here. Something short-circuited and the wire must have struck her. Blew out the whole console." I opened a window to clear the remaining smoke.

"The lightning?"

"Could be." I didn't think so, but I wasn't about to offer up my theory until I had a better idea of who or what I was up against.

She bit her lip. "I can't believe this happened. My father is going to be devastated. Faith . . . was very special."

"That she was." I clenched my fists and took a deep breath.

"Over the past few years, my father . . . I think he was in love with Miss Robner."

The look on my face gave me away. She waved her hands quickly. "I mean, they weren't an item. She never saw him that way. She was moving to San Francisco. This was just, you know, a way station for her."

She looked down at the ground. Her face puckered and turned red and tears started rolling. I held myself stiff, not moving a muscle. The room was silent, and it felt as if the entire world was standing still, waiting to see what would happen.

I turned away from her and took a step to the open window. A moment later, I felt a hand on my back and the warmth of it pulsed through me.

"Are you okay," she asked.

"It's the smoke."

"Did you know her?"

"Yeah. We just met.

"What?"

"I mean, ah, she seemed like a nice—"

"Oh my God."

"I told you, I didn't kill her."

"You!"

"No, I didn't—"

"You came back for her."

I grabbed her arm. "Why'd you say that?"

"She said she'd had her chance at finding love, but something happened and . . . she never got over it."

Looking at Beverley, she resembled her mother even more. I thought about what Amy Hugo had told me. Faith was a part of this. She always had been and always would be.

"I loved her." I raised my hand. "I swear I didn't do this."

"Didn't do what?" Jordan entered the room and looked around. "What the hell?"

"Electrical fire," I said.

"There's been an accident. Miss Robner is dead," Beverley said.

"Jesus Christ," Jordan said. "What the hell is happening here?"

I shook my head. "I was too late."

"Beverley," Jordan said, "go get Sergeant Duff. And no one touch anything."

I explained my theory, or at least my sanitized story, of Faith's death. I could tell that Jordan wasn't buying it. I'd screwed up. I didn't belong here. I'd tried to go back in time to save Jordan, and it had cost Faith her life. I was the loser in a twisted O. Henry story. I had to find a way out before I destroyed everything.

CHAPTER 28
It Never Happened

Jordan leaned into me hard as we walked back to Hugo's office. "What happened back there?"

"What do you mean?"

"You said something to Beverley Hugo."

"Did I?"

"You said it wasn't your fault. Why did you say that?"

"She came in after I found the accident and the body. She screamed and I . . . I didn't want to alarm her."

"You didn't want to alarm her?"

"I had blood on my hands from examining the body."

"Come on, Jack. We're here to do an insurance job. We're not the police. What's going on?"

"We've got to look into Faith's death. It's not what it seems."

"What do you mean?"

"It's all connected. Schuler, Panzinger, Mittelwerk. That's what's going on."

"You're not making any sense. That's all in the past. It's got nothing to do with us."

"Jordan. There was a time—"

"There was time what?"

"When you gave a damn."

He stopped and pointed his finger at me. "I got Sergeant Duff to the scene and that's what you should have done in the first place. It's a police matter. It's in their hands."

"I think it's connected."

"Connected how?"

"Panzinger's teletype message."

"We've been through that."

"Someone else knew about the message. It wasn't expected until the morning."

"So what? How could that have any bearing? This was an electrical accident; probably the storm."

"No. You saw how the equipment had been smashed."

"What?"

"Faith didn't die of electrocution."

Jordan squinted, his mouth upside down. He wasn't biting.

"Her skull was bashed in," I said. "She died of smoke inhalation. It's not an accident—it's murder."

"Why would someone murder Miss Robner?"

"I told you. Because she read the message on the teletype."

"The message you stole."

I shrugged, palms up. "You're missing the—"

"Stop," he said. His eyes were wide in disbelief.

"Well, then what do *you* think happened?" I asked him.

We'd been walking back toward Hugo's office. I stepped in and Jordan followed. The desk was covered with Jordan's work files, some insurance forms, case notes, and pictures. Jordan picked up a photo. I thought it must have been something from the war. Maybe Jordan was finally getting the picture. But then he turned it toward me.

It was an old black-and-white that he had saved from outside the tunnel entrance at Mittelwerk. There we were, two brothers. I was smiling, my arm around him. Jordan had his arm in a cast, a cigarette clenched in his mouth.

"Do you remember this," he asked. "It was a couple of days after we'd been rescued from the tunnel. We went back because the press wanted a positive story, and we were it."

I recited the heading from memory: "Brothers rescued from death camp tunnel."

"That was the headline to the news story, wasn't it? I owe you . . . how you got us out of there. But it hasn't been easy for me. I promised mom and dad I'd look out for you. They were worried about you, when you came back. The booze and all that."

"Look, I appreciate everything you've done for me. And I'm sure the folks do, too. I haven't seen them in ages."

He looked at me coldly. "Jack, they're dead."

Everything was coming apart. It felt like the whole world was conspiring against me. Everything was gone. And it all came back to Mittelwerk.

"Jack, are you so out of it that you don't even remember?"

"When I was trying to get you out of the tunnels, I didn't even know if you'd survive, if you'd ever recover."

Jordan's face tightened.

"It was like that time when we were kids and you had convulsions. I didn't know if you'd ever return to normal."

He shook his head. "Where'd you come up with that? I never had convulsions. I think I'd know if that happened."

"You were six. You nearly died."

"That never happened. Jack, you're not—"

"What happened in the tunnels when I came for you?"

"Five years after the fact, now you want to talk about it? Forget it."

I slammed my hand on the desk. "I need to know what happened."

"Jack, it's the same thing I told the doctors. I honestly don't know." His eyes were wide. "I was inside, sticking to my cover as the Dehomag technician. I convinced them I could fix the IBM machines in another day or two. I got Schuler to build replacement parts that would never quite work. I was stringing them along. They got orders to clear out with all the guards, and I assured them we were so close that they stayed. But they were suspicious because of the air raids. They tied me up and threatened me, accused me. I didn't break, I didn't say a word. I stuck to my script: '*Ich bin Techniker.*' But Panzinger found the photo, the two of us. And then everything changed.

"The next day, Panzinger knew all about you, your rank, your unit, everything. They knew you were coming. I don't know how. Everyone knew the German army was finished, but they had some other plan still. Panzinger had packed suitcases full of files, papers, punch cards, research notes. He told Schuler that was their passport out of Germany. There were other files they burned. They had a dozen prototype machines, and they destroyed all but one.

"Panzinger kept talking about how important the experiment was. He said I was going to be famous as 'Patient A,' but they needed you, too. I remember everything up to the last day. Then it's all blank. Like it never happened. I just remember waking up in the hospital."

"What about the dreams you mentioned? Of being in the tunnels at Mittelwerk?"

"They don't mean anything."

"Maybe not. But tell me what happens."

His body tensed. He shook his head.

"It's important," I said.

"All right. But then it's over."

I nodded.

"It's always the same. I'm down in the tunnels, exploring. Trying to find my way out. There's no one, nothing around. I've got a flashlight and I'm wandering through the main tunnels where they're making the rockets. But there's nothing there. The chambers have blown up and there's just a bunch of debris. Water has flooded into different areas, but I have to wade into it, to try to find a way out. And the strange thing is I know all the tunnels. I know my way, because I've . . . "

He hesitated. And then his voice cracked. "I've walked the tunnels for years and I can never find my way out. Everyone left and I was still there. Sometimes I find my way to an opening. I crawl up a narrow space, clambering over rocks, and I can see a crack of daylight. I push apart these heavy boulders, they weigh hundreds of pounds. I'm dirty and sweating, but I think if I can just get out of the tunnels, I'll be okay. And I finally create a gap of about six inches. I look out and I can see for miles. And I'm thinking I should be able to see some farms, maybe the town of Nordhausen, trains, something. But there's nothing. It's all gone. It's just rock and dirt. There isn't a stick, a tree, or anything. Just a white fog. And I realize the whole world has disappeared and you're never coming for me."

Jordan's face was dark and his mouth was tightened like he was seeing it all now. He collapsed into a chair, exhausted.

"Jordan, I'm sorry." I leaned forward.

"It's not your fault. I mean, it's just a crazy dream, right?" His eyes were shiny, wet.

I nodded. But it wasn't a dream. It was a side-effect from the experiment at Mittelwerk. It was a spillover from some other dimension where things had gone wrong. Very wrong.

"I'm sorry for what you went through."

"I thought I was going to die, I was sure of it. That was the worst part. I thought if the 104th didn't arrive, they'd leave me there in the tunnels and blow everything up. It was a code

Boxer all right." He let out a wheezy breath. "I was praying you'd make it before the Russians, but I didn't want to put you through whatever sick experiments they had planned. Thank God you and Frederic made it."

"He was never there," I said.

"Then how did you find me?"

"I had your map. I got rid of a couple of guards, and I waited until I could get the jump on Panzinger. I always felt like I . . . I failed you. I screwed up the mission. Panzinger and Schuler fled and it was my fault."

"Jack, Jesus Christ. I was a goner and you got me outta there. If that doesn't get you to heaven, I don't know what would. Sometimes I wake up in the middle of the night and I'm frozen in panic, back in that tunnel." He wiped one eye. "You've had enough to deal with. You don't need to worry about my life, too."

I pulled in closer and lowered my voice. "I don't know how to tell you this. But it's not just a dream."

"Jack, what are you talking about?"

"I've seen what you described. The same thing, exactly."

"You never told me that."

I had to explain it to him in such a way he didn't think I was crazy. Finally, I said, "What I saw was . . . from a different time."

"When?"

"I mean, it's like a different version of what happened. In the evac hospital, I was in a coma. And *I* was in the tunnels, looking for *you*."

"What? You had a helluva headache, but you weren't in any coma."

"Look, I'm not doing a great job explaining this," I said. "All those things that happened after the explosion in the tunnels, they happened to you. But they didn't happen to me."

"What?" Jordan put the picture down on the desk and stared at me.

"You were lost in the tunnels in a dream," I said. "I was lost in the tunnels in a coma. I saw what you saw."

"That doesn't make any sense," Jordan said. "You're saying we both—"

"We had the same experience."

"But it's just a dream."

"No, that's the thing. It wasn't a dream for me. It was real. The Z-machine opened up a portal to a different world for you. And after that, our lives diverged. I've never seen that photo before."

"But . . . you were there." He grabbed the photo off the desk and waved it at me.

"No. I was in a different world. I ended up in a coma. And you were gone. They never found you."

Jordan stared, his mouth wide open.

"I never stopped looking for you, Jordan. Five years, I kept at it. I got called to the accident at Blakely Lab. Schuler was there. And I used the Z-machine so I could find you."

He shook his head slowly. "This is too weird."

"It's beyond weird. It's what they were working on at Mittelwerk."

"And here at Blakely Lab?"

"Exactly.

It clicked for him. I could see his brow crease. That was one of the advantages of being twins. We thought the same way. "We've got to do something."

"We do."

"What?"

"Jordan, you really want to know?"

"Absolutely. You got me out of the tunnels."

"You're going to have to trust me on this," I said. "I'm not the screw-up brother you had to rescue from a shooting gallery. I'm the brother who never stopped looking for you. I know about the dream world you've been stuck in. And I can get you out again."

"How?" he asked

"We have to fix it—"

"In both worlds."

"Exactly."

CHAPTER 29
Bloody Well Don't Forget It

It felt good to finally be a team again. I had missed Jordan over the last five years. Seeing him, knowing he was okay, that he trusted me . . . It was like a weight had been lifted off me.

Jordan didn't say it, but I knew he had doubts. Still, he was willing to try.

I'd been thinking about what Amy had told me. I'd deviated from the plan and maybe that's what sent me to this other dimension. I couldn't change what had happened in this world, but if I could get back to where I'd started, I could still put things right.

I was trying to put together all the different pieces from different dimensions. It was like recording a band of musicians who couldn't hear each other. I wondered whether my pack of Hermanos had come with me but thought better of it. I needed a clear head.

"You, there. Jack, right?"

It was Alan Hugo, short as ever, waving the top of his cane to get my attention. His eyes were red and his hair was tousled in a way that suggested he'd pushed it back repeatedly in a losing battle for orderliness.

"I'm sorry for your loss, Mr. Hugo." I extended my hand to him. "I know you were close to her."

"Yes, well, thank you. Miss Robner was . . . a very good, ah, administrator." For a moment it seemed he'd let down his guard, but then he bounced his cane on the floor. "We've had two accidents now. You, your brother, and Sergeant Duff need to get to the bottom of this or there'll be hell to pay, you understand?"

I smiled at the irony of it all. "Of course, sir."

"What is so goddamned funny to you?"

"People don't change, do they?"

"In my experience, a great deal of the world's problems would be solved if people accepted what their roles were and stopped trying to change things."

"Except for you and Blakely Labs, you mean?"

"I have studied this field for twenty years, and if there's a man, or woman, who knows fusion better than I do, then I'd gladly let them lead the way. But the sad fact remains, we're on the cusp of a scientific breakthrough that few people are capable of understanding. And as for the rest . . ." He waved his hand dismissively.

"They get what they deserve?"

"Waters, I don't need your insubordination." He looked around the room expectantly and nodded toward a man coming down the stairs. "You were supposed to question Edmond Asheton. I suggest you get on with it."

Upon hearing his name, the man nodded to Hugo and then proceeded toward me. It was Asheton all right, walking with the rigid gait of a British army officer. He shook hands stiffly in one hard stroke. "What is it you want?"

I tried not to stare, but I suppose he was used to it. Along the left side of his face from behind his ear and across his neck, there was a long patch of shiny, waxen skin. Another patch cut across it from his cheek down, the skin unnaturally taut. His ear was white and mangled. It had been reconstructed none-too successfully. I'd seen my share of wounded soldiers, but it still came as a shock to see Asheton disfigured.

"Didn't mean to frighten you," he said. "My Victoria Cross." He turned to give me the full view and gestured to his face with his left hand. He was missing two fingers. He gave a thin smile. "Never forget, I always say."

I nodded with what I hoped was suitable sympathy.

"I know you've gone over some of this already with the sergeant, but I'd like to hear it again in your own words."

"All right, then." He walked toward the window and leaned against the sill.

"You're here doing a story on German companies?"

Asheton raised an eyebrow. "Nothing of the sort." He opened a cigarette case and retrieved a Player's Navy Cut. I reached over with my lighter and he cupped his hands around the flame, like an old soldier. He inhaled a lungful and then leaned back again.

"It's a profile on Hugo. A puff-piece, actually. See how the great inventor lives among the Hollywood elite. A few snaps of the mansion, his daughter, the local scenery. It'll run in a Sunday edition. Make everyone wish they were in California."

I moved toward the other side of the room, past the coffee table and couch. "And where were you when the explosion happened?"

"Explosion?" he asked. "With your flare for the dramatic, maybe you should be the writer. I was with Alan Hugo in the living room when we heard the bells go off. That was the fire in the lab. I gather there was also a fire in the communications room." He looked at me with unblinking eyes. "A damn shame." He tapped the ash of his cigarette on the sill. "I'd met with Dr. Schuler in the lab yesterday. The fire did a lot of damage, not to mention the water. It's a big setback."

I looked up from my notebook. "That lab is strictly off limits."

He made a face. "Whatever gave you that impression? They do small group tours every day at three o'clock. Of course, the visitors are mostly in the upper-level viewing area behind Perspex, but they can see the scientists running their tests. And I was grateful to get a private session with Dr. Schuler."

I flipped through my notebook, trying to recall who had told me the lab was off limits, but there was nothing.

My head felt woozy, like I was in an airplane that had suddenly dropped altitude. I'd been here before, asking these same questions, but everything was coming out different. It was like watching a movie based on a book and halfway through, the director fires the writer and takes it in a different direction.

"Are you all right, Waters? You look a little peaky."

"I'm fine." I leaned forward and in a low voice, I asked, "How did you end up here anyway?"

He seemed surprised by the question. "After the war, I didn't want to be cooped up as a manager in some office. I started writing little travel stories and that got the attention of a few editors. Next thing you know, I've got my 'Thrilling Cities' column for the *Sunday Times* and everything's tickety-boo. It's taken me all over the world: Paris, Chicago, San Francisco."

"And how do you like it here?"

"Loma Vista has all the charm of a picnic in the rain."

"Well, that's something. Are you traveling with your wife?"

"Never married. Well and good for others, but I can't see anything in it for me. And with this boat race . . . " He turned the left side of his face toward me.

"And where's your photographer?"

"He'll be coming out in a few days. They wait until the story is filed and then hire someone locally."

"Save on expense, is that it?"

"I'm just happy to be out of Blighty for a while. I'd had enough of rationing, what? America has recovered so much better from the war than England."

"Look, I was a captain in the 104th Infantry in the war. I worked with plenty of intelligence officers."

"Is that right?"

He left his perch and walked toward the center of the room. He bent down at the coffee table and flicked ash from his cigarette into a heavy glass ashtray.

"The *Times* doesn't send a Brit to cover a story like this."

"For an insurance detective, you have a curious line of questioning."

Asheton grabbed the ashtray, sprung up, and hurled it at my head. I ducked and it smashed on the wall behind me. But it was just a diversion. He leaped forward and pushed me hard with both hands in the chest, knocking me against the wall. By the time I could regain my balance, he was sidled next to me with a knife at my throat and his other arm holding me in place.

"You've got three seconds to make an impression before I do. Who are you working for?"

"I'm an insurance detective, with my brother."

"Don't play me for a fool. You were at Mittelwerk. What are you doing here?"

The inscription on the lighter, of course. I had to wind him up and fast.

"My brother was OSS in the war," I said. "We were trying to get Panzinger."

"The OSS were bloody amateurs. Without British support they were nothing."

I could feel his breath on my face. I tried to remember what Asheton had told me, what seemed a lifetime ago.

"Bob Lamphere, FBI, told us to check on Schuler. Make sure Black Sun wasn't re-activated."

He took the knife away and shoved me hard. I had to put my hand out to right myself on a chair.

"All right, Waters. Very few people have heard of Black Sun. I'm going to assume you're in the clear and hope to God I don't regret it. These are dangerous times."

"You don't need to tell me," I said. "You're the one with the knife."

"And bloody well don't forget it. Just like Lamphere to send in one of his own without telling me."

I rubbed my shoulder. "To be fair, he didn't tell us about you, either."

He seemed to relax at that piece of embellishment. He closed his flick-knife but didn't put it away.

"And how do you know him anyway?"

"I told you, Jordan was OSS. He worked for Dulles."

"Truman shut down the OSS for a reason. He said he didn't want to create an American Gestapo. But there was more to it. Too much had gone wrong in Germany. Typical of the OSS to send your brother in without the tools or training to do the job. It's a wonder he managed to hang on until you got there."

I must not have seemed like a threat as Asheton finally pocketed his knife. "Of course, now the CIA are back into world adventure. And Hoover has his secret police on the home front."

"You seem to know a lot about American intelligence."

"It's my job, man. Chief Liaison. Lamphere, Hoover, Angleton, all the agency directors are worried about what the opposition is up to," he said. "It's the only thing they agree on."

"You mean Panzinger?"

He nodded. "I've been keeping tabs on the scientists who were part of the Thule Society for the last five years. They've scattered to the wind: America, Australia, Brazil, and worst of all, Russia. We didn't get Panzinger, but at least *they* didn't get Schuler."

He lit another cigarette. "This place is falling apart and quickly. Schuler's harmless. And Hugo's out of money. Very convenient fire, wouldn't you say? I bet the old man does a runner once he gets his insurance money."

"Doesn't leave you much, does it?"

"Like I said, good to get out of London."

"But what about Faith Robner?"

"Wrong place at the wrong time. You and the local coppers can sort that out. For us, it's a dead end." He put his hand to his chin. "Lamphere and I heard some stories. Whispers from the opposition. Secret cities filled with scientists. What they're working on defies description."

"The A-bomb?"

"Far more powerful than that. Imagine the ability to bend the rules of physics, time, space, all of it. If the Nazis had got Black Sun working, it would have changed the course of the war. They would have conquered Russia and from there, who knows? The Russians don't have it, but that's what they're after. You'd be surprised the cables we've been able to decrypt from Moscow."

He puffed on his cigarette.

"Thank God Hugo's running the show. He's the new American, a con man in a tailored suit. Barely understands the science, but wants to take credit for everything. The whole place is an accident waiting to happen."

CHAPTER 30
One Way Out

Churchill and Roosevelt had a special relationship during the war, but it didn't always make its way down to the rank and file. Asheton was running his own operation. I couldn't get a read on what he was really after. And certainly, I didn't trust him. I was running out of options.

Schuler was my only bet. He knew how the Z-machine worked and I had what he needed.

I passed by the machine room on my way to find him. I peered at the wreckage. It looked the same as what I'd seen before. Broken equipment, glass fragments, fire and smoke damage. Of course, the big difference was Panzinger wasn't dead on the floor. He was alive, thousands of miles away. This time Faith died, for reasons I didn't understand.

As I stepped into the hallway, I bumped into a big man. He didn't budge, but I almost fell over. It was Charlie. He was wearing stained, dark coveralls, but his hands were immaculate. He radiated calm confidence. If there was a mechanic from the heavens, it was Charlie.

"You're back?" he said.

"No, that was my brother. I'm Jack."

"I know who you are." His eyes looked right through me. I shook it off. "We haven't met?"

"No." He had that same penetrating aura that Amy had. A calm glow. His lower lip pulsed for a fraction of a second.

I knew he was lying. DeHoCo had taught me that much. But he didn't care that I knew. He was signaling. Charlie seemed to know a lot more than he let on. I would follow up with him, if I got what I needed from Schuler.

"Jordan told me about you." He leaned in close. "He said you got him out of a jam."

"He would have done the same for me."

"Not many could do what you did. It takes courage to confront such darkness."

I said nothing.

"You can't change the past. Your path lies elsewhere. In ancient times, the Rabbi Shimon bar Yochai was persecuted and sentenced to death by the Romans. And so he fled the world, living in a cave. When he emerged, after thirteen years, diseased and covered in sores, he praised God for the wisdom he had gained from his study of the Torah. And now, I see that you have gained wisdom, too. You must leave the caves."

"What do you mean?"

"It's not your time."

I nodded and moved past him.

I found Schuler alone in his office, a large-windowed affair. He'd come a long way from his days as chief lab rat. He wore a blazer and his tie was loose, but it was the same guy. Now he was surrounded by books. Three telephones sat on his desk. He looked especially meek, dwarfed by the giant desk. His hands were in his lap.

"Dr. Schuler, I'm from Pacific All-Risk. I'd like to ask you some questions," I said.

For a guy who'd been promoted to run the whole lab, he didn't seem any happier than the Schuler I'd met previously. "*Ja,* of course," he said. "Sergeant Duff said somebody would come by."

He didn't budge from behind the desk. Some things never change. I crossed the room and shook his hand. I held it until it was uncomfortable, not letting go.

"You remember me, don't you?" I asked. I kept a hold of his hand.

"I don't think—"

"And my brother, Jordan?"

He shook his head.

"Come now," I said. "You remember Mittelwerk, *ja*?"

He yanked his hand from my grip like he'd had an electric shock. The color drained from his face. I was going to twist him until I had him where I needed him.

"Look, we're all friends now. Jordan and I made it out of the tunnels, thanks for asking."

"Yes," he hesitated. "We saved your brother. That was the agreement."

"Not exactly, but I'm not complaining. You seem to have done well."

"We . . . I got free and took the route you spoke of, across the forest. Dr. Panzinger was hurt in the explosion. I got to the other side, but he didn't make it over."

"Shame, you were a good team."

"I did what I had to. You understand? Conrad was like a brother to me."

"I know what that's like. Still, better one of you made it out than for both of you to be captured."

He sat up. "He broke his ankle in the explosion." He reached down with his right hand and lifted his left arm onto the desk with a heavy thud. A stainless-steel hook stuck out from the sleeve of his blazer. And then, a half-hearted shrug. "I found Hugo. But it was a long drive to Spandau, and when we got there they had to amputate."

"Still, you have a new team. Worldwide."

His mouth gaped. "How do you know?"

"It doesn't take a genius to know you're not one, Schuler."

"I am the director of Blakely Labs. I built all of this." He waved his good hand in triumph.

"You aren't any closer than you were in 1945."

I had to let him come to me.

"We have a new approach, but it takes time."

"Look, I don't care about that. I'm working with Sergeant Duff on the fire. Smells like arson to me. How did you and Hugo set it up?"

"I would never!"

"Jordan has the evidence."

"Blakely Lab is my life."

"Who you think Duffy will believe? Me and Jordan, or you?"

"All right. What are you after?"

"Tell me about Panzinger."

"You have learned nothing. He is alive and well. Teaching. What else?"

I crossed my arms.

"I was at a conference this spring, in Helsinki. My work these days is on the theory of multi-dimensional timelines. I had published a paper raising more questions than answers. I thought younger minds might plough this field better than I had.

"When the session was over, there was one man at the back of the room, still sitting in his chair. He looked up at me and said 'What if Tillinghast was wrong?'"

"He took a different approach," I said.

"Exactly so." He blinked twice. "I couldn't believe it. His hair had turned white and he was thin. But his mind. Always so sharp." He tapped his finger to his temple. "He knew exactly the questions to unlock my thinking."

"A nice reunion for the two of you."

"*Ja*, to you it's a big joke."

"Couple of Nazis talking about the good old days."

"I was never a Nazi."

"It's amazing how many Germans say that."

"He has his own lab now, too, in Nizhny Novgorod. A political officer accompanied him to Helsinki, but he was more interested in the nightlife than in watching the two of us work on equations. We found new ways to think about the problem. I thought we might jointly publish a paper. Make safe the technology we'd developed so many years earlier."

"But you can't un-ring that bell, can you?"

"It takes time to make things safe. Perhaps a long time. And as you can see, there are setbacks."

"That's your plan? You're just going to run down the clock?"

"This isn't a game. The Z-machine is dangerous."

"And what about Beverley?"

"She's young, impetuous. But she will learn to be patient. Perhaps one day, it really will be safe enough."

"What's Panzinger's role in all of this?"

"I've shared with him everything so that we can work on this together. We can contain it."

"Oh, Christ," I said. Could he be so naive that he didn't understand what Panzinger was after?

"Conrad is my mentor. Together we can set this right."

"Your mentor runs a Soviet weapons program."

"No, he teaches at the university. He told me so. He helped me set up the network so we could work with scientists in other labs."

"You poor sap. And you've nothing to bargain with. Not like Greenglass or Fuchs. They could name names. But you're stuck. You're the last guy in the chain, with nobody left to rat out."

"I'm not a spy. Conrad is a colleague, a friend."

"I'm sure he was happy to remake your friendship. The Russians weren't too easygoing with the Germans they found. He's lucky he made it out alive. It would be hard not to feel betrayed."

Schuler looked puzzled for a moment and then his face went ashen.

"What is it you want?"

"I want you to put me on the Z-machine."

Schuler looked flustered. "I told you it's not safe. We have never run an experiment with a human test subject."

I glared at him.

"We did what we had to do during the war, but it's not like that now. We don't know enough about how to get you through the stasis zone. You of all people should understand the danger."

"You listen to me. You're going to take me to the Z-machine, and I'm going to determine once and for all whether you know what the hell you're talking about. Frankly, I don't even think you've got the balls to do it."

"I won't do it. I made a vow after the war never to—"

"You'll do it for this." I extracted the teletype pages from the pocket of my jacket and held them just out of his reach. They were enough for an FBI arrest on espionage charges. Twenty to life, certainly. If the politicians had their way, the electric chair.

"How did you—" He started out of his chair. "You are a thief. Whatever you think the Z-machine can do for you, you're wrong. It's not some rich man's toy. It's dangerous."

I folded the pages up again and put them away. "I can turn this over to the feds. Or you can use it to help me. And then you can continue with your containment research."

He looked from me to the phones to the bookshelves, as if the equations would show themselves.

"Your threats don't scare me. Beverley and I will figure it out with or without Panzinger. It'll take more time, that's all."

"I'm afraid time is what I don't have."

I pulled out my roscoe.

"You either take me now, or I'm going to blow your ankle off and then you're still going to do it, but you're going to be in a lot more pain."

He slammed his steel hook on the desk. "You think you know what you are dealing with? You're a dangerous fool. If the machine fails, you would end up stuck between two worlds, a living hell. Enough have died. I won't have one more death on my conscience. Not for Beverley and certainly not for you." His right hand massaged his left arm, just below the prosthetic. "Your threats won't change a thing. I vowed I would never put another human being on the Z-machine."

"It's too late. You already have!"

He blinked twice. "Never."

"You did it all right. You told me all about your little convergence area, where the stars disappear. You were thinking of writing it up for a physics journal. And then you sent me to the vanishing point, where the dimensions intersect. Did I get it right?"

"Gott im Himmel!"

"You had to convince me to use the Z-machine so you could test your breakthrough. And now I'm begging you to send me back."

"But . . . I don't have a breakthrough. I've been stuck for months."

"You built on Panzinger's ideas, just like he's building on yours. Well, here it is."

I handed him the teletype message. He snatched it and placed it on his desk, his nose just inches from the paper. His eyes went back and forth as he studied the formulae.

"That's it, right?" I asked.

"Shush. Give me a moment." He leaned his head back to take in the whole page. Then he scribbled onto a blank piece of paper.

"Well?"

"This is . . . nothing. It's just a way to limit the power to the Tillinghast resonator. But the Z-machine will never achieve the force it needs. It's like attaching a heavy trailer to a sportscar. It solves the problem, but . . . " He shrugged. "The issue was always with the overheating. It made the Z-machine so dangerous. We could never calibrate it safely. It only worked the one time." He lowered his head. "So many lives destroyed."

"You told me you developed your breakthrough walking to the convergence area, studying the birds. You observed how the birds flew, how they communicated. Could two birds come up with the same sequence independently?"

"Yes, I have often wondered about that." Schuler removed his glasses and wiped them on his tie. "You know, it is the behavior of the flock that matters, not the individual bird."

"That's it! That's what you said."

"It must be a strange sensation," Schuler said. "I think we've had this conversation before. Have you ever had that feeling?"

I felt a shiver down my spine. My vision started to blur, the color fading. It was one of those moments Amy had warned me about.

"You said you created a fan-out design. Everything in parallel."

"Did I?" He placed his glasses back on his head and he turned back to the papers on his desk. His eyes passed back and forth and he scribbled furiously. I approached the desk and his arm flew up to keep me quiet. He muttered to himself for what seemed like a long time. Finally, he put his pencil down and turned to me.

"Well?" I asked.

"I must say, it's quite brilliant." His face beamed. "We can control dozens of small resonators in parallel. Each component part is quite simple, but together it's like—"

"A symphony," I said.

"Yes, quite so. It's unconventional, but—"

"But what? You can calibrate it properly, right? It's safe?"

"Yes, the calibration is no problem. The danger is not in the Z-machine. The danger is the temptation. You know how badly we failed in the war. Our pursuit of power destroyed Germany and everything it stood for. Why would it be any different now?"

"That's why I have to go back. I have to finish this from the other end. When the last experiment is over, Jordan will help you tear it all down."

PART IV

CHAPTER 31
A Doorway

Loma Vista, California
June 27, 1950

As my vision cleared, I saw a ripple in the air, blinked, and then all was quiet. The room was lit yellow and bright like a sunrise. The desk, the straps, the machine, everything was clear and brilliant. I knew immediately that I was back. It was like the feeling I got the first time I smoked reefer. One instant, nothing was happening, and then the next, it was like someone tapped me on the shoulder and everything had changed. I felt calm. Everything was okay.

I took off my goggles and listened. I heard water dripping from the roof and windows rattling in the wind. I was alone.

I undid the straps and got up quickly. I grabbed my gun and ran the path to the house. It was past the time to be cautious.

As I approached, I saw a group in the kitchen. I had to see if she was there.

I entered the room and Duffy turned to me. "Alan Hugo wants to see you," he said. "And he's not happy." I pushed past him.

"Where's Faith?" I asked.

Duffy stepped back and shrugged. "Last I saw, she was in the living room."

I caught sight of myself in a hallway mirror. My hair was wet and disheveled, and my eyes were like pinwheels.

He called after me. "You don't look so good. What's going on?"

"Find out where Schuler is," I shouted as I raced down the corridor.

The room was dim, lit only by a green-shaded lamp. Faith was seated on the sofa, shuffling papers into a folder that sat on her knees. She looked up as I entered the room.

"Thank God you're all right," I said.

"What happened?" She stood up and came to me. "You're soaked." She put her hand on my chest and stood so close, I could feel her warmth. "You're shaking."

"I was worried."

"About what?"

"About you."

"I'm perfectly capable of taking care of myself. Don't worry. Sergeant Duffy isn't trying to make time with me."

"That's not what I meant." I softened my tone. "I know I've messed up. I want to make things right."

"I called the insurance company."

"I thought I lost you."

"I said we'd get the preliminary paperwork to them—"

"I had this vision that you—"

"—by Monday."

"You died."

Her mouth opened, but she said nothing. She put her hand to her cheek and looked away.

I turned her face back to me. "I don't want to lose you."

"You're scaring me, Jack."

"You mean everything to me. All I'm asking is for you to give me a second chance."

A moment passed.

I held my breath while my resolve intensified.

She took my hand.

"Please. Don't do this. Not here."

"Just think about it."

"Where did all this happen?" she said, letting go.

"I was following up with Schuler. He's built another Z-machine."

"I don't understand."

I took her hand again in mine. "I know it sounds strange, but it's all true. I made it back."

Her mouth trembled. "Back?"

"I saved him."

Her face flushed and she turned away.

"Jordan was alive. We made it out of the tunnels together." I stood up. "Don't you understand?"

"Jack, I can't do this."

"Listen to me: it really happened."

"You were only gone a few minutes."

After a long moment, she looked up at me. She spoke slowly. "I know for you it seems real. We'll get someone who can help."

I flung her hand away, more forcefully than I had intended. I could feel anger welling up inside me. "Look, I know what I saw. I was there."

She turned away and leaned forward, her body crumpling, drawing inward. She was silent, holding it in best she could. And then when she couldn't hold it anymore, the dam burst. She sobbed quietly into her hands.

Why did it always end up with me hurting her? "Faith, you need to believe me." I rested my hand on her shoulder. She took my hand and her breathing steadied.

I fished a square of paper out of my pocket and placed it on the desk in front of her.

It was another long moment before she looked at it.

In a soft whisper, she said, "Where did you get this?" She picked it up like it was a delicate object and cradled it in her hands.

"It's really true?"

I nodded.

She looked at the photo of me and Jordan outside a tunnel entrance. We were in clean uniforms and shaven, posing like victors. So it must have been taken a few days after our escape. I had no memory of being there with Jordan, and I don't know who snapped the picture. She flipped it over. On the back, there was a note in pencil: *Me and Jack, Mittelwerk—April 13, 1945.* She flipped it back and examined the picture more closely. "At least you smiled for the camera."

"There's definitely a connection between Amy Hugo's death and what happened to Panks."

"How's that?"

"She planned it. As a way to shut down her research. She'd figured out what the Z-machine could do, and she was afraid of it. So she destroyed it all. But it left her trapped."

"Trapped? But she died."

"She died. That's in our world. But she still exists, in a dimension outside our world. She called it a temporal limbo."

"You make it sound like purgatory."

"That's as good an explanation as any. And I think Jordan is trapped, too."

"How is that possible?"

"They each died while they were using the Z-machine, between worlds. Amy had a purpose, a plan she was carrying out."

Duffy appeared in the doorway, surveying the scene, but not quite a part of it. "Everything all right?" he asked.

Faith forced a smile that was almost convincing, the damp of her eyes suggesting otherwise.

"I wanted to make sure Faith was okay," I said.

"Missy?"

"Thank you, Sergeant." She blinked twice. "It's been a night full of surprises." She gathered up her folder and touched her hand to my shoulder. "I'll see what else I can find."

Duffy's eyes followed Faith out. "What's going on with you two, anyways?"

"It's complicated."

"'Cuz you're partners? I would think that would make things easier. Common bond and all."

"If I want advice—"

"A lady like that, you need to take care of her."

"What are you, filling in for Ann Landers now?"

"So, what did you find from Schuler? You weren't gone twenty minutes. I didn't even have time to update the captain on the radio."

"Good," I said. It felt like I had been living in some crazy dream-world for months. But for Duffy and everyone at home, only minutes had passed. It was hard to keep straight. "We need to keep this to ourselves for now."

"Keep what to ourselves?"

"You remember what Asheton said?"

"About the Black Sun and all that?"

"What they're working on is dangerous as hell."

"That was during the war."

I shook my head. "Black Sun, the Z-machine, it's the same thing. They've been working on it the entire time. They figured out how to make it actually work."

"But it was burned in the fire."

"Schuler's got a whole other workshop. Not quite as polished, but it works."

"It works? How?"

"You don't want to know. Panks was killed over this, and he wasn't the only one. Schuler's in danger."

"If this is related to the case, I gotta radio the captain."

"No."

"Jack, this is my job."

"Give me an hour. That's all. After that, we open it all up."

"What does this Z-machine actually do?"

"You really want to know?"

"Uh-huh."

"It opens up a doorway to different worlds. The past, maybe even the future."

Duffy blanched. "That ain't right. You can't change the past."

"I lost my brother in the war. I went back and saved him."

"Jesus Christ, you almost had me for a minute. You make choices in life, you live with it. I oughta know." He shifted his weight onto his good leg.

"If it *did* work, isn't there something in your life that you wish you could do over?"

"Forget it. You're talking nonsense." Duffy slumped down into a chair. His voice was barely above a whisper. "We can work the case, but don't talk to me about this other stuff."

"Panks's death, Amy's death, they're tied up in this."

"How is that possible?" Duffy put his hand to his head. Beads of sweat were breaking out. "What about Asheton? Does he know about Schuler's workshop?"

"What he knows and what he's saying are two different things."

"But he's working with the feds. We're just a couple of—"

"Asheton isn't looking out for you, me, or anybody other than himself. It's just us. You, me, and Faith."

Duffy's head wobbled. I'd seen men fall apart in battle when they couldn't get past their own fears. I reached out my hand.

"Look, Duffy, there's one other thing. The explosion in the lab? The same thing happened in the tunnels in the war."

"That place, Mittelwerk?"

I nodded. "You remember that smell in the lab? It was there both times. There was an accelerant, alcohol and gunpowder."

"You just remembered that?"

"I need your help. I can't do this without you."

He looked up and sat straighter.

He thought for a moment. "Asheton's not FBI. He's not even American."

"Exactly," I said.

"What'd the English ever do for us, anyways?" Some of his color had returned. "Warm beer and a lot of hot air."

Just then we heard a loud noise.

"That's a gunshot outside," Duffy said, suddenly alert. He stood up and drew his 38. "Quick, out back."

CHAPTER 32
Caveat Venditor

We ran toward the lights of the barracks and lab buildings, the rain making it hard to see. I looked back at the house and I saw lights appear on the second floor.

"I'll get the barracks," Duffy said, panting badly. He jerked his thumb to the farther building. "You check the lab."

Where the hell is Schuler, I wondered. Duffy had slowed to an uneven trot, but I kept my pace steady.

I ran to the lab, scanning the horizon for any motion. As I approached the door, I heard a click. I stopped in my tracks. I held my breath and waited. A latch closed. With the rain, I couldn't tell where it came from.

I counted silently to three and then entered the lab, my gun leading the way. I moved quickly, staying alert for any sound that might indicate an intruder.

I moved as quietly as I could to the entrance of the machine room. The lights were on in the hallway and the door was open, but the room was dark. I heard a soft rustling sound.

I turned on the overhead light. The room was empty. Ash and debris swirled on the concrete floor where Panks's body had been. Wind was coming in through the broken windows. Only a faint odor of the fire remained, more chemical now that Panks's charred body had been removed.

"Jack, over here!" I heard Duffy call from outside. "The barracks."

I took another minute to check the storage area. It was as deserted as the machine room. No sign of anyone. Once I got outside, I picked up my pace and ran along the stone path to the barracks.

I saw Alan Hugo walking quickly along the grounds near the mansion toward the barracks. He must have heard the shot. He had one hand shielding his face from the rain, the other clutching his cane.

Duffy met me outside the entrance.

"This is a damn mess," he said. He holstered his weapon.

Duffy led me into the barracks area that we'd searched earlier.

I was too late. We were in one of the single bedrooms, no larger than a New York hotel room. There was a body on the ground, its mangled, bloody face looking up at me.

It was Schuler.

Dead on my watch.

Of all the people I'd met in five years, in two countries, trying to find Jordan, Schuler was the only one who came through. He wasn't the rat I'd thought he was. He was a genius. He might have figured out a way to rescue Jordan, to bring him back to our world. Now Amy was dead. Panks was dead. Schuler was dead.

Who was next?

He was flat on his back, with a Walther P38 in his right hand. Bakelite grip, standard issue to German troops, probably the same one he had pulled on me in the tunnel. Half his head was blown off, his face was badly scorched, and bits of brain and bone were splattered on the wall behind him. A thin, dark red pool reflected from the floor. Glass shards and a couple of feathers stuck in the blood. Traces of dark red smeared Schuler's shirt.

With a wound like that, there wasn't much hope. I checked for a pulse to be sure. It couldn't have been more than a couple of minutes since we heard the gunshot, but the body was already cool. What was left of him had a pale-blue tint.

"Seems clear to me," Duffy said, hitching his pants. "Schuler was upset, had a couple of drinks, and decided he didn't want to live anymore."

"I should have gotten to him," I said. "I could have warned him."

"Warned him? Jack, this is self-inflicted. He worked with Panks all those years. I guess it hit him pretty hard."

I pointed to a sheet of writing paper on Schuler's desk. "Was that here earlier?" I asked Duffy.

"Lemme see." Duffy walked toward the desk and picked it up, holding it on the sides. "Looks like a suicide note," he said. He paused to read it. His lips moved silently and then he frowned.

"Well?"

"It's . . . some kind of suicide poem."

He handed the paper to me. It was written in a flowery old-fashioned style, the penmanship uneven.

I see all our search for knowledge is vain,
And this burns my heart with bitter pain.
Then let them hear my death-knell toll.
Then from your labors you'll be free,
The clock may stop, the clock-hands fall,
And time come to an end for me!
Caveat Venditor.
–DS

"It's Faust," I said. "That book of poetry Schuler was carrying around."

"What's he say? My time is up?"

I read aloud: "And time come to an end for me."

"Case closed, right?" he asked.

"What do you mean?"

"It's a confession. He killed himself."

I took another look. The paper was smudged, like he'd written it quickly.

But it didn't all fit together. Like he was saying too much and not enough.

There was a knock, and I looked over to see Alan Hugo in the doorway. "What's going on?" he asked. "I heard gunfire."

"I'm afraid there's been another death," I said. "Schuler." Hugo looked over and then jumped back, his hand springing to his mouth. His head swayed like a bird's nest in the breeze.

Duffy ran over and grabbed him, quickly moving him to one of the chairs.

"Careful there, Mr. Hugo," he said.

"Get your paws off me, you idiot," Hugo shouted. Duffy stood back, waiting for the blast, which came soon enough, both barrels. "This is all your fault. You two morons were supposed to keep an eye on things." He took a deep breath. "How could you let this happen? First Panks's death and now Schuler." His face was an ugly red. "How the hell am I supposed to explain this?"

Duffy's mouth opened, but nothing came out.

"I oughta call Captain MacDonald and have the two of you permanently assigned to cross-guard duty." His eyes glowered and his head rocked back and forth. "And where's that English clown, Asheton?" he yelled, getting to his feet again.

"I thought he was with you," Duffy said. "He said he had some more questions."

Hugo looked up perplexed. "I haven't seen him. I was working in my office, alone," he said.

"Seen who?" The voice came from the hallway. It was Asheton, leaning against the doorway. "I heard a noise. Everything all right?" His eyes went from Alan Hugo to the body on the floor and then he froze. He shook his head stiffly and let out a quiet, "Christ almighty."

Duffy nodded. "I thought you were with Mr. Hugo?"

That's right," Asheton answered. He looked over at Hugo. "I went to your study and then the lab. I couldn't find you, so I walked back to the front of the house to see if you were on the grounds somewhere."

"You said you were in your office." I turned to Hugo.

He didn't blink. "I was. I went upstairs to get my cigarettes, that's all. What's all this about? You people are messing around while my lab is in ruins."

I heard Charlie's booming voice as he and Beverley entered the barracks. "What's going on?" he asked. "We heard a gunshot."

"Dietrich's dead," Asheton told him.

Beverley looked unsteady on her feet. She let out a slow gasp and drew her hands to her face. Alan Hugo stood up and went to his daughter, putting his arms around her shoulders.

"I'm taking her back to the house," he said.

"We may need to ask a few more questions," Duffy said.

Hugo paid no heed and walked out with his daughter under his arm.

Duffy looked over at me. "Do you want me to . . . "

"Naw, let them be," I said. I looked around at Charlie and Asheton. "Gentlemen, we'll follow up with you after we're done here."

"Righto," Asheton said. "We'll be in the main house."

I nodded curtly.

"What a mess," Duffy said, shaking his head slowly.

"Well, at least we kept them away from the body," I said. "Mind if I take a look?"

"Fresher's better."

I crouched down on one knee and went through his pockets. There was a wallet, a small notebook, and a set of keys. I studied Schuler's desk and noticed the drawer was slightly ajar and hanging at an angle. Duffy leaned in to examine it. The lock had been mangled.

"Why would Schuler break into his own desk?" Duffy asked.

"He wouldn't," I said, tossing his keys on the surface. "Somebody else did this."

I reached down and opened the drawer. There was a leather holster in it. I picked it up and placed it on the desk.

"Take a look at the holster."

"Must have got it in the war," Duffy said, waiting for a response. I crossed my arms. "It's for a Walther, says so right on the leather." He looked at me, the student waiting for a hint. "What am I missing?"

"Try it on, Watson," I said.

He picked up the holster with his right hand and started to lower it to his hip and then stopped.

"Schuler's left-handed."

"Exactly," I said.

I bent down and looked closer at Schuler's body. I pulled at the collar of Schuler's shirt. "Look at this," I said. "Bruises on his neck. What do you make of that?" I stood up and dragged the soles of my shoes against the floor to wipe any blood off them. "Must have gotten into a fight before whatever happened here."

"So why the note?" Duffy asked.

"It's a set up," I said. "This isn't suicide. It's murder. Whoever got to Panks also got to Schuler. But Schuler was smart. He was trying to tell us something."

Duffy picked up the note again. He scrunched his eyes in concentration and re-read it. "What's this *'caveat venditor'*?"

"*'Caveat emptor'* means *buyer beware*," I said. "I'm guessing *'caveat venditor'* is the opposite. It means *seller beware*."

"Never heard of that one."

Nor had I. And it wasn't Faust. I folded up the note and put it in my notebook. I took another look around the room. Schuler lived like a monk. Empty desk. Clean blotter. A water glass.

We looked around the barracks, tossing mattresses, emptying desk drawers, working in silence. We found nothing and then headed back to the house. The wind had picked up and the rain came at us in horizontal bursts, stinging our faces.

"I don't buy the suicide note," I said. "Schuler was angry. He wanted to prove to me the Z-machine worked."

"Come on, it's getting late. I wanna wrap this up. He's just another dead Kraut," Duffy said. "What do you care? Anyway, the captain is going to blow his top."

"Schuler was going to tell me what happened in the tunnels at Mittelwerk. I hated him, but he didn't do this."

"Just file your report and call it a day."

"Are you kidding me?" I stopped in my tracks. "This is a double murder."

Duffy kept walking, his eyes on the pathway. "Maybe how you see it, but there's no evidence."

I caught up and stood in front of him. "Look, Panks's death was no accident. And Schuler's wasn't suicide. He's left-handed, the gun is in his right. And where were his glasses?"

Duffy stepped off the path and brushed past me. "What are you talking about?"

"He was practically blind without them. So where were they?" I called after him.

"I don't know. Maybe he took them off."

"I searched the body, the desk, the room. They weren't there." I caught up with him. "Someone killed both of them. The killer is after something, and he won't stop until he gets it. If we're not careful, we'll end up like Panks and Schuler."

"Now you're overreacting."

"If there's something worth murdering two people over, then why not three . . . or four? The Z-machine is at the root of this whole thing. And it ties back to Amy Hugo's death eleven years ago."

"That's crazy. We don't even have proof that Panks was murdered. How are we gonna prove something from eleven years ago? Forget it." We walked the path to the back porch. "I gotta call the captain before Asheton does." He kept his eyes front. "He ain't gonna like this."

I could see how it would play out. There was plenty of blame to go round. I went back to the porch and lit a cigarette. I was well past the halfway mark on the pack. I looked out at the darkness. I could barely see the path we'd been on.

A few minutes passed, and Duffy came back out and jerked his thumb inside. "Captain wants to talk to you." His eyes were down at the ground. I flicked my cigarette butt out on the wet lawn.

"It's not your fault, Sergeant," I said. I clapped him on the back.

I picked up the receiver and answered. "Waters here."

"What the hell happened out there?" I could feel the heat even over the phone line.

"I'm sorry, sir. It wasn't what any of us were expecting."

"Dammit, you were supposed to be helping Sergeant Duff, not running some renegade operation. You let a suspect go back to the scene of the crime and kill himself? What were you thinking?"

"It wasn't like that." I said the words, but it was a lie. It was my fault.

"Waters, I said you could work with Duffy as a test run of what it might be like for you to join the force. Now I've got another DB on my hands. This doesn't look good for either of us."

"I believe this is a multiple homicide."

"In Loma Vista? Are you out of your mind? I oughta come out right now and remove you. It's lucky for you that storm has flooded the roads."

"Sir, if you'll just let me explain—"

"No, I've had quite enough explanations from you. As of now, you are—"

"Sorry, Captain .. I'm ... having .. hearing ... storm ... "

I tapped the hook on the phone a couple of times and, wouldn't you know it, the line had gone dead. *This storm was really taking its toll.*

I walked back outside. The rain was still coming down and thunder boomed in the distance.

Duffy looked surprised. "So, you okay?"

"Some of the roads are washed out."

"Yeah. Anything else?"

"Nah. Phone went dead."

"I hope you know what you're doing."

"Never stopped me before," I said.

"So, you're still on the case then?"

"At least while the road's out. Unless you heard otherwise."

"Between you and the captain, I would think."

"And he's going to be delayed."

"The storm."

"Yep."

Duffy tilted his head. "You got brass balls. I'll give you that."

CHAPTER 33
Venona

Duffy and I walked down the back hall toward the kitchen. The house was quiet. A single light flicked on in Hugo's study. I motioned to Duffy and we moved like shadows. I pushed open the door.

"Quite the reporter," I said. Asheton was sitting at the desk with a folder of papers spread open in front of him. He had nerve all right.

"Gentlemen," Asheton responded.

"What are you doing in here?"

"I could ask you the same thing."

"Yeah, but I've got the gun." He looked momentarily surprised to be staring down the barrel of a gun but recovered quickly.

"Please. I've taken the liberty of plundering the family financials." He was cool all right. Duffy was more agitated than Asheton. "You'll want to have a look at this."

He slid a folder toward me across the desk and leaned back in his chair. I put my gun away and Duffy resumed breathing.

"Your man Hugo seems to be in rather a financial jam. Overdue invoices, dunning letters, banks calling in loans. Looks to me like he's sunk all his money into Blakely Lab and now he's skint."

I rifled through the papers.

"You think he staged the fire?" Duffy asked.

"Hardly my area of expertise." All eyes turned toward me.

"The fire wasn't an accident," I said. "It wouldn't be the first time someone torched a failing business. But it doesn't explain Schuler's death."

"He was caught up in this." Asheton leaned back and heaved his feet onto the desk. "Unlucky fellow, I would say."

"Caught up in what?"

"Let me fill you in. I'm not going to shed a tear that Panks and Schuler are dead. But it would have made my job so much easier if they were alive and kicking."

"How's that?"

"I told you: I've been tracking the Thule Society scientists for some time now. But only to see where it leads. We've got a more formidable enemy now."

"The Russians," I said.

He nodded. "If the Russians ever get hold of this technology, it would change the balance of global politics. This isn't about a couple of stray Nazi scientists. I couldn't care less. Our investigation is much more serious than that."

"What investigation?" Duffy asked, looking over at me.

"It's a little unusual, but, given the circumstance, I think a slight breach of protocol is appropriate. Let me put you in the picture," Asheton continued.

I nodded.

"Our governments have been cooperating on something called the Venona Project."

Duffy rolled his eyes. "Here we go again."

"Lamphere at the FBI can vouch for all of this. Toward the end of the war, the U.S. had rather a lucky break. They've been able to decrypt cables from Russian agents for several years. Seems that when the German army was advancing on Moscow, the factory that made one-time encryption pads got a bit sloppy. They printed the same encryption pad without variation. Not terribly secure. Together, we've been able to decrypt all of their messages."

"What's that got to do with Blakely Lab?" I asked.

"We arrested a Los Alamos physicist, Klaus Fuchs, code named Charles, in England in February. It seems he had been sending atomic secrets to the Russians. Fuchs identified Harry Gold, a chemist in New York, as his U.S. courier. He was running Fuchs's material to a KGB man in New York, Vasily Zagadka, the Soviet Vice Consul. Lamphere's FBI team picked up Gold last month."

"The atomic spies," Duffy said.

"Heard about it on the radio," I said.

"Gold gave a full confession. That led the FBI to David Greenglass in New York. He was a bad egg at Los Alamos. Went pink and started tattling to the reds. Lamphere thinks he can get more names out of him."

"You're rolling up the network," I said.

"Precisely." Asheton stood up from the behind desk.

"The most recent cable from Zagadka was an order to shut down their west coast operation and exfiltrate two soviet agents known as Triad and Raven. That was my green light to pick up Panks and Schuler. They were our last hope to understanding what the Soviets are up to. If we had them, we could apply pressure, just like we did with Klaus Fuchs. Unfortunately, the way things have gone, we're at a stalemate."

"At least they don't have Panks."

"Yes, there's that." Asheton took a step forward. "You know, Waters, you're smart. You could be doing so much more."

I waited for it.

"No offense, but you're wasting your time here in Loma Vista."

Duffy looked at his watch, not invited to the party. Asheton continued on, unabated.

"When this is over, I'd be happy to put in a word for you with Lamphere. They're always looking for good agents. Men who can think on their feet and mind their Ps and Qs."

"Not really my style."

"Give it some thought."

"If Panks and Schuler were thinking of defecting, how would they do it?"

"There's a dogsbody working out of the Russian Embassy in Mexico City named Valeri Meretzki. The defectors would make their way to Mexico and from there, use the Russian embassy to get out under diplomatic cover, through Cuba or Latin America."

Duffy's eyes lit up. "Mexico City?" he asked.

"We found train tickets on Panks." I pulled out my notebook, opened it up, and handed Asheton the tickets. "There was also twenty thousand in cash in Panks's room. Hundred-dollar bills, wrapped in elastics."

"There was that torn hundred-dollar bill, too," Duffy said.

"They sometimes use half a banknote as a way to identify an operative," Asheton said. "Panks was likely meeting someone he didn't know. His contact would have the other half, like a claim check."

"Seems like an expensive way to do things," I said.

"Oh, not to the Russians." Asheton's head bounced lightly. "They've been printing their own currency for years. They do a good job, but your people can spot the difference. Something to do with the paper."

"We can check on that," Duffy said.

"The Russians have been after the Z-machine since news reports leaked in '44. You Yanks waltzed right in and took it from under their very noses. Bloody lucky that Hugo was able to pick up Panks and Schuler north of the camp, keeping them out of Russian hands. They still thought they had something coming to them when the Americans made Nordhausen part of the Soviet Occupation Zone. They left some V-2 rockets and the engineers living nearby, but the brains were long gone. Hugo saw to that."

I cast my line. "The Russians were outmaneuvered."

"You could put it that way." Asheton's face tightened.

"So they're still after it," I said.

"Given Panks's death, everything here is moot. But I need your discretion on the matter."

"Of course. And we'll have your cooperation on the murder investigation?"

"Trust me," Asheton said. "We're all on the same side here."

CHAPTER 34
Limbo

I still didn't trust Asheton because I knew what he was after. I didn't have much time, so I decided to throw a bomb and see what happened. There were two pieces I had to bring together and I had to time it just right.

I found Alan Hugo alone in the living room, his head perched on his right hand. A cigar had gone out in the ashtray, but the smell lingered in the air.

"What do you want?"

"I'm afraid I need to ask you a few more questions," I said.

"Can't this wait until tomorrow?"

"I'm sorry, sir, not with what's happened to Schuler."

"This whole fiasco is your fault."

"Sir?"

"If you and that bonehead Duffy had half a brain between you, I wouldn't be in this jam. My two best scientists dead, my lab in ruins."

I pulled out my notebook and flipped the pages. "We found train tickets in Panks's possession. Seems he was headed to Mexico City."

"So he had a holiday coming up. Nothing to do with me."

"Well, sir, it would have been a holiday, as you put it, for two. He had two tickets. And he was scheduled to leave tonight. Had he told you about this?"

"My men don't punch a clock."

"But he cleared it with you?"

"He mentioned it."

"Who was he going with?"

"What?"

"He must have mentioned who he was traveling with."

"With Schuler, of course. It's a holiday weekend, a few days sightseeing."

"Okay. Thanks for clearing that up." I wrote, *Mexico sight-seeing* in my notepad. "Still, not a bad haul."

"What?"

"Half a million insurance. I'd say things have worked out nicely for you."

He looked away from me. "Without Panks's breakthrough, it's a big setback."

"Half a million dollars—get yourself some new friends, eh? Maybe Americans this time."

"Waters, you're patriotic, I'll give you that. But a relic like you can't stand in the way of progress. We're in a different time. America doesn't have a lock on progress anymore."

"You know a guy named David Greenglass at Los Alamos?"

"Some beatnik Army friend of yours?"

"Hardly. It was on the radio. He was a machinist. Arrested for passing documents to the Russians."

"Not even a scientist. What would he know?"

"He's naming names. Harry Gold ring a bell?"

"Never heard of him." He looked down at his watch.

"Just thought it was interesting: you, Panks, and Schuler, all at Los Alamos."

"Of course, we were all there. That's where we began work on the new Z-machine. We'd still be there if the pencil-pushers there weren't so short-sighted. But I'll prove them wrong. It's just a matter of time."

I closed up my notepad and put it in my jacket pocket. "Your wife figured it out."

"What?"

"She solved the power problem, same as Panks and Schuler, but eleven years earlier."

"Waters, you're lower than I thought. All her work was lost in the fire."

"She knew what she was doing. Wrote it all down."

"How the hell would you know?" Hugo asked.

"And then she hid it."

"What?"

"She figured out how to create a . . . what was it again? A *temporal limbo*."

"That's a crackpot theory if there ever was one. The stuff of graduate students with over-active imaginations."

"She engineered her death to prove its existence."

Hugo's whole frame bolted upright. "Why the hell would she do that?"

"It's a good question. Maybe she was tired of your company."

"You're bluffing. You don't know a thing."

"I know Schuler figured out the same breakthrough as your wife. And without Schuler or the lab book, you're sunk. I could hardly blame you."

"For what?"

"The fire in the lab, for one. I'm no scientist, but it seems like a pattern. Same as eleven years ago. And you know, that could tie up the insurance settlement."

He glared for a moment and then reached for his cane and squeezed it until his knuckles whitened. "You think I care about the insurance money?"

He slumped in his chair and let out a sigh. It seemed like a full minute of silence passed.

"For me, it all comes down to the science." Hugo's hand slipped into his pants pocket and he jangled coins, as if he had a compulsive scratch. "It's too bad we can't prove the temporal limbo theory just yet." He was now jangling the coins in a faster rhythm and he looked at me. "Imagine what it must feel like." He slowed it down. "To be trapped like a bug in a bottle. For eternity." He snapped his hand against his thigh and whispered, "It's just a theory, you know." He shrugged his shoulders and smiled. "But if it were true . . . It would be interesting to consider how one might bring someone back from that hell."

His look turned to a glare. "So, you listen to me, Waters. You get those missing pages from the lab book and you bring them to me."

CHAPTER 35
Legend of the Hummingbird

Charlie was still on my list for a follow-up conversation. He had too many connections to the Z-machine to ignore. Duffy said he wanted to check on the patrolman, which was a good enough excuse for both of us. Charlie wasn't the forthcoming type and it was better for me to meet him on my own. I found him in the kitchen, his head in a cupboard.

"I wanted to ask you a few questions."

"I'm getting an aspirin for Miss Beverley."

"Is she all right?" I asked.

He shrugged. "It's been difficult for her. A lot for a young lady to deal with."

"For anyone. I appreciate you taking care of her," I said. "Back to what happened earlier. What caused you to run to the barracks?"

Charlie frowned. "We heard a noise. I wanted to make sure everyone was safe."

"And where were you?"

"I was watching over Beverley for a while, to make sure she fell asleep. She's still a young girl to me."

"Notice anyone else?"

Charlie watched me pull out my deck and light a Lucky.

"Alan was ahead of us, I think. I'm sorry you are being dragged into all of this." He looked at me expectantly. "Could I?" he asked, nodding to the Luckys.

I pulled the pack from my pocket and offered it to Charlie. He plucked one and I lit it.

"Didn't think you smoked," I said.

He took a deep draw like a longtime smoker, who'd given it up. "Only OPs," he smiled.

I shrugged. "It's a complex case."

"No."

"No what?"

"You're the one making it complicated." He seemed to look through me. "You've seen things, but you don't understand."

"Tell me," I said.

"My family has been here for thousands of years, protecting the sacred area."

The words echoed in my mind. "The vanishing point?"

"There are powerful forces here."

"I'm trying to determine what happened to Dr. Panks and now Schuler."

"This is a special place. It's always been that way. It will always be."

"Look, I'm running an investigation."

"It is bound in your past and mine." He brought his large hands together, intertwining his fingers. "But I wonder whether you can see it."

"See what?" I was getting exasperated.

"How your brother fits in."

Before I could think straight, the words fought their way out. "What do you know about my brother?"

"I know he is gone." He exhaled smoke and then put out the cigarette. "But also not gone."

"How do you know any of this?"

"You have seen things from the lower world. To look upon the *nunashish* is dangerous, especially for a novice."

"Spare me the lecture. What's going on here?" I wanted to shake him, but I jammed my hands into my pockets instead.

His gaze was fixed upon me, his eyes darkened. He laughed.

"You and your brother are entangled. You are a part of this, as much as I am. What you do will determine both of your fates."

"What is this mumbo jumbo?"

He gave a short huff and looked at me disapprovingly. "You're better than that, Jack Waters. You know very well this is forbidden knowledge. That is the problem and also the solution."

"The serpent eating its own tail."

He raised his eyebrows. "I'll have to remember that. You understand more than you show."

"I don't mind being underestimated."

"Another thing we have in common. People see me and they see only one thing. But people are more complex than that. Blake Hugo was an exception. He worked hard to understand our ways. But Alan . . . " His lips tightened. "He doesn't care about our past. Times have changed and there aren't so many Chumash left. Hardly anyone speaks the language anymore. When you lose that, what's left? I wonder what our ancestors would think. They settled a vast area. They lived with nature. Now, we're the hired help."

"Yet, Blake Hugo—"

"Mr. Hugo did great things for the Chumash," he said. "The mission was sacred to him. He protected the Chumash." That word again. "But Alan cares nothing of the past. He would destroy it all to achieve his goals." He paused, his eyes clouded over.

"Alan knew he would never be like his father. He had polio when he was young. Did you know that?"

I shook my head.

"It made him tough. But not in a good way. He cared only about the mind—not the heart. Do you understand?"

"I think so."

"The pain Alan suffered stayed with him. He wanted to be great, but he didn't hold himself to greatness. He didn't care about people the way Mr. Hugo did. Alan became interested in the upper and lower worlds of our Chumash stories, but it was just fuel for his desire."

He paused in reflection.

"After Mr. Hugo died, it all changed. Alan decided he needed to develop his own reputation, so he built this big operation. At one point, we had fifty people working here. Can you imagine? Alan wanted to prove that he was as important as Mr. Hugo." He exhaled sharply.

"It can't be easy to live in the shadow of a man like Blake Hugo," I offered.

"Until his father died, Alan never tried. He had the lab out east. But that was Miss Amy's doing. She was careful in her work. Mr. Hugo was always afraid of what Alan would get up to. That's the reason I went east. To make sure Alan didn't get into trouble."

"What kind of trouble?"

"Alan was born into a rich family. He had more ambition than ability. Always looking for short cuts. Alan acted as if his success was pre-ordained."

"He seems to have done well."

"Outwardly, yes, he's a success." He brought his hand to his chest. "Alan's father was concerned with the inner spirit. He lived modestly here in Loma Vista. He could have lived like a millionaire in New York or Los Angeles. But he liked the life he had. He was a friend of the Chumash, an honorary in our tribe. He took the sacred Datura with the elders when I had my passage. That had a profound effect on him. The *moymoy* gave us a bond."

"How so?"

"It opened him up to a different view of the world. How we are connected to the upper world and the lower world. But he had a vision that also scared him."

"How?"

"We have a legend of a time in our past, long ago, when man fell out of harmony with nature. The Creator cast a blanket over the world plunging everything into darkness. Mr. Hugo believed that one day the underworld would fold into our world and everything would be in darkness again. Forever.

"I think you have seen this also." He looked at me gravely. "He left for several days and stayed at the mountain beyond the meadows, to contemplate these visions. When he returned, he had made peace with it." He paused. "That fall, Alan went to study at Miskatonic. I went with him. I studied the science of theology, looking for answers across all the religions. It was a great help to me. So that I could understand my quest."

"Which is what?"

"I told you. To protect the sacred area."

We were going around in circles. "Charlie, I'm trying to understand why someone would kill Panks or Schuler."

"All the usual reasons I should think. Jealousy, envy, greed, betrayal."

"Okay, let's try this on for size. You've resented Alan Hugo all these years and decided to settle the score. You took your vengeance on Blakely labs by killing Panks and then Schuler."

Charlie laughed. "Don't be ridiculous. Could you hurt Jordan?"

It took me a moment to process what he said. "Charlie, are you saying Alan is your brother?"

"We're half-brothers. My mother, Anacapa, was Mr. Hugo's housemaid after his wife died."

"Does Alan know this?"

"Alan Hugo sees only what he wants to see. Mr. Hugo told me this before I went east and I made a vow to keep Alan safe."

I didn't know what to make of this story, so I waited for Charlie to resume.

"Your brother, Jordan, you've seen him." It was a statement, not a question.

"Yes."

"We believe that when a person dies, they are reincarnated. But sometimes it takes many years before their work is done. You understand?"

I nodded.

"In the legend I told you, when all is darkness, the tribes argue on how to restore the world. They try and try but they can't find a solution. Then a hummingbird appears as a messenger to the others. He's not brave like a bear or swift like an eagle, but he has an idea. Hummingbird stands on the shoulders of the crow, who stands on the owl, who stands on the eagle." His hands animated the story. "Eagle flies as high as he can to Father Sky. Then owl flies even higher until she is tired, then crow. Finally, hummingbird flies to the top of the upper world, higher than anyone can fly on their own. He pokes a hole in the blanket that covered the world and now there is a tiny amount of light that shines through. That is how the stars were created to end the darkness. But hummingbird has flown so hard, he can fly no more and falls to earth."

He looked directly at me and his eyes showed a fear I had not seen before. "Until today, I always trusted that Mr. Hugo found a reason to be at ease with his vision. But you arrive like the hummingbird, a messenger. What you saw in the lower world, you can't unsee it. There's no going back for you. The hummingbird dies."

CHAPTER 36
A Moment with Beverley

I headed to the kitchen, still processing what Charlie had said, when I ran into Beverley.

"I thought you had gone to bed."

"Couldn't sleep," she said. "Too much going on up here." She pointed to her head. She was clutching something by her side. She looked flustered.

"I have that sometimes," I said.

She looked down for a moment, thinking. "Is that why you . . . " She pinched her left thumb and finger together and brought her hand toward her mouth, miming.

"I suppose so," I said. "It calms me when things get to be too much."

"That's what adults always say." She seemed disappointed. "Does it work?"

"Sometimes."

"You're one for answers, aren't you?"

"What about you? What have you got there?"

She looked down again, embarrassed. "It's a picture of my mother." She showed it to me. It was the photo from Hugo's office of Alan and Amy Hugo on their wedding day. Charlie was on the left, wearing a suit, and a third man was on the other side.

"Who's that?" I pointed.

She looked at the photo. "That's my mother's brother, Uncle Harry. It's an old photo."

How could I have missed it? The resemblance was obvious. Harry was the connection.

"Did you know him?" I asked.

"When I was a kid, he used to visit my mother. And then a few years ago, Harry started coming back. He'd come over for dinner when he was in town. He traveled a lot. He always brought me something. I think he felt bad that he hadn't been around."

"When was the last time he was here?"

"I was in school. He left a book of poetry for me. It was a couple of months ago."

"Where were you taking the photo?"

"I just wanted to have it, in my room."

"Could I borrow it?"

She furrowed her brow. "I don't know—"

"It's just until tomorrow. I'll bring it back."

She handed it to me. "That's okay. I'll get another." An awkward silence. "Is this about what happened to Schuler?"

"It's all related. Panks, Schuler, the Z-machine, your mother."

"Do you think she was . . . " She looked down, self-conscious. "Was she as good as the others?"

"Your mother is the smartest scientist ever."

She nodded, placated. She walked toward the door, but she turned when she reached the doorway, her head over her shoulder, looking back at me.

"You saw her."

"Pardon me?"

"You said 'is.' You said she *is* the smartest scientist ever."

I winced inside.

"No, no."

"You met my mother."

"I—"

"I heard Schuler talking about his new fan-out design. I thought it was just a theory. How did you do it?"

"Schuler has been working on some alternate prototypes. He had them hidden away."

"I knew she was alive." Her face beamed with excitement. "We talked. I'm not crazy. And you talked to her, too. What did she say?"

"She told me to protect you."

"Tell me more. My God, I haven't seen my mother in eleven years."

"I can't say anything else. I promised Amy I would keep you safe. She has a plan and I trust her."

She looked at the ground. It wasn't her first disappointment.

"Did Faith see you with the photo?"

"No, I don't think so."

"And where is she?"

"I thought she was with you."

CHAPTER 37
Schuler's Warning

"Duffy, you seen Faith?"

He was unfazed. "Not since we came back. Said she wanted to check on something."

"What exactly?" I asked.

"I told her about Schuler and the suicide note. She didn't buy it, either."

"Where'd she go?"

"She's not in the house?"

"I didn't see her."

"She must be out by the barracks or gone back to the lab or something."

I'd been out to the barracks already and there was no sign of her. I reminded myself that Faith had been a war correspondent long before she was my partner. But it didn't offset my growing uneasiness.

"There's something that's been bothering me about Schuler."

"What's that?" Duffy asked.

"Remember when we first heard the gunshot? What did you say?"

Duffy rubbed his chin and his gaze tilted upward. "Jeez, Louise, I don't know . . . " He rubbed his chin. "Maybe something like, *Was that a gunshot?*"

"What you said was 'That's a gunshot outside.'"

"Okay, so what?"

"You thought it was outside. We heard it reverberate off the walls of the courtyard. And when Hugo came into the barracks, he said the same thing."

"But Schuler was in the barracks."

"Exactly."

"He couldn't have been moved, not with all that blood on the floor."

"He was killed in the barracks. But whoever shot him muffled the sound. Later, they fired a second shot, outside. They wanted us to hear that and come running."

"Why would they do that?"

"Let's see what we can find outside."

Duffy looked out the window. "It's really coming down."

"You want to explain to the captain why you didn't search the grounds?"

I turned on the outside lights. We grabbed our coats and hats and headed into the rain. It wasn't the best idea I'd ever come up with, but it was a start. We started at different ends of the open space looking for any evidence we could find.

I could see a couple of people in the dining room, silhouetted, but it was hard to make them out. I stopped to get a better look, to see if I could spot Faith.

Lightning flashed in the sky, followed by the crack of thunder.

Duffy shouted, "Jack, over here. By the cellar."

I came running. "What did you say?" I asked.

"I found something," he said. Water was dripping off his hat and onto his face. "When the lightning flashed, I saw it." He bent down and picked it up. "It's a bullet casing."

I shouted over the rain: "No, not that. You said, 'the cellar.'"

"Yeah, that's the cellar over there." He pointed behind us to an old-fashioned cellar door with a few steps leading down into it. "I figure our shooter might have wanted cover to run back inside the house."

"*Caveat venditor*," I said. "That's what Schuler was telling us. Beware of the *cellar*."

"But what about the bullet?" Duffy asked. He held it in front of my face.

It was what was left of a 9-millimeter shell, a Parabellum. The name came from the Latin motto of the German factory that made them: *Si vis pacem, para bellum*. If you want peace, prepare for war.

I turned it over to look at the markings on the bottom of the brass. "We're looking for a Luger," I said. "A black widow."

"Where are you going?"

"I'm going into the cellar. That's what Schuler was telling us."

"Jack, he wasn't telling us. He was warning us."

"Look, there's something I figured out. Remember that photo of Hugo, his wife, Charlie, and the other man in the suit?"

"I'm here in the rain and you want to talk about family photos?"

"The other man is Amy Hugo's brother, Harry."

"So what?"

"Harry Gold."

"I'm not following."

"Harry Gold, who was arrested."

"What?"

"He's Hugo's contact for the KGB."

"Jeez. So now what?"

"Go back inside and keep an eye on everyone. And if you see Faith, stay with her." I looked at my watch. "We don't have much time. Give me fifteen minutes to check my theory."

The cellar had an old wooden door at the bottom of concrete steps. When I walked down the steps, I was out of the wind and rain and out of sight from anyone in the house. If someone were trying to sneak back along the side of the house, this was the perfect cover.

I opened the latch and gently pushed the door open. It creaked, so I left the door ajar rather than pull it shut.

Then I saw the red-and-blue scarf on the ground. It was Faith's. I kept still for a moment, listening to the rain and waiting for my eyes to adjust. I couldn't hear a sound other than the steady drumbeat of my heart over the rain. There was a narrow, dimly lit hallway. It was cramped and smelled like rotten vegetables. I moved with caution, aware of every step and every scrape of shoe leather.

An interior staircase led up to the kitchen, but that wasn't what interested me. There was a newer stained oak door at the end of the cellar hallway. I opened it quietly, but it was too dark to see what was on the other side. I heard a faint rustling and the squeak of wood. I fumbled around until I could find a light switch and turned it on. Then I saw her.

Faith, mouth gagged, was tied to a chair. Her eyes were pleading, nervous, her face pale.

A sharp intake of breath came from behind me. Before I could turn, something hard came crashing down. I saw a bright flash and then I was falling like a sack of potatoes from a grocery truck.

My last thought: *I was right about the Luger.*

CHAPTER 38
Dirt Nap

I smelled dirt. That's how I knew I was alive. I was cold and the musty smell made me think I was back in Belgium crawling through the forest. But it was too quiet for that.

I could tell that my hands were free, because I was lying face down on top of one of them. Another good sign. The siren in the back of my skull needed to restrain itself before I could think. I pushed myself up from the dirt floor.

The room was vast, and as I moved, the sounds echoed off the stone walls. I looked up and the ceiling must have been fifty feet above me. I was back in the tunnels. I shivered and I realized how cold I was. I could see my breath.

"Mickey Mouse," a voice whispered. I looked to my left. It was Jordan, ten feet away, walking down the center line to the next chamber.

I heard a roar of thunder. "What the hell?" I asked. "Is that storm never gonna end?"

"Jack, they're bombing the place." A sprinkling of dirt fell from the ceiling. Even down in the tunnels the sound was unsettling.

"Where's Faith?" I asked.

"Don't worry. She's back in Loma Vista where she needs to be," Jordan said. "I found a way out."

He handed me my revolver and a piece of paper. It was my mission orders for Mittelwerk. Enter the tunnels. Rescue Jordan. The SIS will take care of the rest. Get in and get out.

"Jordan, what happened in the tunnels? Why did it blow up?"

"You were there. Think back." He tapped his temple. "It's all there."

It came back in a flood. It wasn't a memory. I was reliving it. Moments before the explosion, I'd heard scraping, then a click. I caught a whiff of burning tobacco, the woosh of kerosene igniting.

I could see it. It was just a color at first. And then the image hovered above me, just beyond my grasp. The map of the tunnels, with the location of the meeting. I saw Schuler with his pistol and Panzinger tapping his finger on the cover of the Audubon book. I saw myself from above, overwhelmed, my eyes darting from Schuler to Panzinger, but missing the obvious. There was an energy that told me what my senses couldn't. Now I knew: there had been a third man hidden in the shadows.

"You need to get out of here," Jordan said. "There isn't much time."

"What about you. You're coming with me, aren't you? That was the whole point."

"Jack, I'm sorry." He shrugged, embarrassed. He was holding it in. "I can't leave here. It's not safe for me out there." There was another explosion on the surface and the ground shook like an earthquake. "You need to finish what was started. You need to destroy it all. It's the only way to make it safe again. I can't do it. Do you understand?"

I nodded. I put the gun away and patted my pockets. I couldn't find my lighter, just my old Hermanos. Didn't that figure.

When I looked up, Jordan was walking away. He gave me a nod and turned. Behind him, I saw the old German officer in the SS great coat. His skin was so thin and transparent that I could almost see the bones of his skull beneath it. It was Panks, or some version of him. He turned to me, pointed his pistol my way, and laughed. *"Zwillinsgrbuder,"* he called out.

The sound echoed and made my head hurt so much I wanted to split it open to release the pressure.

I took my revolver in my hand. It felt solid, heavy.

I sat down on the ground and put my head in my hands, hoping everything would just stop. I could think of only one way out. I closed my eyes.

I'd failed. I'd failed everyone.

I felt something cold envelope me. I opened my eyes again. Everything was white around me, like a fog had rolled in.

Then I felt a hand on my shoulder. It was Faith. She looked calm and her eyes shone bright. She crouched down next to me.

"Where were you?" I asked.

She leaned into my arms and said, "Everything's going to be okay."

I held her close, savoring the moment. She took the gun from my hand and she shook her head. Then she pushed back away from me. She turned and the air in the room rippled and the colors ran like a fresh painting. It wasn't Faith anymore; it was Amy. She was in the same luminous long dress as before. But her face was pale and the dress was faded.

She leaned forward and she whispered into my ear: "All will be unveiled."

She turned and the fog cleared a path. I could see Jordan at the far end of the chamber, calling her. The sound was lost to the fog. She reached forward one last time and touched my cheek.

And then I saw all of it. All of time and space was laid out in front of me. Every possibility was laid out flat, with every branch, every connection exposed, vast spools of player piano rolls. I was floating above it all, and I saw the dimensions undulate like waves. One path glowed like a discordant musical score. I could see and hear every instrument and every wretched note that still needed to be played.

And I would have to play it.

PART V

CHAPTER 39
Out on a Ledger

I jolted awake. It was like slamming on the breaks in a dream to stop from driving over a cliff. I stood up. Everything hurt and my mouth felt like it had been repaved. The chair where Faith had been lay on the ground, knocked on its side.

I knew Amy and Jordan weren't actually here, but I blinked twice and scanned the cellar just to be on the safe side. I felt my head to make sure it was still in one piece. The lump on the back of my head thundered and my hair was damp and sticky. But I was electrified. I'd found Jordan and he would be okay.

I had to find Faith. I had to assume she was alive. For how long, that was a different question.

Working with Duffy, I had a shot at pulling everything together.

I did a quick check of the room. There was a small desk and several file cabinets. On the desk was a two-way wireless telegraph with a small earpiece. It was warm as a loaf of fresh bread. A long wave setup like that had a range of over a thousand miles.

I slid open the desk drawer. Nothing but scraps of papers and a few pencils. As I slid the drawer shut, it stuck. I pushed harder and it went back in place. I opened the drawer again and reached underneath to feel around. I pried loose a thin, pocket-sized notebook that had been taped to the bottom of the drawer.

I flipped through the pages. It was a ledger. Every page had entries with payment dates, descriptions, dollar amounts, and sources. At least half the payments going back to 1942 were marked VZ.

It all made sense. Hugo had a source of funding for his lab all right.

He was working for the Russians and Vasily Zagadka was his handler.

I hobbled outside to the back of the house and into the kitchen. I heard voices down the hall. Sergeant Duffy walked into the room when he heard the door open.

"All right, Jack. What did you—" His eyes bugged out when he saw me. "Are you okay? You look like you got run through a printing press."

"I had a run-in in the cellar, but it's okay. I got something for Asheton. Where is he?"

"He's in the living room with the others."

"Has he been there the whole time?"

"I think so. I stepped out for a minute to radio the captain. But otherwise, sure."

I put my hand to the back of my head. It was starting to throb. I had flashes in my eyes, the onset of a migraine. I looked around the room and it was like I was watching it on TV, the color draining out of my vision.

Duffy tilted his chest forward. "You were gone a long time, Jack. I had to call the captain. He's on his way."

"Go get Asheton," I said.

Duffy left the room and walked back in with Asheton a moment later.

"Sergeant Duffy said you found something?" Asheton asked. And then with more alarm, "What happened to you?"

"Well, I figured out what Schuler meant when he said 'Caveat Venditor.' Hugo has a wireless in the cellar."

"I should have realized." Asheton put his hand to his forehead. "The Russians would never give up."

"I found a ledger he kept. It details every transaction he made with the Russians. It goes back to before the war with names, dates, and places for every secret he sold. Triad wasn't a person—"

"That's enough!"

We all turned in unison. Alan Hugo was standing in the doorway, brandishing a gun. It was the Luger Black Widow semi-automatic. His cane was in the crook of his arm, and he held Faith in front of him. Her hands were bound and her scarf was tied around her mouth.

CHAPTER 40
Man with a Gun

"Get away from the window. Sit down," Hugo ordered. The winds were picking up outside; the trees were swaying and the shutters were banging.

"Faith, this will be okay," I said. I tried to sound confident, but my voice was hollow, even to my own ears. Her eyes were wide and she gave me a tentative nod.

"Shut up, Waters. My train is leaving in fifteen minutes and I have every intention of being on it. Now hand over your guns."

I took out my revolver and put it on the table. Duffy did likewise with his snubnose. There was a flash of distant lightning outside and then the skies opened up and the rain came down heavier than before.

"You, too, Asheton," Hugo said, this time louder over the rain. "All your questions about how the Z-machine works, I knew you weren't a reporter." He motioned his gun at Sergeant Duffy and me.

Asheton removed his holster and slid his gun onto the table.

Hugo leaned his cane against the wall, scooped the guns up with his left hand, and then put them on the counter behind him. His eyes were fixed on us the entire time.

"Even if you make it to Mexico, the FBI will be onto you," Asheton said.

"Once I get to the Russian embassy, I'm beyond your reach," Hugo said. "Unless you want to start World War III."

Lightning cracked the sky, followed by a retort of thunder. The storm was closer. The noise resounded in my ears, like giant gears grinding.

"Doctor Hugo, please," Duffy said. "Let's just talk this through." He took a tentative step forward but stopped in his tracks when Hugo swung his gun toward him.

"Panks and Schuler abandoned me. Now it'll have to be me and Beverley. We'll rebuild the Z-machine in Russia. It'll take longer, but we'll get there."

"Russia?" Asheton asked. "Do you know what they do with people like Beverley there? She'll be put in a prison hospital."

"I can take care of her."

"Hugo, how did you know I'd go to the cellar?" I had to get him talking. The walls were starting to shimmer. I looked down at the floor and it was pulsing like a muddy river coming to a boil. Everything was in stark black-and-white, like a low-budget movie.

"I know Latin as well as any undergraduate. *Caveat venditor*, indeed. As soon as I heard you talking about that, I knew you'd find your way to the cellar. When Sergeant Duffy went to his patrol car, I went down the stairs and waited. Then Faith came snooping around."

The bells in the town square started ringing. They were hard to hear over the rain, and the sound came out distorted, like a distant air raid siren. Duffy turned to me and I knew he heard it, too. We had less than fifteen minutes before the train left.

"So the Russians bought you off?"

"Don't make me laugh. It's not about the money. It's about the science. The Russians are the only ones with the vision and the guts to see it through."

Asheton said, "You won't control a bloody thing. You're out of your mind."

"I've already talked to the assistant minister of science. He's going to propose it as part of their five-year plan."

He turned toward the door. "Beverley, Charlie, get in here," he shouted.

Charlie entered the room. "Yes, Mr. Hugo," he said. He didn't seem to be bothered by the sight of Hugo holding court with a gun. Beverley was tentative, peeking at everyone from two steps behind him.

"Charlie, get some rope. Tie these men up." Charlie braced, then his shoulders slumped. He grunted and went to the pantry. "Beverley, remember that plan we talked about?"

"Daddy, I've been waiting for years."

"Beverley, you're ready to lead the work. Go get your things."

Beverley went upstairs.

"They're going to rip this from you and give it to the Russian military," Asheton said. "You'll be the showpiece they trot out once a year at the May Day parade, the American scientist who sold out his country. You're just a political tool to them."

Hugo said, "I don't care about politics. I've never believed in any of that. And so what if their army has it? They paid for it. And if they use it to show up the Americans, well that's just what this country needs, a little more competition."

Asheton shrugged. "They've sold you a bill of goods, Hugo."

"What about your courier, Harry Gold?" I asked. Hugo's look hardened. "Was your brother-in-law a believer?"

"The man was contemptible." He spat on the floor. "The only thing he believed in was saving his own skin."

"We can work something out," Asheton said. "The FBI would take into consideration any assistance you provide."

Hugo wheeled on Asheton. "You Brits can't even feed your own people. The sun is setting on the British Empire, Asheton."

Charlie came back with a large coil of rope.

"Thank you, Charlie. I knew there was a reason I kept you around. I'll need you to stay here when Beverley and I leave for the station. You can say I forced you to tie them up; that's true enough." He pointed the Luger at Charlie.

Then he waved his gun at Faith. "You get over there with the rest of them."

Her eyes filled with panic.

"I need the pages from Panks's lab book," Hugo said. "I've looked all over for them and I figure the only reason I haven't found them is because you got them first."

"Asheton, you better hand it over," Duffy said.

"I don't have it," Asheton said.

"I've had enough of your games, all of you," Hugo said. "Where is the design?"

"I swear, I don't have it," Asheton said. "There's nothing in the lab book."

"Hugo, let Faith go, and I'll give you the missing pages," I said.

"You've got them, Waters? Well then this should be easy." He took a step forward, cocked the Luger, and pointed it at Faith's head. She squeezed her eyes tight and held her breath. "Why don't you just hand them over then?"

"I don't have them on me. They're hidden." I felt calm.

"Don't mess with me or you'll be picking pieces of this girl's skull out of your hair."

"Let her go first. She's got nothing to do with this."

Hugo stepped back but kept his gun trained on Faith. "All right. Charlie, untie her." Charlie came forward, undid the scarf at her mouth, and untied her wrists.

"Jack, what are you doing?" she whispered to me.

"Just get out of here," I yelled.

She got up and ran toward the door, but as she passed Hugo, he grabbed her shoulder with his left hand and knocked her to the ground.

Hugo was agitated now. He was shouting over the down-pour. "Don't take another step. For the last time," he spat. "Where are the missing pages?"

Beverley walked back into the room, this time with a small valise that she put down at her feet.

"Beverley," I said. "You need to give your father the photo of your mother." Beverley looked at me and blinked. Then she turned to Faith. Asheton looked on, his face tense.

"It's okay, honey," Faith said. "It's going to be all right."

Beverley looked down at her bag and then to her father. "I wanted something to remember her."

"Give it to me," Hugo barked. "Now!"

Beverley picked up the bag and clutched it close to her body. "Daddy, no."

"This is how we're going to rebuild the Z-machine," he said. He was speaking slowly, in a deliberate manner. His eyes focused on her like a hypnotist. "We'll work together. Just like your mother wanted. This is what you've studied for."

"Leave her out of it," Charlie said, his voice like thunder over the rain.

"What the hell are you talking about, Charlie?" Hugo said.

"Daddy, don't speak to Charlie that way."

"Beverley, be quiet and give me the picture. We've made a brilliant discovery. Do you understand? We're building on your mother's work. You and I will do it together."

Charlie spoke calmly. "Alan, I can't let you. Panks's work, the breakthrough. It puts everyone in danger." His body was still, his eyes intense.

"In danger of what?" The veins on Hugo's neck were pulsating, his voice loud as a drum.

"I made a promise."

"A promise?" Hugo repeated, outraged. "Goddamn you! You work for me, Charlie."

"I promised to protect the forbidden knowledge of my ancestors."

"Charlie, don't give me this two-bit Chumash crap. Beverley and I are leaving. We've been preparing her for this her entire life. I think she might finally be up to the task."

Charlie shook his head. "I can't let you use Beverley the way you used Mrs. Hugo or Dr. Panks. It destroyed them both."

Beverley's eyes jumped from Charlie to Hugo and back again.

"What is wrong with you, Charlie?"

"I'll stop you if I have to."

Hugo shouted at his daughter. "Beverley, give me the goddamn photo!" Beverley reached into her bag and pulled out the framed picture. It was the wedding photo that showed Amy Hugo in her veil. The photo with the hidden secret.

A light flashed outside, but it wasn't lightning; it was the headlights of a car as it turned into the driveway. A car door slammed, and Alan Hugo turned toward the window.

Faith sprang up and pushed Hugo hard with both hands, away from Beverley and directly in front of Charlie.

Charlie put his massive hands together and took a backswing aimed at Hugo's head. At that moment, the room lights flared like flashbulbs and then fizzled into darkness.

The image of Charlie, frozen in the wind-up, the anger in his clenched jaw, was seared into my brain. Charlie must have connected because I heard a powerful punch, followed by something wet and soft thumping against the wall and sliding to the ground.

I heard the photo crash to the floor, glass shattering. Something metal skittered across the tile and came to a stop. Everyone scrambled. There were shouts and Beverley screamed. I took a step back and saw Duffy feeling his way along the wall to the back counter. There was a low buzzing, then the lights flickered like a neon sign and came on. I sprang forward and grabbed the Luger.

Duffy had his snubnose pointed at Hugo on the ground. Hugo was still, his cane by his side. I leaned down. His neck was bent in a way that a neck shouldn't be. No breath. No pulse. Nothing.

Charlie stepped back. "I didn't mean to . . . I just wanted to stop him."

"You stopped him all right," Duffy said.

"He must have broken his neck in the fall," I said.

"Charlie, what have you done?" Beverley screamed. She ran over, crouched down, and kneeled over Alan Hugo's limp body, crying.

A second later, Captain MacDonald entered the room, soaked from the rain. "Duffy," he said. "What the hell's going on here?" His eyes moved from Duffy to Alan Hugo's body on the floor and then to Charlie and the rest of us.

Faith moved quickly to console Beverley. She bent down and put her arms around Beverley and held her. Neither spoke.

Charlie sat down. He wasn't going anywhere. I lowered my gun. The color was slowing seeping back into the world.

CHAPTER 41
Final Crescendo

"Turn around, Charlie," Duffy said. "I need to put the cuffs on." Charlie was almost a head taller and had seemingly killed a man, but if Duffy was nervous, it didn't show. He was in full control. Charlie turned around with his hands behind him, not saying a word. Duffy slapped the bracelets on with his left hand, then holstered his gun and turned Charlie back around to face the room.

"Somebody tell me what's going on here," MacDonald said, putting his hands on his hips.

Sergeant Duffy stepped forward. "It's complicated, Captain. This man, Charlie Cordero, is under arrest. Involuntary manslaughter. But as to the rest of this . . . " He shrugged.

MacDonald turned to take in the room. "And who is this?" he asked, gesturing to the floor.

"That's Mr. Hugo," Duffy said.

Before MacDonald could react, Faith stood up and shook his hand. "Faith Robner, insurance detective." She gestured to me. "My partner, Jack Waters. And this is Beverley Hugo, Alan Hugo's daughter." Faith had her arm over Beverley's shoulder.

"I thought this was a simple insurance accident."

"Captain, I can walk you through this, if you'll allow me." I gestured toward Sergeant Duffy who held my gaze. "Sergeant Duffy played a vital role tonight, though he's too modest to say so."

Duffy nodded his head ever-so-slightly, his eyes bright. Charlie looked on.

"This was supposed to be a straightforward case. A scientist dies in a lab explosion. But the more we dug into it, the more layers we uncovered," I said.

MacDonald slid off his cap and ran his hand through his hair. His eyes wandered to the liquor cabinet.

"Would you care for a drink?" Asheton asked. "You may need it before we're finished."

MacDonald nodded. "I'll take a scotch." Then looking to Duffy. "Sergeant, you're permitted." Duffy went over and poured drinks for both of us.

"Of course, everyone had alibis," I continued. "The more we talked to the suspects, the more it was clear they were lying to us. Alan Hugo had a motive to collect on the insurance."

"Half a million," Duffy said.

"Hugo was a desperate man, out of money. I think Panks's death really was an accident. Hugo set some kind of timed explosive device to cause a fire in the lab, so he could use the insurance money to buy some time. But he didn't know Panks would be there that evening."

Asheton looked up from his glass.

"Things take rather a strange turn from there. To explain why Hugo was so desperate, I have to back up and give some context to who Panks and Schuler really were."

"I'm dying to hear," the captain said, taking his scotch from Duffy.

"Panks was the head of research at Mittelwerk, a Nazi lab in Germany during the war. They experimented in fusion and other ideas about energy. Some of it was pretty strange. During the war, the Germans called their invention Zeus. When they came to America to continue their work, Panks called it the Z-machine. Schuler was his protégé. It was Schuler who came up with the most recent breakthrough, what he called a fan-out design. It enabled them to boost the Z-machine to a higher voltage than ever before. It was what Hugo needed to make the system fully operable.

"Panks took the credit for the breakthrough and Schuler felt slighted. They might have argued about it, but Schuler would never have killed Panks. He admired him too much. But then the pages from Panks's lab book went missing." I took a sip of my scotch.

"Schuler didn't believe Panks's death was purely accidental. That set him investigating on his own, going back to the bar-racks. He's a scientist. He figured out the cause of the fire and then it was obvious."

I was laying it on a little thick. If I had to paint Hugo as a bigger villain than he was, so be it.

"That brings us to Mr. Asheton," I said. "The man who isn't what he seems. What was an English reporter doing here in Loma Vista? Hugo first put me on to him. His line of ques-tioning didn't make sense for a reporter."

"Go on," MacDonald said.

"In fact, he's a foreign agent."

Asheton flinched momentarily.

"Our English friend is here on behalf of MI5 and working with the FBI. The arrest earlier this year of Klaus Fuchs led to the capture of two other atomic spies." I motioned for Asheton to elaborate.

"We were looking for two agents codenamed Triad and Raven," he said. "With the arrest of Harry Gold and David Greenglass, Triad was ordered to shut down his operation." He shifted in his seat and caught my eye. He might have been worried about how much I would say.

"Actually, there would have been four defectors," I said. "Triad is Russian for trio, meaning Hugo, Panks, and Schuler. Panks had two train tickets, so Hugo must have the other two. One for himself and one for Raven, meaning his daughter, Beverley."

Beverley looked up at the mention of her name.

"Well done," Asheton said, but his tone negated the words.

"I'm sure you would have gotten there," I said, pleased that he hadn't.

"The case took a turn with Schuler's death, shot with his own pistol and leaving a cryptic note. The obvious interpretation was that Schuler killed Panks and then himself. But it was too neat. Schuler was left-handed, but the gun was in his right. He was telling us something in the note, but he was mindful of Hugo. Duffy helped me figure out that '*Caveat venditor*,' which Schuler had written in the note, wasn't actually 'seller beware' but 'beware of the *cellar*.'"

"When Schuler learned that Hugo was shipping them all off to Russia, that was too much for him. Schuler hated the Russians. I'm not sure he would have gone along with that plan, even if Panks were alive. And either he knew or he guessed that Hugo had a radio in the cellar."

"So that's what they argued about," Beverley said.

"Hugo shot Schuler inside the lab and then fired a second shot outside so that everyone would come running to the barracks. Then he snuck back in through the cellar, circled back, and joined us."

Beverley sobbed openly at what I'd said and I felt bad for that.

"He said he'd gone to get his cigarettes," Duffy said.

"That's right. You'd been looking for him. Isn't that right, Asheton?"

"I knew there was something off about that," he said.

"We got there in the end. All sins are forgiven." I looked at Charlie while I said it. He bowed his head slightly. That's all I needed.

I turned to MacDonald. "It was in the cellar that Faith discovered Hugo's wireless. And I found a ledger that showed he'd been working with the Russians for years."

I lit a cigarette and inhaled deeply. "Charlie, I understand what happened here with Alan Hugo. It was an accident. It wasn't your fault."

"I didn't mean to . . . " he mumbled.

"Duffy needs to take you in; you understand that," I said. He nodded.

"There's one thing I never figured out though, Charlie. What happened eleven years ago?"

He didn't move a muscle, he didn't blink, he didn't even seem to breathe. He looked right through me with those piercing eyes of his. The room was silent.

Duffy finally broke the silence. "Jack, how could that matter," he said quietly.

I turned to Duffy. "No, Sergeant, the details always matter." I looked at Charlie. This time, I softened it. "Charlie, shouldn't people understand what Amy Hugo wanted?

"I did what had to be done," said Charlie.

The room was silent and all eyes were on Charlie.

The silence nudged him forward.

"I did it and I'm proud of it."

Charlie's eyes were fixed, as if he were looking inside himself. "Amy," he said and then corrected himself. "Mrs. Hugo had told me about the Z-machine. It would unleash a power no one could control."

Beverley leaned in.

"She knew she couldn't do it by herself." Charlie's face was hard. "She worked it all out, down to the last detail. She needed help and I gave to her." His chin rose, defiantly. "I would do it again."

Beverly jumped up and started to lunge toward Charlie, but Duffy restrained her.

"How could you?" Beverley shouted. "You killed her! You killed them both." She dropped to her knees sobbing. "You rot in hell, Charlie."

It unfolded exactly as I expected.

I made the sign of the cross. For me, for Jordan, for Amy. We were all damned, but at least Charlie would be out of it.

CHAPTER 42
Morning Light

I put down my scotch. I'd had enough. Enough booze, enough dope, enough lies for a lifetime. There was a pencil line of red coming on the horizon and it underscored how tired I was.

I did what I could for Charlie. Manslaughter five wasn't so bad. He'd made his promise years before and he saw it through. He had real courage. I wondered if I'd be able to do the same when my time came.

Captain Macdonald took Faith home. Now it was just me and Duffy alone in Alan Hugo's office.

"Come on. There's one more thing we have to do," I said.

He picked up his glass and drained it.

We zigzagged down the trail, same as I had with Schuler. The sky was beginning to lighten. As we got to the vanishing point, I looked up and everything was black and silent, just as it had been before. Duffy didn't seem to notice.

I slid back the door and we stepped inside the workshop. Schuler's Z-machine gleamed in the light, like some half-finished science project. It didn't look like much. But I understood its power.

Duffy sidled up to me. "It was just a Ponzi scheme, right? That machine doesn't do anything. Does it?" he asked.

"Sergeant, when you were coming home from the war, I bet you saw new recruits, shipping out. They must have asked you what it was like, being in battle."

"They couldn't understand it." He looked down at the ground. "I hoped they never would." He raised his eyes. "I gotta tell you something—"

"No. You don't owe me anything."

"Not you," he said.

"Sergeant, you don't owe anyone."

"About Okinawa. I'm not like you, Waters. I was yellow. How do you think I managed to get shot in the leg?"

"We all paid. But you only have to pay once. That's the mistake, to keep on paying." I nodded to the Z-machine. "Listen, we're going to clear all debts. Understood?"

"And what about you?"

"We'll both be in the clear." I put my hands on my hips and nodded to the Z-machine. "We've got to destroy it."

"What? Jack, I can't do that."

"Didn't you ever bury some inconvenient testimony? Lose a piece of evidence?"

"Never. This isn't Detroit."

"Look, the Z-machine is a weapon. It's a ticking bomb. I'm going to disarm it, permanently. You do what you want."

I went back outside and walked around the building. There was a separate storage shed with some equipment, a gas pump, and some Jerry cans.

When I got back, Duffy had found some old rags and pushed all the equipment toward the center where the Z-machine sat. We doused the rags and threw them on the pile.

I heard a metallic click and turned.

"Hold it there, gents."

Asheton was leaning against the doorway, pistol in hand. He set down a briefcase that had been in his other hand.

"What's this then?" I asked.

He walked forward. "You know what it is, so step aside."

"I want to hear you say it."

"I can't let you destroy this. It's too important."

"Come on, Asheton. You know how dangerous this is."

"We can't let the Russians get ahead of us."

"They don't have anything."

"They have everything Hugo shared with them, and they'll build on it. They'll put a hundred scientists on it. Sooner or later, they'll figure it out. That's a risk we can't afford."

"And what about your friend Lamphere at the FBI?"

"I radioed him already. Told him everything was destroyed. This is for King and country, I'm afraid."

"What?" Duffy asked slack-jawed.

"No longer a joint operation, I take it," I asked.

"Don't be dim. You Americans are worse than the Russians. Surely, you can see the damage that's been done? Businessmen running the government, technology for sale to the highest bidder. It's a disgrace."

"Why'd you do it? Why kill them?" I asked.

"No one crosses me. Ever. Panks and Schuler had their chance at Mittelwerk. But they chose wrong. And I wasn't about to let Schuler's breakthrough fall into the hands of your government. Anyway, I got what I came for. And Hugo, well, he got what he deserved."

"Strangled was it?"

"I thought I'd have to shoot him." His lips curled into a smile, relishing the thought. "But when the lights went out I used his cane to crush his windpipe. One must improvise, when the situation demands. Your little story about Hugo, I almost believed it myself. Too bad your friend Charlie has to take the rap for Hugo's death, but that's the way it goes." He pursed his lips for a moment.

"You don't get it, do you?" I said. "He was keeping the world safe from the likes of you."

"Well, no matter." He beamed. "I'm impressed you figured out my little ruse. I meant what I said earlier. You're a smart man. You could be a real asset." He looked away for a moment and half his face was in shadow. "You should think about which side you want to be on."

But I knew the answer to that one.

"What was it that put you on to me?" he asked.

"You did, Captain Frederic."

"How's that?" His eyes narrowed.

"You were Jordan's contact. You betrayed him, you son of a bitch." I couldn't control myself. "He died because of your bomb in the tunnel."

He shrugged. "It was just another OSS cock-up. I mean, it was a shame all 'round. I was ready to take Panks and Schuler, and then you lot arrived. What could I do? Jordan was in the wrong place at the wrong time."

I looked over at Duffy. "Sergeant, how's your leg?"

"My leg?" Duffy responded.

Asheton turned toward Duffy and as he did, I surged forward with a flying leap. I used the momentum to windmill my fist straight into his face, knocking him to the ground. Before he could get up, I kicked over the Jerry can, sending a stream of gasoline toward the rags at the center of the equipment. I ran to the switch on the console and pulled the lever to power up the Z-machine one last time.

There was a loud thrumming noise as the machine built up its power. The air shimmered.

The Z-machine had been the target from the beginning. First a nightmarish invention, then a scientific miracle. It had never been put to use in any way that could benefit society, and now it never would. I stared at the metal structure. It gleamed in silence, holding its secrets. All I knew was that I'd never see Jordan again.

Asheton pushed himself up off the ground, getting to his feet with the grace of a fallen toddler.

"You bastard," Asheton called out. He scrambled on the ground for his gun, but I was ahead of him. I scooped it up and dropped it into my pocket. I was done with Asheton and all his conniving. I pulled out my lighter, the one I'd carried with me through all of Europe. I flicked it to draw a flame and tossed it gently amid the rags, like a street performer with a flame-throwing trick.

The noise of the Z-machine continued to build momentum and I wondered if I'd miscalculated. The rags smoldered for a moment and suddenly flames shot up. There was a sizzling sound with tubes popping like fireworks. In a moment, the Z-machine was engulfed in flames. It loomed large in front of me, almost holy. I grabbed Asheton's briefcase and threw it into the center of the fire. Did he even have the missing pages?

"Run," I called to Duffy.

We sprinted as fast as we could out of the building. I glanced past everything, trying to memorize it. It was all a blur. We were about thirty yards clear when the ground trembled and we dove behind a clearing. The explosion was louder than I expected. It ripped through everything. Glass shattered and smoke poured out. Flames surged, like waves in a tropical storm twenty, thirty feet in the air. The beams cracked one by one. In a few seconds, the roof would collapse.

I watched the years of engineering experiments and equations with passing respect as they crumbled. Blakely Lab would never be created again. A vision swam past of Amy and Jordan watching from a distance high above. I wondered what they would think of all this.

Asheton emerged, silhouetted by the flames of the building. His face was black from soot. His jacket was gone and his shirt and pants were blackened. He scanned the horizon, turned, and saw us. He had a look of surprise on his face. Then he ran, his long limbs trailing, clutching his briefcase.

"You'll pay for this," he shouted hoarsely.

We had all paid.

CHAPTER 43

The Mission

San Moreno, California
November 22, 1950

I sat on a bar stool. Music played from the jukebox.

It would be Thanksgiving tomorrow. People walked past the window, carrying home their last-minute groceries and trimmings in bulging paper bags. That sort of life was still a long way off for me. My fingers drummed on the table in front of me. But the moment was quiet and that felt good.

Following the strange case of multiple homicides and a spy ring at Blakely Labs, nobody in these parts seemed interested in probing into what lurked below the surface. Blakely Lab was shut down, the FBI put a clamp on everyone, and soon the story faded completely.

The Hollywood Stars started to rally in September. If they didn't win the season, they'd finish well ahead of the Los Angeles Angels, and that was enough for most people.

But not me.

Manny came by and refilled my coffee. A stifled grin emerged from the corners of my mouth and soon spread across my face. I was thinking everything over. The carpet was stained and the place was deserted. Sitting here, I could be anyone daydreaming the day away. Just another guy killing time. I felt tired, but in a good way. There was nowhere I'd rather be.

The Wurlitzer in the corner bubbled away, casting orange-and-blue lights across the empty room. Today was straight, no reefer. No strange colors. That wasn't completely in my control.

I let the sound of Billie Holiday's "God Bless the Child" from the jukebox wash over me. I loved the way Eddie Heywood's piano followed the contours of her voice in a perfect arrangement. It was sacred and profane, but God bless the child that's got his own.

Sure, money made a difference. It gave you freedom. But to me, she was singing about doing things your own way, the best you could. The past didn't matter.

The words reminded me of Beverley. Faith was worried about her. But Beverley was tough and smart. She'd make something of her life. Still, she was a loose puzzle piece that wouldn't fit properly.

No matter how many times I replayed the scene in my mind, dealing out fates to strangers like cards in a rigged poker game, I could never get a better hand for Beverley. Amy Hugo knew what she was doing when she put the plan in motion for Charlie and me.

I played my part, as did Charlie. I couldn't have asked for a better teacher.

Charlie took the rap for Hugo's death. There was no way out of that. There was a prospect for appeal and, given a sympathetic judge, he could come out the other side in a few years. That's what I hoped for.

I got Pacific All-Risk off the hook for the insurance claim. They were relieved to hear the news, though I spared them how Hugo had died.

There was one thing that surprised me. There really was something hidden behind the glass of Amy Hugo's wedding photo. It wasn't the missing pages. It was a letter for Beverley. Nothing more.

Asheton remained a wild card. He disappeared from the coast that morning. A few months later, I telephoned Special Agent Lamphere at the FBI, but got nothing. He didn't acknowledge knowing anyone by the name of Asheton, said he couldn't speak on any joint work with MI5 and said he was unaware of any British intel ops in the United States. I think it hurt him to say hello.

And Duffy, God bless him. He and Captain MacDonald were spirited and generous in their exhortations to join the San Moreno PD. "You solved the worst crime wave we've had in fifty years," Duffy said with a sigh. "From here on, it's all downhill." I still remember him saying that, his mouth stuffed with a Danish pastry, as he reached across his desk to phone his daughter and tell her goodnight.

Duffy could go back to the way things were. But I couldn't be a cop again. Not with what I had to do. I had to live my own way. The way I'd only dreamed of before.

"All right?" Faith asked.

I startled. I didn't hear the bell over the door. "Wait, sorry, yeah."

She laughed.

She said she'd meet me at the San Moreno, but as often happens, I got so deep in my own thoughts that I didn't notice her come in.

She was fully decked out, camel-hair jacket over a white blouse and pinstriped pants, blazing-red silk scarf loose around her neck to match her lipstick. "So why all the mystery today on the phone? And why, of all places, did you want to meet here?"

I took a deep breath.

I had made my peace with a lot of things. With Jordan. With what I'd seen. With the mission. Sometimes at night, I still saw the skull man in his SS coat and that was okay, too. What I hadn't settled were things with Faith. She had gone to San Francisco and stayed there when the *Chronicle* gig had dried up.

Legally, we still had a business together, though we weren't taking any new cases. We were both in limbo between San Francisco and San Moreno. I had no particular place to call home. Nothing was decided. I had to change that.

"Faith, you know there are things about me—"

"Jack?" She took my hands in hers.

"Things I see, ways I do things, that other people don't—"

"You don't need to do that," she said. "I know who you are."

In the days following the Blakely case, I told her about my visions, about what Amy Hugo had shown me. About the mission. I had to say it again, but differently.

"I don't want to do this on my own."

"Jack, I've always been with you," she said. "You only had to ask."

She leaned forward and kissed me and I felt the heavy presence of that small velvet box in my pocket. I'd pull it out and open it for her when the time was right.

We left the San Moreno and ran back to the car ahead of the rain. With the fees from the Blakely case, I'd bought a new Hudson Hornet convertible—sleek, metallic gray, low to the ground. It was a beautiful machine.

As we approached the car, I jumped ahead to open the passenger door. As she slid in, I caught a sight behind me. A man in a dark suit ducked into the bar at the San Moreno. The wind was blowing, and I didn't hear the bell.

I started up the car and it roared. A familiar song came on the radio.

There's a man down in the alley
He's got a Colt 45 . . .

"Hey, listen to that." I turned to Faith. Her eyes were bright. Mick and Jerry must have gotten their record deal after all. I tapped my hands on the steering wheel and pulled into traffic. As I cruised onto the coastal highway for the long drive to San Francisco, I smiled.

There's one thing that's certain in this world . . .

Our mission was just beginning.

THE END

EPILOGUE
Now and Forever

June 30, 1939
Miskatonic, Massachusetts

Dear Beverley,

If you get this letter, I will be a distant memory. All will have worked out. Read this carefully so you understand.

To have a daughter, to love you, was everything to me. But the lure of science and the higher dimensions was strong. What I saw was strange, beautiful, and terrifying. It nearly engulfed me.

Strange things inhabit our world, between the dimensions. Now, I realize it was a world we are not meant to see. I made the decision to shut the door to those terrors. To hide what I discovered and destroy the tools that made it possible.

Only one way would keep you and the world safe. It will not be easy. You will face many traumatic events, but I know you are strong and you will prevail.

That is what gives me the strength to do what I must do.

One day, you will understand why I had to leave. It's not easy to say goodbye. There lives in my heart a promise—that while creating something evil, I gave birth to something good. That was you.

Venturing forward, I know you will do great things. I have seen a view from high above and I know that you will be on a better path. Your protector will see to it.

Even now, some things will unfold in terrible ways. I wish I could hide those things from you.

Remember all that has happened and forgive Charlie for what he did. He kept his promise to protect the higher dimensions. This was the most complex thing I have ever willed into being, and if you are reading this letter, there is nothing left for me to hope for. The mission is complete. I hope you will understand the part that each of us had to play without me having to spell it out. I love you now and forever.

—Amy

AUTHOR'S NOTE

My brother and I traveled to Germany in the summer of 2019 to retrace the steps of the 104th U.S. Infantry, which liberated Mittelbau-Dora and captured Mittelwerk. We visited old town Antwerp, had lunch at Quinten Matsys, which seemed much as it would have seventy-five years earlier for Jack and Jordan. We took a train to Cologne and visited the massive cathedral. We imagined what the area would have looked like when the Allies had leveled the city with their nightly bombing raids. We drove to Nordhausen, visiting the KZ memorial at Mittelbau-Dora. We saw the site of barracks, the parade grounds, the front gate, and the crematorium, a tiny two-room building that still stands.

Then we entered the tunnels of Mittelwerk, to walk where Jack Waters would have gone on April 11, 1945. It had fallen into disrepair after the Russians attempted to seal off the facilities by blowing up the entrances in 1948. The tunnels still contain the partial remains of rusted V-2 rocket engines, gyroscopes, and other detritus.

The summer of 2019 was also the fiftieth anniversary of the lunar landing, powered by Wernher von Braun's famous Saturn V rocket. Von Braun emerged in the 1950s as a Disney-fied all-American hero and a major force at NASA.

No doubt, von Braun *was* a great American. But he was also a *Sturmbannführer* in the SS. He designed the V-2 rockets that bombed London and Antwerp. He visited Mittelwerk more than a dozen times during the war. When he found progress lacking, he went to Buchenwald and requisitioned thousands of slave laborers, an almost-certain death sentence. More than twenty thousand slave laborers died in the making of the V-2 rockets at Mittelwerk; more than five times the number that were killed as a result of V-2 bombings.

This book never answers the question as to whether the United States *should* have recruited Nazi scientists, but it is a parable of what can happen if, as Amy Hugo might have said, you open that door. The characters are fictional, but Mittelwerk, T-Force, the Osenberg list, Operation Paperclip, and the Venona Project are all real. For more than thirty years, the CIA and FBI employed former Nazis as spies and informants in the fight against communism.

There are several good books on The Venona Project. The best is *The FBI-KGB War* by Robert J. Lamphere, a fourteen-year FBI agent who launched the project to decrypt top-secret Russian cables and shared the work with MI5. Lamphere helped break Klaus Fuchs, leading to the arrest of Harry Gold, David Greenglass, and the Rosenbergs in the summer of 1950. His book reads like a thriller. Sadly, it is out of print, though used copies abound on eBay.

For readers who would like to know more about the recruitment of Nazi scientists to the United States, I highly recommend *Operation Paperclip* by Annie Jacobsen. No Paperclip scientists were ever found guilty of war crimes in America or

Germany, though a handful were forced to leave the country under dubious circumstances.

There is a lengthy section in the book about Major General Harry G. Armstrong, a pioneer in the field of aviation medicine and inventor of the pressurized air cabin. Dr. Armstrong recruited German aviation doctors to the United States, including his counterpart, the director of Aeromedical Research of the *Luftwaffe*, Dr. Hubertus Strughold, whom he had met at conferences in the 1930s. Armstrong and Strughold had similar careers and became lifelong friends. Armstrong was promoted to Surgeon General of the Air Force and Strughold became Chief Scientist of NASA's Aerospace Medical Division. Strughold was the subject of three separate investigations into his suspected involvement in war crimes committed under the Nazis. He remained a controversial figure even after his death in 1986.

By the most unlikely of coincidences, Harry G. Armstrong was my wife's grandfather.

—*Zack Urlocker*
Traverse City, Michigan
mzurlocker@gmail.com
www.mzurlocker.com

ACKNOWLEDGEMENTS

Writing a book with a historical fiction element feels like traveling through a dark tunnel. You're not at all certain where you're going, but you're deeply appreciative of anyone who guides you. That this was a first novel and a collaboration between two stubborn brothers made the path at times seem even less clear. But many people did shine their lights for us, and we would like to thank them.

At Inkshares, we'd like to thank CEO Adam Gomolin, who believed in the project, and Noah Broyles, the operations manager who acted as sherpa. Diane Young helped us tremendously in developing the story, and Pam McElroy did a brilliant job coaxing just a little bit more clarity and intention in her edits. We were supported by approximately 500 early sponsors on Inkshares, without whom this book would not exist. Thank you for all your patience!

We were guided by many beta readers, including Thom Allen, Vic Allen, Charles Ardai, James R. Benn, Tal Klein, Mark Stay and Frank Zinghini. On the ground, we were supported by the staff at the Mittelbau-Dora Concentration Camp Memorial near Nordhausen, who took us underground twice and answered all our questions, and by kind, generous people in Antwerp and Köln. Thank you all.

GRAND PATRONS

Matthew Neil Asay
Matt Talbot
Michelle Rizor
Nicholas Soulliere
Oisin O'Connor
Patrick M. Garrity
Peter E. Baker
Peterjohn Marquez
Patrick Moran
Puneet Agarwal
Rich Nigro
Robert A. Mc Donald
Robert Castaneda
Robin Vasan
Roger B. Mc Namee
Rory A. Mcdowell
Ruoting Sun
Ryan Denehy
Stacey Curry Bishop
Stephen Blum
Stephen J. Harrick
Steve Robert
Tal M. Klein
Tel K. Ganesan
Todd Greene
Vinay P. Joosery
William E. Savage Jr

INKSHARES

INKSHARES is a reader-driven publisher and producer based in Oakland, California. Our books are selected not by a group of editors, but by readers worldwide.

While we've published books by established writers like *Big Fish* author Daniel Wallace and *Star Wars: Rogue One* scribe Gary Whitta, our aim remains surfacing and developing the new-author voices of tomorrow.

Previously unknown Inkshares authors have received starred reviews and been featured in the *New York Times*. Their books are on the front tables of Barnes & Noble and hundreds of independents nationwide, and many have been licensed by publishers in other major markets. They are also being adapted by Oscar-winning screenwriters at the biggest studios and networks.

Interested in making your own story a reality? Visit Inkshares.com to start your own project or find other great books.